The House of Envy

Book One
The Dark Mountain Chronicles

Jennifer K. Johnson

Dedication

To the martyrs, thank you for having a faith that surpasses this life, and inspires all of us to examine how we live.

*Greetings to all who know the truth of our world,
and to all those still trapped in the darkness.
This book contains no ordinary story.
There is something powerful buried within its
written words.
The truth hidden in these pages has the power to transform you.
Those with a discerning eye will never see their world
the same again.
As soon as you have read the first page, your journey
has begun.*

You have been warned.

~ Chapter One ~

With dirt and small stones cutting into her palms, Angeline pushed herself up from the ground; her eyes widened in horror, as the carriage faded from view and descended farther into the depths of the dark mountain. Abandoned and alone, Angeline clutched her heart while a thick darkness enveloped her. Shades of paint dripped down her face, guided by a steady flow of tears. She cradled her head gently in her hands and wept. Soon, her glorious color would be nothing more than a memory; just an ashen face of gray, like the skin of a true commoner. Emptiness and fear descended upon her: starting at the very tips of her butterfly-like wings and moving all the way down to her ornately decorated toenails.

Angeline glanced up from her cupped hands to gain some hope from her surroundings: nothing; even her hands were invisible in the darkness. Nearby, she could hear water droplets hitting stone and resonating on the cavern walls. Angeline was certain she heard something scurrying across the gravel. Was it moving towards her? Her heart began to race.

Inwardly, she recited the Code of Glamour, hoping it would give her courage:

> ### Code of Glamour
> *There is no one who matters but you.*
> *Be the best, no matter the cost to others.*
> *Eat and drink from the fruit of your own vanity; it will give you power!*
> *You deserve to be worshiped and admired by all those lesser than you.*
> *Bask in the beauty of your own glory.*

As she meditated on each word, Angeline could feel them stirring deep within her. They were a part of her, pushing her closer to her desires. She cherished this code more than any beings of mere flesh and blood. Angeline felt her strength returning, as she whispered, "I have the power to regain my station and I don't need anyone else. I am the creator of my own destiny."

However, the code was only able to distract her for a moment. She brushed a long, dark curl from her face, as her mind focused with rage upon the one person who had ruined everything: Julia. It was by Julia's stricter adherence to the code that her position as Supreme Madam had been revoked. Her golden wings quivered as she fixated on this painful revelation, along with all that had transpired.

Still deep in thought, Angeline had failed to notice the sound of rolling gravel getting progressively closer. A giant centipede was now making its way, gradually, up her leg. The light, feathery sensation of the creature's legs caused beads of cold sweat to form on the back of her neck. Her fear of touching this massive insect was not as strong as her desire to remove it. She reached under her silk dress, grabbed the creature's thick, scaly body, and threw it high into the air. The centipede hit the cavern wall with a loud shriek and a crunch. Angeline felt her stomach churn in response to the repulsive sound. Her body shook, as she curled herself into a tight ball; her wings fell around her, as she fainted from fear and exhaustion.

Adlar and Kenrick sat like stone statues in the royal carriage, as it jostled and bumped along a rocky road. Both men were dressed in royal blue capes, with impressive feathered wings looming uncomfortably behind them. Kenrick shifted uneasily in his seat. Leaning forward, he clutched the hilt of his blood-grooved, long sword; the cold metal felt smooth and familiar in his rough hands. The hilt bore the traditional insignia of the House of Envy, a woman with emerald eyes and head turned upward. In the dark carriage, a sliver of light escaped from the small gap between Kenrick's sheath and metal hilt. His silver blade glowed naturally from the phosphorescent inlay, the work of Marcos, the master swordsmith.

Kenrick's eyebrows furrowed, as he broke the awkward silence. "Alright, Adlar, tell me again why we didn't silence that old she-serpent? Personally, I would have enjoyed finishing her off nice and slow."

Adlar gave him a look of mild annoyance and gruffly muttered his reply. "It was my decision to make, not yours; because I am in charge and you are not. This is based on the simple fact that I have the ability to think before I act. You are a reckless toddler who would rather tear the legs off a lizard than follow the instructions of your superiors." Adlar roughly poked his finger into Kenrick's chest as he continued. "We didn't kill her because killing someone when not expressly told to is foolish. It would have led to a slow and painful death for both of us. Do you understand now, you stupid little boy?"

Kenrick was infuriated by Adlar's response and was seriously contemplating giving his old mentor a quick stab, and pushing him out of the carriage. He slowly reached down toward his boot, which housed a well-known secret: all royal guards carried a poison-tipped dagger to execute all those deemed unworthy of life. Kenrick gradually retracted his hand, after catching a glimpse of the smirk on Adlar's face and the deadly gleam emanating from his right eye. He knew that Adlar was a well-seasoned assassin and would make quick work of him. With this in mind, he buried his damaged pride and mumbled something to Adlar about now understanding. Kenrick shifted his gaze to the window. He watched as shapes and light flickered by for hours, until he saw the familiar glow of Hawthorne City; they were finally home.

~ Chapter Two ~

A small light bobbed in the darkness, leading its owner down a highway shadowed by death. The glow from the lantern fell upon a still form. It hovered over the body, blanketing it in a circle of light; this was not the first time the light had revealed a lost soul, and it certainly would not be the last.

Angeline awoke to a damp cloth on her forehead and the pleasant sound of someone humming. She had almost forgotten that she had been abandoned; her mind had tricked her into thinking she was being pampered by one of her servants. Angeline's eyelids fluttered open, revealing a little girl with sparkling, hazel eyes looking down on her. For a moment, she felt warmth pass through her heart, but it was soon ruined by her pride.

The little girl had washed Angeline's face, gently cleaning the minor cuts and scrapes. Sadly, by performing this generous act, she had made an innocent mistake. With the water, she had not only washed the blood and the dirt away, but also most of the remaining paint.

Angeline touched her face and peered into a nearby puddle that was reflecting light from the lantern. The image that greeted her caused her to scream, "You stupid, worthless child! Look at what you've done to me! You've taken the only thing that I had left, my beauty!"

The child took a step back, as Angeline's angry voice echoed throughout the empty cavern. She waited for the quiet to return before responding; her voice was small, but surprisingly bold. "I'm sorry, but your color wasn't real; it was broken. I had to wash it away to make your face better. I was sent here to help you."

Angeline fumbled for a response, unable to grasp the meaning behind the girl's odd proclamation. Quickly, she decided that the girl was either insane or of extremely low intellect. Bearing this in mind, Angeline rose from the ground and lifted her wings, in order to intimidate the small girl. Dwarfed by Angeline's dominating posture, the girl stood just slightly above Angeline's waist.

Angeline poured all her thoughts out on the child. "Help me? How dare you speak to me? I could tear your wings off and leave you here to rot. Of course my color isn't real, you senseless girl. But it was the most beautiful, luxurious paint that only real power can afford to buy. I never had to wear that watered-down spit and dye you have on your face and hair. You are the kind of girl that is disposable. You can only dream of being as beautiful and powerful as I am. Now go away and play with the dirt you're so fond of, you little pretender!"

The little girl stood straighter and lifted her head proudly. "My name is Ellie, and my color is not broken. It will never fade or wash away with water. I have been painted with the love of the Creator, and He personally thinks I'm beautiful." A smile immediately spread across her tiny features, while she daintily twirled her little yellow dress in a circle. As she moved, she lightly flexed her pale, blue-and-yellow wings.

Angeline felt sick; her words had not affected the girl. Even worse, they had made the child happy. There was a time when just looking at one of her servants could reduce them to tears. Had she lost all of her power over people? Her body responded by slumping back to the ground. She turned her face away from Ellie, trying to hide her fragile emotions and protect her damaged pride. She began to whimper and cry softly.

Ellie instantly stopped her elegant display and carefully knelt beside Angeline. She placed a soft blanket around her new friend's shoulders, along with a tender arm. Her small heart hurt, and she started to cry out of pure empathy. Ellie hummed a sweet melody, as she cried and rocked Angeline to sleep.

The carriage came to a stop in front of an enormous, columned cathedral, constructed out of a beautiful, black marble. The mammoth structure had a dark, almost living presence to it, as the glowworm lanterns cast their lights over its five enormous statues. Their jeweled eyes glared down on the two robed figures exiting the royal carriage and swiftly moving through the large, iron gate. Their black boots made a subtle tapping noise, as the two men walked down the main corridor and came to a stop at a marble archway, with a sheer, blue curtain that sparkled with real gold dust. A female servant peered out from behind it and ushered them in.

The room was furnished extravagantly in royal blue and gold; in the center of the room was an impressive marble fountain. The fountain's base was diamond in form: and in its center stood a beautiful female statue with outstretched arms, a delicate face tilted upward, and water flowing from her palms. The men were led to the base of the fountain and told to wait for Madam Julia.

Adlar and Kenrick only had to wait a few minutes before Julia appeared from her private chamber. She glided down the stairs; her face devoid of any expression. Kenrick felt a chill run down his spine, as she stood before them. Julia dramatically lifted her hands and clapped three times. In response, all of her servants quickly disappeared from sight.

Julia turned to Adlar. "Good, now we are alone. I want you to tell me everything. I must know exactly how much she suffered, and don't leave out any of the details! Make me feel as though I was there." She sat on the fountain's edge and shifted into a more comfortable sitting position. When she was ready, she gave Adlar a quick nod to proceed.

Adlar personally thought this was an utter waste of his time and a small blow to his ego. He had never been fond of stories, and he was even less fond of telling them. At this moment, he wished that Kenrick had been chosen to be Julia's little performing animal; but for the sake of protocol, he swallowed his pride and spoke. "Madam Julia, on behalf of the royal guard, we congratulate you on your recent ascension to the elite position of Supreme Madam, the sole ruler of the House of Envy. As a display of the honor we hold for your office, we obtained all the jewelry and coins the vanquished had on her."

Adlar proceeded to pull out a black satchel, that was tied to his belt, and carefully emptied its contents into Julia's waiting hands. The jewels only caused her desire to hear the story to grow. Julia waved her hand impatiently, indicating for Adlar to continue. His jaw twitched before he began to address her. "Early yesterday, I was given an official order, which stated that Madam Angeline was to be removed from power. In response to this decree, I assembled six guardsmen and proceeded to prepare for a traditional removal ceremony. I summoned a black carriage to wait at the front gate, and for it to be drawn by the best of the iridescent salamanders. I then gathered the necessary tools and brought my men to this very chamber.

"Once here, we found Madam Angeline in the process of berating one of her servants, completely unaware of our arrival. Two of my men seized her arms and held her in a fixed position. She squirmed fiercely, enabling her to momentarily break free from their grasp. She even drew blood from one of my men, when she savagely raked her fingernails straight down both sides of his face. In response, the guards acted quickly by twisting her arms behind her back. They kept her subdued in a forced kneeling position. I now had her full attention; the fear had settled in, and her right eye began to wander. As I stared at her, she knew that her secret had been exposed. The time had come to reveal our intentions." Adlar removed the royal parchment from his left breast pocket and read it out loud.

"It is the official ruling of the Supreme Royal Council that Madam Angeline Tattersall should be removed from her position, due to a recently discovered weakness. In the House of Envy, we hold a high standard of beauty; perfect eye symmetry being one of our basic requirements. This defect was revealed to us by the accused's very own sister, the beautiful Lady Julia Tattersall of the Chamber of Crimson. We believe that Lady Julia understands the very spirit of the Code of Glamour, which is to be the best, no matter the cost to others. Therefore, Lady Julia Tattersall has been found to be more qualified to lead the House of Envy, based on her exquisite beauty and her willingness to make the proper sacrifices. She shall replace Angeline immediately! The execution of these orders is to be assigned to the able discretion of Adlar LeCreed, Captain of the Royal Guard.

Official decree declared by:

Lord Julian Radcliff, Head of the Supreme Royal Council"

Adlar quickly handed the decorated parchment over to Julia and continued talking. "With our intentions now revealed, we continued with the rest of the ceremony. She was still in a forced kneeling position when I walked over and pushed her head down, forcing her to bow before her servants. Then, all sixty of them filed in and formed the line of burden. The line started right here and went all the way out into the hallway. The first servant walked right up and spit in her face. She screamed, 'You have failed as a leader, and your time in the House of Envy will be easily forgotten.' The second told her that when she would get upset, she would slur her words like an ill-trained child. It continued on like this all the way down to the last servant, who merely laughed in her face and stated how weak and unattractive she looked. They had all burdened her with her flaws, and by the look on Angeline's face, each word had wounded her. These statements are just a sampling of what was said. If you desire to see the entire list, I had Kenrick make proper documentation of everything."

Kenrick knelt before Julia and offered her a stack of organized papers. Julia's large, sapphire eyes gazed hungrily upon them, quickly snatching them from Kenrick's open hands. She giggled with excitement and implored Adlar to continue.

"Her mind had now been permanently poisoned by the piercing words of her servants. We tied a rope around her neck and bound her arms behind her back. Then we paraded her through the House of Envy, ensuring that all could see her fall from power.

Eventually, we arrived at the carriage, where we placed a burlap sack over her head and tied a rope securely to the floor of the coach. Making sure that she was fully humiliated, Kenrick made use of her as a footrest.

"Throughout the remainder of our journey, she talked incessantly. One moment, she would scream at us, calling us traitors, and the next, she would be pleading for her life. She displayed all the signs that the ceremony of burden had been a success. With her current symptoms, I would be surprised if she survives a week before she destroys herself.

"After a full day's journey, I found the perfect spot to dispose of her. It smelled damp and stale, and I could taste the bitter flavor of death. It was as if a voice whispered in my ear, telling me, "This is it. Stop". I immediately ordered the carriage to halt. Once the coachman had pulled off to the side of the road, we untied her, removing the sack from her head. She kicked and screamed wildly as we pulled her from the carriage; neither Kenrick nor I said anything to her. We ripped off her jewelry and took the last of her remaining possessions. She begged us to spare her life, and we, in respect for our positions, remained silent. When we had finished, I signaled Kenrick to go back to the carriage. We turned our backs on her, leaving her to die alone in the darkness. That, Madam Julia, is all that I have to report."

Madam Julia smiled contentedly, as her fingers stroked the papers nestled beside her, pondering all the details of her sister's countless inadequacies. Adlar stood for a long time observing Julia, patiently awaiting her response. He coughed to gain her attention. Julia's head slowly turned to look up at him. "What are you two doing? Why are you still here? You have completed your job; now I am through with you. Leave me!" Julia raised her hand to wave them out. Once alone, she stood, clutching the papers. She glided quickly to her chamber, preparing to relish every detail.

~ Chapter Three ~

*E*llie's quiet humming had soothed Angeline's nerves, and now she was completely relaxed. Her mind was emptying itself of all the painful thoughts she had been having; she finally felt at peace. Angeline was growing attached to this little girl without even thinking about it, which was extraordinary, because the only person she had ever been fond of was herself.

Ellie's gentle tune stopped abruptly, forcing Angeline's painful thoughts to come flooding back. She instantly opened her large, almond-shaped eyes to see what had ruined her escape from this harsh, new reality. She tried to get Ellie's attention, but the girl's gaze was fixed elsewhere. Angeline turned to see what Ellie was looking at, and what she saw terrified her.

A man was running, animatedly, towards them. He had wild brown hair that was so dark; it was almost black. He was unusually tall with well-proportioned wings that were white but dingy. His clothes were well worn. The light reflecting from his lantern cast shadows all around him, which added to his crazed appearance.

Angeline stood up awkwardly and ran down the road in the direction the carriage had traveled. She disappeared into the veil of darkness, stumbling clumsily over her enormous silk dress; she hoped the wild man would get to Ellie before her. Even with having to constantly pick herself up, she kept a watchful eye over her shoulder to observe how close the man was to catching up with her. Angeline knew the darkness would protect her; whereas the child's light would expose her, making her an easy target. Breathlessly, she slowed and watched as he made his way straight to Ellie.

He quickly came upon Ellie and scooped her up into his arms, holding her in a loving embrace. From her safe vantage point, Angeline looked on in surprise: as the man gently set the child down, knelt on the ground in front of her, and began to talk with her face to face. He placed his hands directly on her shoulders, and his posture gave the appearance that he was focusing intently on every word the child said.

While they talked, Angeline assessed her situation. She took a long look into the black abyss and realized that running away was hopeless. Then she looked back at her other option and decided she would rather be with people than by herself; at least then she could attempt to manipulate them for her own survival. She slowly started making her way back to them.

When she reached them, the man carefully stood up, obviously trying to appear less threatening by his careful movements. Angeline felt small in the shadow of this giant man. He gently extended his hand as he addressed her. "Hello, my name is Aristus, and I am Ellie's father. I want to apologize for startling you; I was thinking only of my daughter's safety."

Angeline was glad to be speaking with an adult. She thought it would be nice to converse with someone on the same intellectual level as herself. It also pleased her that Aristus was not unpleasant to look at, and, with a little grooming, he could easily pass for a warrior in the Coliseum of Power. She stood more poised and focused on keeping her language and tone refined. "Greetings to you. I'm sure that your child has already informed you of my social standing. I am the Supreme Madam Angeline Tattersall of the House of Envy. There has been a grave misunderstanding, and my position has been seized from me by my sister. I am in need of your assistance to guide me back to Hawthorne City. If you do so, I have the means to ensure that you will be well compensated. You will never have to wear those hideous clothes again, and people will respect and fear you. I would like to leave as soon as I have been provided the opportunity to fix the horrendous damage that your child has done to my face."

Aristus had displayed a variety of different facial expressions as Angeline made her speech. What began as a concerned, somber expression eventually hardened into a disgusted frown as she finished her monologue. He was mildly offended by her assumptions regarding his character, but it was her conclusion that he would be motivated by things, such as money and power, that annoyed him the most.

Despite his obvious irritation, he intentionally chose to ignore her words. "Miss Tattersall, you look as though you could benefit from a good meal and a comfortable bed. Would you honor us by accompanying Ellie and me home for dinner? I'm sure my beloved wife, Honna, would be pleased to have another empty seat filled."

Aristus unwittingly had boosted Angeline's ego; she concluded that he had wisely accepted her proposal to improve himself. She took the offer of his wife cooking for her as his attempt to show respect for her high social position. These thoughts were what produced her egotistical reply: "I would love to accept your humble offering."

Aristus nodded and motioned for her to follow. He looked visibly annoyed by her words, but he honestly couldn't bring himself to waste time trying to explain what he had meant. Ellie picked up her small medicine bag and led the way with her father. As she reached his side, he lovingly took her tiny hand into his. Angeline made a mental note about how odd it was for a parent to show so much affection for a child; this family was the strangest she had ever seen. Children, to her, were nothing more than an unnecessary obligation; a responsibility with which she had never seen the benefit of burdening herself.

The two of them walked steadily, while Angeline purposefully walked slowly, enjoying the fact that they had to periodically stop and wait for her. They hadn't walked very far when Aristus did something rather unusual. He walked directly up to the solid rock face that ran all along the road and began talking to it. Angeline couldn't hear what he was saying, so she stepped closer, hoping to catch a part of it. She began to snicker at how absurd Aristus looked speaking to an inanimate wall.

All of a sudden, the ground began to shake. Angeline felt a fierce rumbling under her feet. The ground was moving, and the stonewall in front of her was opening to form an extravagant archway with an ascending stairway. She roughly grabbed Ellie by the arm, while Aristus walked through the opening and began climbing the stairs. Angeline couldn't form words; she just shook and stared wide-eyed, with her mouth hanging half open.

Ellie did not seem to notice the extent of Angeline's fear as she spoke to her enthusiastically. "Now, don't be scared. The rocks obey all those who serve and believe in the Creator. I will walk behind you, so that they don't squish you as they seal behind us."

"Squish me?" Angeline squeaked.

Ellie thought Angeline truly did not understand what she meant, so she took a small piece of bread from her bag and put it between her fingers. She squeezed the bread flat, so that it oozed between her fingers, and she looked back up at Angeline. "That's getting squished, and I think it would hurt a lot."

Angeline did not wait another second. She sprinted up the stairs after Aristus; Ellie followed right behind her, thinking how fun it was to play chase up the steps. As they climbed, the loud crashing of rocks behind them caused Angeline's adrenaline to surge. She was running so fast that she caught up to Aristus, who had been climbing at a fairly brisk pace himself. He knew that his wife was worried sick over Ellie not coming home last night. In fact, he was concentrating so hard that he hardly noticed when Angeline came up behind him. In her increasing panic to get up the stairs, Angeline tried to climb over Aristus, pulling out several of his feathers in the process.

Aristus shouted in surprise, and abruptly turned to face a very terrified Angeline. Taking a deep breath, he carefully locked eyes with her, keeping his voice calm and even as he addressed her. "Miss Angeline, calm down. You are going to be just fine. Hold on to my wing, and Ellie can hold your other hand. We're not going to leave you."

Angeline felt a little calmer with Ellie's warm hand in hers. She felt safer knowing that they would not allow her to get squished. Angeline walked in sync with them until the stairs came to an end, and they had reached a steel trap door located directly above their heads. Aristus' height forced him to crouch beneath the door, where he knocked forcefully.

In time, the door responded by opening upward. A delicate hand appeared and pulled him through the opening. Angeline was now directly under the door and was looking into the green eyes of a smiling, freckle-faced woman, with curly, red hair tied back in a ribbon. Her eyes were pink from crying, but her whole demeanor was warm and welcoming. Angeline reached up to clasp her hand and was gently lifted into Ellie's home.

Once through the door, she began to take note of her surroundings. Their home was much larger than she had anticipated; although nothing about these people had been anything like what she had expected. Angeline quickly realized that she was standing in a kitchen. The room smelled sweetly of a variety of homegrown spices. She casually rested her hand on the cold, stone slab that made up the kitchen table; it was, by her standards, crude, but surprisingly intricate. The sides of the table were carved with unique runes woven in, between countless exotic plants and animals. They were all beautiful, unlike anything she had ever seen before.

Gradually, her gaze moved from the table to a large sitting room. All the walls in this room were covered with bookshelves. Aside from the shelves, the room contained four stone couches, chiseled into the center of the room. Each bench had large, yellow-and-red embroidered pillows to make them more suitable for sitting.

There were two new faces occupying this area of the house. The first was an elaborately dressed man about her age, curiously rummaging through his pockets while enthusiastically flipping through the pages of a book. The light in the room reflected off his golden hair, and Angeline welcomed the sight of a well-painted face. In the far corner of the room, an elderly woman was sitting alone on the floor, wrapped in a brightly decorated quilt. Angeline could not see the woman's face, but she was able to see her deformed and aging hands protruding awkwardly from the patchwork blanket.

Angeline's mind was swimming with questions. She stood motionless, trying to make sense of everything, while watching as the family prepared for supper. With her left hand, Honna was stirring a pot filled with a mushroom sauce, and with her right, flipping fish in a pan. Ellie was setting the table, while Aristus gathered up everyone for dinner. Angeline had begun to feel at ease with her surroundings and decided she was ready to take a seat at the table. She sat in the chair nearest to where she had been standing.

One by one, they gathered at the table to eat. Ellie sat next to Angeline, with the chair next to her presumably left open for Honna. Aristus led a small toddler, whom Angeline had not observed earlier, to sit next to him at the head of the table. The little boy was slightly pudgy, with solid, white hair that puffed like a dandelion around his small, round head. While everyone was getting seated, Honna busily moved from the table to the stove, filling everyone's plates. She set a hot basket of rolls on the table, as Aristus politely led everyone into formal introductions.

"This strong, young man next to me is Bowen. Now Bowen, would you like to tell our new guest anything about yourself?"

A proud smile spread across Bowen's face, as he proclaimed, "I three and eat . . . um . . . rolls all up! Grrr..."

Aristus smiled affectionately at Bowen and playfully ruffled his feathery hair. Then, he turned his gaze toward the stunning looking-gentleman Angeline had seen in the sitting room. "Here before you is a man who is accustomed to introducing himself. I will allow him the pleasure of addressing you personally."

The man stood up and made a dramatic, sweeping bow with one hand. Then, with the other, he gently placed Angeline's hand in his and kissed it. "Greetings, my rare jewel. I am Trinzic the traveler; seeker of all things beautiful and wonderfully mysterious. As a professional seeker of beauty, I must say that yours surpasses even some of the more impressive gems." He gave her a noticeable wink and relaxed back into his seat.

Aristus rolled his eyes and exhaled an exasperated sigh. "Ah yes, so that's Trinzic, and the woman sitting in the corner is Melora; she prefers to eat her meals over there. Ellie has brought us a new friend, and she has expressed a desire to introduce her to all of us."

Ellie stood up for her announcement. "This is my new friend, Angeline. She's sick. Her color is broken, and her heart is very sad. So I brought her home to serve and take care of her."

Angeline felt heat rushing to her face. She stood up, rage surging through her blood. "How dare you have a child introduce me," Angeline screeched. "She made me sound like an old, confused hag. Do you think I'm a helpless old woman who depends upon the charity of fools to survive? No! I am still young, only three years aged since being a youth." Her voice broke. "I am still beautiful! I am still worthy of worship!" Angeline turned her face away from the awkward stares, because she could feel her eyes beginning to grow moist with tears. She wanted to crawl under the table and disappear. Embarrassed and confused, she started to walk away, when Aristus spoke. "Angeline, stop! We are here to serve you, along with all others who are lost, or in need of rest. If that makes us fools, so be it! Ellie has the honor of willingly serving you until you no longer have need of her. Please sit down, so that we all may enjoy the meal my wife has prepared."

Angeline's mood instantly changed. She turned around dry-eyed; she was fashioning a satisfied smirk, as she glided back into her seat. "Now that is the way to properly address someone of importance. Thank you for establishing your place."

Aristus looked as though he was being forced to swallow a rock, but he politely remained silent. The rest of the meal was rather uneventful. Honna had mashed up some food and was spoon-feeding it to Melora. As she fed the old woman, she hummed the same melody that Ellie had sung to sooth Angeline. Everyone at the table was fairly quiet, excluding Trinzic and Bowen. Trinzic was excitedly telling Angeline about all his roguish exploits and adventures, while Bowen tried to steal the spotlight by finishing all of Trinzic's sentences, whenever he paused to breathe. This caused Trinzic to talk faster and faster, so as to take as few breaths as possible.

Trinzic talked for such a long time that after a while, it was only the three of them left at the table. Bowen, meanwhile, had fallen asleep, with his little head resting heavily on his dinner plate. Even with Bowen asleep, Trinzic's speed had not slowed throughout the one-sided conversation. Angeline mustered in a persistent effort to pipe in her desire to go to bed, but he continued talking over her.

Honna eventually came to her rescue. "Trinzic, I'm sure Angeline would love to hear your complete life story, but it is getting very late. We would all like to get to bed. Allow me to show her where she can get a nice bath and some rest. Also, Trinzic, if you don't mind me saying so, it wouldn't hurt you to bathe once in a while."

Trinzic was obviously embarrassed. He quickly mumbled a goodnight to Angeline and briskly walked to his sleeping quarters; everyone then set about preparing themselves for bed.

~ Chapter Four ~

Julia was lying comfortably on her stomach in the middle of her enormous four-poster bed. She was thoughtfully caressing the silk sheets with her fingers, as she meditated on her own personal genius and physical beauty. In front of her were two stacks of papers: one pile contained love letters and praises from her countless admirers; the other contained the names and painted faces of possible male prey.

"One of you will prevent me from suffering the same fate as my dimwitted sister," she whispered to herself, as she examined each picture carefully. "I refuse to be carted out of here like some dirty animal. I will use my unmatched brilliance and exquisite beauty to keep gaining power. Oh, Julia, what mere man could possibly deserve your hand in a joined union?"

Julia stared down at the profiles and sorted through them by appearance. All those not considered stunningly handsome or youthful were immediately discarded without a second thought. Next, she pushed the love letters onto the floor, and arranged the remaining profiles by rank and position across her bed. Once the top five had been selected, twenty more pieces of paper glided to the stone floor. Now, she had to decide which of these five men she could easily manipulate and use to gain the most power. Julia bit her lip, trying to visualize with whom she would look the best standing next to in the grand banquet hall. She was fairly certain that she could beguile any one of these men with her feminine charm, but it had to be effortless. There could be no mistakes; slip-ups, in these matters, often led to a death sentence.

Three of the men were obviously physically strong and had reputations for being shrewd, intellectual businessmen. She helped them to their places with all the other rejects resting on the floor. Now only two men remained: Lord Balin Alric and Lord Denham Fontaine. The Lord Balin was an ambitious miner who had worked hard to obtain power over his co-laborers. He earned his title through bribery and personal charisma, whereas the Lord Denham was from an old aristocratic family. He had never worked to earn his power, and was known for his charm and wit.

"Hmmm," Julia whispered. "He appears moldable." She closed her eyes and tried to visualize who would make a better statement publicly. With that, she decided on the Lord Denham; she needed someone more settled in his position, not a man she would be competing with for power. She did not need or want a partner, but rather a simple puppet she could easily control. The Fontaine family was known for socializing with the elites of high society;

they were the ideal family to get her established in a position of lasting power.

Julia's mind was made up; she unceremoniously tossed Lord Balin's profile from her bed. Now that she had finished the selection process, she summoned her head servant. A slender, young girl obediently glided into the room, stopping at the side of the bed with a curtsy.

Julia gave her orders. "Krenna, I have a special task for you. I would like you to gather all the information you can on the Lord Denham Fontaine. I need every detail, down to his favorite color. If you do this task to my satisfaction, you may select any item you fancy from my belongings. Also, I would like this whole deplorable mess picked up and destroyed." Julia waved her hand over the scattered papers lying on the floor as she continued. "Burn it! I don't want anyone rummaging through my personal business. That is all that I require from you; now be gone!"

The girl nodded and quickly gathered the mess of papers on the floor. Krenna disappeared from the room, and Julia took a moment alone to gaze thoughtfully at the picture of the Lord Denham. "You poor fool! You can't even imagine the snare that I am preparing for you: mind games and trickery, all wrapped up in a pretty face — the perfect tools to catch a mate."

Honna was helping Angeline get ready for bed, while giving her a short tour of their home. Honna talked as they made their way to the bathroom. "I'm sorry I wasn't able to sit with all of you at dinner, but Melora is my gift from the Creator. I have been chosen to care for her. She needs a little extra love and care sometimes; tonight was one of those nights. She hasn't spoken a word since she was brought to us, but I just know that she will say something any day. Look at me carrying on like Trinzic. I'm sure you're not really interested in Melora's progress. I bet you're more interested in a refreshing bath and a warm bed."

Angeline was exhausted, but a bath still sounded wonderful. She felt stiff and grimy; it would feel so good to be clean. With a voice near pleading, she expressed her desire to take a bath. Honna smiled sweetly and led her to the bathing room.

They arrived at a thin, stone door, which opened into a unique washing room. Against the far side, the rock wall opened, and water from a cavern stream was entering from the uppermost corner. The water flowed into a shallow, rounded whirlpool. From there, it continued down a gradual slope, disappearing through the adjacent rock wall. On the wall, near the entrance, hung a modest-sized mirror that was stationed right above a rounded, stone basin for washing one's face and hands. As they entered, Honna grabbed some items from a nearby shelf that had been hidden behind the open door.

"Here are some clean clothes for you to sleep in, and a modest outfit to be worn tomorrow morning.

I know my clothes may not be the same style that you are accustomed to, but it appears we are a similar build, so at the very least they will fit you. Your clothing has many layers, but I believe I could have it washed and mended in about a week's time."

Angeline shuddered visibly, as she looked at the white pantaloons and matching blouse. They were not at all like the garments she was familiar with, but she was slightly intrigued by the unusual material. The fabric was not made up of silk, fur, or leather, which was the only kinds of material she had ever seen or knew existed: it was not as shiny as silk nor as smooth. Whatever it was, it would have to suffice.

Facing Honna, she answered. "Your clothes are not at all satisfactory, but I obviously can't sleep in what I'm currently wearing. Therefore, I suppose, if I have no other options, I will have to make do with these things."

Honna tried to be understanding. She casually retrieved some soap, along with a large sponge for Angeline to dry herself. Honna handed them to Angeline, as she replied, "If there is anything else you require, I will be staying awake for a while. Just open the door and call for me; I'll be happy to get you anything you need."

With that, Honna left, closing the door behind her. Now that she was alone, an unnerving chill ran down Angeline's spine, as she stood in this unfamiliar place. The silence of the room rang in her ears, causing her to miss the welcome distraction of other voices. The only voice that could be heard was the one in her head, along with the gentle trickling of water. Angeline turned to the mirror; hoping it would bring her some comfort, perhaps even lighten her deteriorating mood: but the sight that greeted her brought neither an improved mood nor comfort. Instead, it evoked sheer terror. Fear shot through her, like lighting in her veins, and she was beginning to feel sick.

Her once neatly ribboned hair was now loose and sticking up in all directions. Streaks of blue paint, both light and dark, ran from her forehead to the base of her neck. Her right eye was encircled by a large bruise. It felt as if a hideous stranger was inhabiting her body. She leaned closer to the mirror to get a better look at her damaged face, and cursed when she examined the extent of the destruction. Her eye lenses were cracked and needed to be removed. Angeline winced, as she pulled each jeweled lens out roughly. She looked down at the decomposing fish lenses and then back at herself in the mirror. Her eyes were no longer white with a blue sapphire in the center, but solid black. Staring into her natural, dark eyes, her only thought was why Ellie didn't scream and leave her to die; she couldn't believe how hideous she had become.

Angeline turned away from the mirror; her body seemingly moving of its own accord toward the whirlpool. She stepped out of her heavy gown and cautiously entered into the cool, swirling water. The water shocked her out of her painful trance. It revolved around her sore body. Her head fit perfectly into the stone behind her, and her ashen body relaxed, allowing her to think sensibly. She slowly reached for the small sponge and soap that Honna had left for her. Angeline wiped the sponge softly over her face, pausing over her right eye; the cool water felt good on her bruise. Sitting with her eyes closed, Angeline continued to dwell on positive thoughts to motivate herself to action.

She spoke to break the silence. "You are still a beautiful leader. All you need are the right cosmetic tools to repair the damage they have done." In saying those last few words, her mind instantly brought her back to the removal ceremony. She could hear them labeling all her mental and physical imperfections. It felt like they were in the washroom, berating her all over again. Listening to their screaming and condemning words, her body began to convulse. Angeline was fighting a losing battle with her mind and body. She felt trapped, and she screamed out in pain. Everything went dark, as she slid under the swirling water.

Two feminine hands struggled to lift her out of the water. Honna strained against the stone, and finally managed to pull Angeline from the whirlpool. Once she had Angeline out of the water, Honna hit her squarely in the center of her back. Angeline's wings twitched, as water came sputtering out of her mouth. Honna quickly covered Angeline with her apron and the clothing she had brought for her to sleep in; her timing was perfect.

Aristus and Trinzic burst through the door. Both men looked a bit startled and slightly embarrassed. "We heard a horrible scream," Aristus stammered uncomfortably. "Is everything all right?"

Honna gave Aristus a stern look. "You both should know better than to rush into a washroom when a lady is indisposed. Now scurry off to bed, so our guest can get dressed in peace. She is supposed to be resting, not being rushed or bothered by a couple of excitable men." Honna winked at Aristus to let him know that she wasn't really mad at him, and that she had the situation under control.

Aristus understood and smiled. "Come on, Trinzic, Honna probably just saw a spider, and you know how much she hates them. Let's get back to bed." Trinzic seemed confused and interested in the rest of the story, but Aristus ushered him out and closed the door.

Now that the two women were sitting alone in the dimly lit washroom, Angeline spoke. "Honna, thank you for saving me and protecting my dignity." Angeline looked broken and physically exhausted; Honna was puzzled by this new woman who sat before her. Angeline appeared and acted differently than the woman she had brought in to bathe. Her eyes were now solid black, and her face a pale gray. Honna felt a deep sorrow in her chest, as she stared into those empty, black eyes. They called her back to a time she had almost forgotten; it wasn't that long ago that her own eyes were once the same dark color.

A tear ran down Honna's cheek, as she silently uttered a quick prayer. *My precious Creator, thank you for loving me and washing the darkness from my eyes. I owe you everything. All the joy in my life is a credit to your transforming gifts.*

Honna handed Angeline a drying sponge, as she explained, "It really had very little to do with me. It is the Creator who deserves all the credit. He is the one who made my heart unsettled about you to let me know you were in danger."

Angeline was beyond exhaustion and wasn't interested in what Honna was saying; all she cared about was going to sleep. She looked up into Honna's eyes. "Could you get Ellie? I need her singing to help me fall sleep. I just need the distraction."

"I will wake her and get you a dry set of clothes to wear," Honna politely replied, then hurried out. She returned moments later with the clothes. She quickly handed them over to Angeline and moved outside the room, allowing Angeline to dress.

Angeline was finally dry, with a growing desire to be warm. The stone floor was cold against her feet, as Honna escorted her to her room. The room was smaller than she was used to, but that didn't matter. All she could think about was getting into bed. Ellie was waiting for her in a chair next to the bed; her eyes opened and closed, fighting her own need for sleep. Angeline fell roughly into the bed and pulled the covers up to her chin. Honna quietly withdrew, as Ellie began to sing.

The wind blows over the Crystal Lake,
A voice calls to all those who have ears to hear.
It is the Creator. He calls to you. He sings . . .

Let my healing waters restore,
Let my love make a home in your heart,

Let my truth open your blinded eyes,
Return, my child, to your father's arms,
Return . . . return . . . home.

The place you dwell is dark and cold,
Enter his warm world of light,
Hear him sing his song of love,
For you he sings . . .

Let my healing waters restore,
Let my love make a home in your heart,
Let my truth open your blinded eyes,
Return, my child, to your father's arms,
Return . . . return . . . home.

As Ellie sang, Angeline felt a comforting peace wash over her, and she drifted into a deep sleep. Ellie stopped singing; then watched Angeline for a moment as she slept. She quietly thanked the Creator for sending Angeline to her, then curled up in her chair and closed her eyes.

~ *Chapter Five* ~

A large crowd had gathered in the House of Envy. Winged figures moved like bees, swarming around the nine different palette stations: each person looking for eye lenses, paints, clothing, and portraits of their favorite palettes. Most were visiting the stations of Madam Julia and Lady Ember. Lady Ember had just been chosen to fill Julia's old position in the Chamber of Crimson. Male and female alike were excited to see the debut of the two women; all the palettes were adorned in their finest silk gowns, designed by their new madam.

Madam Julia sat perfectly still, as she leaned dramatically on her marble fainting couch. People of all types gathered below her pedestal window to marvel at her beauty. Her admirers called to her, causing Julia to feel empowered by their worship. While maintaining her stunning display for her audience, Julia suddenly felt a small piece of parchment slide between her slender fingers. Julia stretched elegantly to read the note; the message stated that Krenna had completed her task. Julia had to fight the desire to leave her post. Her gaze shifted slowly to find the servant who had given her the note. Once eye contact was established, she rapidly fluttered her eyelashes to signal the servant girl to come. When the servant had reached her, she leaned with her ear next to her mistress's mouth.

Julia whispered, "Go immediately to Krenna. Tell her to meet me in my private chamber. I will join her when I have completed my duties here; I should be there within an hour's time. That is all for now. Leave me." The servant left to do as she was told. Julia bit the side of her lip, trying to contain her excitement.

It had taken Krenna only a week to gather all the information she needed on the Lord Denham. Her pace was quick as she walked to her mistress's chamber; all the while hoping that Madam Julia would notice how hard she had worked on this assignment, and then finally realize how much Krenna did for her. She imagined how impressed Madam Julia would be with all that she had done. Krenna felt confident as she moved down the narrow hallway, clutching her precious assignment tightly to her chest. She turned the corner and entered the lavishly decorated room of her mistress.

As she entered, Julia greeted her with an abrupt request. "Krenna, I am glad that you are here. I need for you to deliver a brief summary of all the information that you have put together for me. When you are done talking, I will take what you have in your hands and look at it privately."

Krenna was taken off guard. She had planned to give a long, detailed report to show how much she had done and all that she had collected. Thankfully, she had grown accustomed to having to think on her feet, due to her mistress's constant change of moods and desires. With the intent of gaining more time to rethink her speech, Krenna spoke. "Madam Julia, before I begin, may I offer you a beverage to refresh yourself and some food for you to eat?"

Julia merely nodded her head. Krenna immediately set about filling a goblet and putting small, decorated pieces of candied fish on a golden tray. She worked quickly to get everything ready, while her mind raced to put the right words together. Once the food and drink were prepared, Krenna gracefully brought them over to her mistress.

Then Krenna began. "This is the heart of the information I collected on Lord Denham; I hope that it meets your complete satisfaction. The Lord Denham Fontaine is known for being extremely generous. His personality is one of a lighthearted, boyish jokester. He often showers his many close friends with expensive, rare jewelry. Denham and his family reside in the central city of Crossford, the home of the Coliseum of Power. His best friend, Julian Radcliff, with whom you are well acquainted, is in charge of all his personal finances and social engagements. The Fontaine family makes all of their extensive wealth through their production of luxurious weaponry; all of their weapons are known for their light handling and unique design. The family should be able to sustain themselves indefinitely, based on the fact that they have multiple facilities with hundreds of workers. Not only is Lord Denham very wealthy, but he has been known to be very popular with women. Within the past year, he has had at least five known marital prospects. At this time, a rumor has been circling that he has become interested in his longtime childhood friend, Lady Celestra Penteon, and has plans to propose to her within the week."

Julia interrupted. "That will do. Now hand me the papers, and leave me to my thoughts." Krenna was flustered and very disappointed. She had a lot more to say. However, she obediently turned and exited the room.

Julia felt foolish; she had not planned on nor anticipated any competition. What would she do now? Go back and sort through the pictures? Just then, she was struck with the perfect solution. A grotesque smile began to spread across her face. In her mind, it was if the last piece of a puzzle had just fit into place. She knew what needed to be done. She shouted for Krenna, who had only left the room seconds before.

Krenna re-entered, looking frazzled, though her voice sounded calm. "Yes, Madam Julia? What is it that you desire?"

Julia responded, "I need you to fetch Kenrick for me immediately. I wish to speak with him within the hour, or I will be very displeased with you. Now go!"

Within half the amount of time Julia had allowed, Kenrick was standing in her chambers. He had come without a moment's hesitation. Julia was an exceedingly powerful woman; having her call for him was a boost to his ego. Kenrick stood before her, attempting to look as professional and composed as possible.

Observing their entrance, Julia spoke. "Krenna, leave us. We have important things to discuss." Krenna quickly departed, leaving Julia and Kenrick alone. Julia smiled almost lovingly at Kenrick as she addressed him. "Kenrick, I am pleased that you could meet with me on such short notice. Come, sit with me here on my bed, and we shall discuss some important things."

Kenrick's feet shifted uneasily. He was surprised by her request, and he moved cautiously to the bed and awkwardly climbed up onto it. Julia pulled the silk curtains down around them, so they could talk privately. She looked deep into his eyes.

"I have called you here to discover if you would be interested in destroying someone for me. I need you to carry this out quickly and quietly. I had thought about Adlar, but I need someone younger and stronger. Adlar confessed that you had wanted to end my pathetic sister's life; that proves to me that you have the right stomach for the job I am about to offer you. Before I continue, I must be certain that your heart is in this. I am sure you understand that I can't just tell everyone about my plans to kill; it would be a foolish mistake on my part. So do I have your word that you will take on this job, or do I need to find someone else?" Julia looked at Kenrick with pleading eyes.

Kenrick was beaming: this was his opportunity to steal business away from Adlar, and perhaps get even with him for making him feel like a half-wit. At this point, he would have killed just about anybody, maybe even his own mother, if the price were right. "Yes," Kenrick blurted out, "I'll do it."

At that, a sinister grin slowly spread across Julia's face; it stayed there, firmly planted, as she continued. "I was expecting more than just a simple yes, but that will do. Thank you for accepting this assignment. This is what I have planned for you to do. I need you to kill a woman by the name of Celestra Penteon. She lives in the central city of Crossford. At this moment, Krenna is gathering all the information you will need to find and dispose of her. I will give you until the end of the month to finish this job. If it is not done by then, I will be forced to find someone else. I have already made arrangements for you to be released from your regular duties, starting immediately. All that is left for you to do is to gather up your belongings."

Kenrick was feeling a bit rushed and was curious about how much he would be getting paid. Inwardly, he gathered the courage to voice this concern. "Before I leave, I would like to know how much you will be paying me, and by what means you would like me to dispose of her."

Julia's voice squeaked girlishly. "Money is no object. Feel free to name your price; that price could even include Krenna. I have seen the way you look at her. I am sure she would make a fine wife. If you think you'll grow tired of her, you could always have the union severed, or kill her, for all I care. Basically, if you can imagine it, I will provide it to you as payment. If you do this job well, I can be extremely generous. However, if you fail, I promise that I will make sure you die very unpleasantly." Her tone had changed, and her eyes narrowed as she glared down at him.

Then her gaze lifted, and her voice returned to its previously sweet tone. "As for how you kill her, I don't really care. I will leave that up to your creative, natural talent. Also, you can have my sister's old jewelry to sell; I think it is tacky anyway. I am sure it will bring you more than enough money for food, lodging, and supplies. One last thing: you must not tell anyone of our arrangement. It has to be done in secret. If you don't follow my instructions exactly, you will not get anything, and anyone you tell will die. That should be all the information you require. Wait one moment while I collect the jewelry."

Julia got up and walked around the room, gathering up a large bundle of jeweled bracelets, ornate necklaces, and glittering earrings. She dropped them into a decorative silk satchel and handed it to Kenrick, placing a single kiss on his cheek. "A stolen kiss for luck, along with my sincere gratitude."

Kenrick felt like he was floating, as he turned to walk away. He felt as though he could conquer the world. Finally, someone had noticed his talent.

Angeline had been with Ellie's family for over a week. In the short amount of time she had been living with them, they had made her feel like family. She had almost forgotten about her hunger for power, until today. Aristus sat at the breakfast table, discussing his plans for the week.

"I know that sharing unpleasant news at the table may be considered poor manners, but what I have to say must be said. Later tonight, or perhaps tomorrow morning, I plan to head out to work in the rice fields. Trinzic has agreed to come with me. We will probably be gone for a couple of months."

Angeline, who had spoken very little over the past week, looked inquisitively at Aristus. "Aristus, I have two questions concerning your travels: first, why would you need to work in the rice fields? From what I have seen, your family appears to have an adequate supply of food. Also, you don't seem like the type of people that would use coins or gems to purchase anything lavish. So why work if you don't have to?"

Aristus cleared his throat and answered, "I have no intention of earning any money. The Creator ensures that all of our needs are met. Out of thankfulness for all He has done for us, I am going to the rice fields to do His work. The fields are filled with those who work very hard to earn a living; many die in the process. My goal is to ease their load, and bring them the peace that only the Creator can give."

Trinzic chose this moment to voice his own reasons for going. "Well, now we know that Aristus is crazy, and, as always, gives the strangest answers to the simplest questions. Yet, in spite of those odd social behaviors, he has rescued me from quite a few dire situations. He is my good luck charm, and where he goes, I follow. Isn't that right, my lucky comrade in all things mysterious and wonderful?"

Trinzic gave his signature wink to Aristus, who, in turn, blushed in embarrassment. Aristus tried to keep the conversation moving by shifting the focus back to Angeline. "Um . . . thank you, Trinzic, for your personal take on the situation. Angeline, I believe you said you had two questions. What was the second?"

Angeline bore a determined expression as she replied, "It is not really a question; I just wanted you to know that I will be going with you. It would have been a question, if I had wanted your permission, but I just realized I don't need it."

Aristus looked taken aback by her blunt, cold declaration. He knew that Angeline wasn't a prisoner in their home, and that she was free to leave whenever she wanted. He was mostly surprised by the timing; she hadn't mentioned leaving since the first night she arrived. The whole table was silent, waiting for Aristus' response. He could feel the silence pressing in on him like a huge, unbearable weight. He just sat there, frozen. All he could do was pray for guidance: *I know that you brought this woman to us for a reason. I just ask that you guide my words, and show us our part in your plan for her.*

Just then, the words came to him. "Angeline, I am not going to tell you that you can't come with us, because you are right; you don't need my permission. I am not your father, nor do I ever intend on taking that role. However, if you choose to come, you will see things that will cause you pain. You will be confronted with the truth, and I guarantee that it will not be a pleasant experience. I think you should reconsider staying here; you need more time to heal. Don't you want to be more prepared? I don't want you to make a rash decision. Why not take a little time to think about it?"

Angeline sat in her chair, taking in everything he had said. She raised her pointer finger to indicate she wasn't finished. Aristus set his head in his hands and waited for her response.

"Aristus, when I first arrived here, you told me that Ellie would be my servant; only you may have called it something else. No matter what the exact words were, I have decided that I will be taking the girl with me, based on our verbal agreement. I will consider what you have said about my leaving, and let you know my decision later."

At that moment, Honna interrupted. "No! You can't just take her. Who knows what kinds of evil could befall her under your supervision. Aristus, you have to tell her no."

Aristus placed his hand over Honna's. "You know that it has nothing to do with the protection that Angeline can give. The Creator is the one who has given her this task. He is the one who is in charge of her safety. Besides . . ."

"But she is only a little girl," Honna cut in.

"Honna, please let me finish. I know that you are scared, but just let me finish."

Honna felt a little ashamed and knew that what Aristus was saying was true; she just didn't want to hear it. She sat staring down at the table, with tears welling up in her eyes.

"We know that the Creator has even used infants to accomplish His plans. It is not about Ellie's ability; it is about our willingness to put our trust in Him. We have to believe that He knows what He is doing. Ellie, your mother will pack up your things, and we will await Angeline's decision."

Ellie immediately got up from her chair, grabbed a roll, and headed for her room. As the door closed behind her, the ground began to shake and rumble. Angeline was frightened, until she realized it was just the stones moving. She remembered hearing that same sound the first day she had come to this strange place. She immediately began voicing her thoughts to the group.

"I know that everyone is probably tired of hearing me talk, but just one last question: was that the sound of Ellie leaving this dwelling, and if so, where is she going?"

Aristus perked up for a moment, as he answered her. "She is doing exactly as she has been taught. She has left to speak with our Creator."

"Oh," Angeline replied.

The conversation had died, but Angeline's mind was still processing. *Aristus speaks like he actually thinks that I understand what he is saying,* she thought. *Sometimes I could swear these people aren't even speaking the same language as me.* Angeline ate the rest of her meal in silence, trying to make sense of this family and their strange way of life.

~ Chapter Six ~

The sitting room was filled with people, as well as numerous rice sacks holding supplies. Bowen was running at the large bags, trying to knock them over. Even with all the tension in the room, everyone was grinning as they watched the toddler play; except Trinzic, who was laughing hysterically. Deciding to join in the fun, Trinzic bounded out of his chair to help Bowen set up the heavy sacks for tumbling. The pile was almost chest high when they had finished.

"Now, little Bowen, prepare to be amazed," Trinzic proclaimed. "Stand back and watch a master at work." Trinzic took a few large steps away from the pile, and then began to sprint towards it. At the base, he leapt into the air, flipped over the rice sacks, and gracefully landed on the other side with a bow. Everyone clapped with enthusiasm.

Bowen was grinning from ear to ear, as he squealed, "Bowen amazing, too!" He ran fiercely at the pile, with his face all scrunched up in a determined furrow. He gained speed as he charged up the incline. Just before he reached the peak, his left foot caught on the tip of the hill, and the whole mountain of sacks came crashing down on Trinzic, with Bowen tumbling after them. "Wee . . ." Bowen squealed, as he sailed down the hill, until he came to a sudden stop on Trinzic's chest. "Ta-dah!"

With that, everyone laughed so hard, their sides hurt, including Angeline. Trinzic moved Bowen and the remaining sacks off his chest. Once the bags were all stacked, Trinzic pounced on Bowen and began teasing him. "Steal the show, will you? Well, here's what happens to little showstoppers." Trinzic began to tickle Bowen playfully; he giggled so hard that tears were rolling down his little, pudgy cheeks. Everyone was still laughing, and Angeline wondered if she ever had laughed so hard before.

Suddenly, the laughter stopped. Angeline looked up from her hunched-over stance and saw Ellie standing before them. She was smiling, and Angeline was certain that Ellie had a slight glow as she spoke with authority. "The Creator told me that I am supposed to go with Angeline. I have been chosen to serve her and aid in her metamorphosis."

Tears of pride welled up in Honna's eyes, as she got up from her chair to embrace her daughter. Aristus came up behind them and held his precious girls. He looked up from the family hug to address the others. "It appears as though Honna, Bowen, and Melora are the only ones who will be staying home tonight. Everyone else will be coming along with me; of course, that is assuming that Angeline still desires to join us."

"I have had more than enough time to heal, and I am ready to enter the real world," responded Angeline, matter-of-factly.

"Very well," Aristus replied. "We need to get going before it gets too late." He quickly called Bowen over to him. The little toddler had moist eyes, as he ran to receive a hug from his father. Aristus took in a long breath and held it, while he lovingly squeezed Bowen. He loudly exhaled and then whispered in his son's little ear, "Bowen, I need you to watch over your mother for me. It's really difficult for her when I'm gone. I need you to be brave and be on your best behavior, so that she doesn't miss Ellie and me too much. Now, please go to your mother and let her hold on to you as we leave."

Bowen obeyed his father and ran to Honna with outstretched arms; she scooped him up lovingly. Aristus walked over to his wife and cradled her head in his hands, as he gently gave her a kiss on the forehead. His final loving gesture was a quick kiss to his finger and a delicate touch to her nose. Honna was still blushing as she heard the rumble of the stone. She watched as her family disappeared through their living room wall; all that was left for her was to wait and pray for their safe return.

Kenrick sat in a dark corner of the Majestic Tavern, holding a chalice filled with a bubbling, hot, green liquid called haze. His hood was pulled up over his head to prevent curious stares from anyone who could possibly recognize him. Under the hood, he was sweating with nervous anxiety, as he concentrated on the information Julia had given him. In looking through the material, he grew increasingly concerned. He was beginning to realize he had no idea where he should start. Every mission he had ever done had been with Adlar taking the lead; this was his first time alone. Kenrick closed his eyes and attempted to visualize everything that Adlar had done and said on those missions. While he thought, he could feel his brain throbbing from the mental strain. In his deep concentration, he didn't notice the serving girl who had been seeing to his table, until she tapped him on the shoulder, which caused him to spring to life.

Startled, his killer reflexes automatically set into motion, and he spun effortlessly out of his chair and stationed himself directly behind her. He grabbed hold of her hair, using it to pull her head sharply back. Kenrick then twisted her arm uncomfortably behind her, causing the poor girl to whimper, while tears began to roll steadily down her light-yellow cheeks. Instantly, Kenrick's mental block cleared. His mind pulled him back to one of the many times Adlar had disrespected him, by scolding him like a disobedient child. Kenrick's eyes closed, as he remembered that day...

Adlar had allowed Kenrick to carry out the kill by himself, but it did not go as expected. He had been given the name of the intended victim and had easily tracked him. Everything had appeared to be going according to plan, until he followed the man into a room with three other people. He was already set on finishing the job, so he quickly disposed of all four of them. He knew instantly that Adlar was going to be angered by the larger than necessary body count, and he had been right.

Adlar had come into the room, figuratively breathing fire. His face was contorted in anger, as he berated Kenrick. "You can't even begin to understand the trouble that you have caused me. You have left a horrible, sickening mess for me to clean up! I gave you an opportunity to prove that you possessed some skill beyond being an above-average guard, but instead you have proven to me that you are merely reckless. You have broken almost every code that an assassin is supposed to follow, along with every rule of common sense."

Adlar closed his eyes and took one long, deep breath before he continued his scolding. "Now Kenrick, you will leave this place and cower in some alley. When I am finished cleaning up your mess, I will come and find you."

Kenrick had no other recourse but to obey; he found a nearby alley to sulk in. After an hour of waiting, Kenrick felt strong hands grab ahold of his shoulders. Adlar's voice rang painfully in his ears. "Careless waste, I have just saved your life; and now you will return the favor by listening carefully to what I am about to say. If you choose to ignore my advice, you will prove yourself unworthy of being an assassin.

"There are five rules that every assassin needs to respect and obey. First, always know everything about the person who is hiring you; never accept a job solely on the amount that you are being paid. Second, remember that an assassin must always be aware of his surroundings, carefully observing his target from a distance before he strikes. During this studying phase, it is vital that you remain detached from the victim; lest you hesitate and die in his/her place. Third, the assassin's name must always remain a mystery. Once an assassin becomes known, he becomes a target for revenge. Fourth, never kill someone who is innocent, like a child or widow, because there is too much guilt and remorse connected with them. The final rule for an assassin is to never let your guard down; never allow yourself to trust anyone. Basically, if you have failed to see how these principles apply to you, let me clarify: killing three extra men draws far too much attention to yourself! Never be this sloppy again, or I promise that you won't be able to live with yourself!"

Kenrick's mind gradually drifted back to the tavern and his predicament. He felt uncomfortable as he looked into the tear-filled eyes of the serving girl; he didn't know whether he should apologize or let her go. Maybe he could make her feel like it was her fault for disturbing him. Kenrick hated social situations; he had no idea how to relate to people, especially females.

While he was standing there, contemplating his next move, his grip gradually began to loosen. As his hold on the girl relaxed, she managed to free herself from his grasp. Once free, the serving girl gave Kenrick a quick jab to his gut, and then forcefully stomped on his foot. He doubled over, barely able to see the girl disappear out of sight. Immediately, he noticed the tavern had become unnervingly silent, and that all eyes were focused on him. Kenrick quickly took stock of his situation and decided he should find a different tavern in which to lodge. He grabbed his leather bag and quickly slipped out the door.

After Kenrick stepped out onto the quartz walkway, he walked until he was standing directly in front of an onyx lamppost. The lamp had four lights spiraling upward; each ball of light set elegantly in the mouth of a ruby-eyed serpent. Kenrick set his bag down at his feet and leaned against the cold stone. His head touched the lamppost; slowly, he arched his head upward to relax under the lights. Gazing at the serpents felt good; it was easy to visualize himself as one of these creatures. They shared his predatory instincts and symbolized his need for power.

In the quiet of the street, Kenrick whispered to himself, "Why have I been so nervous about this? I know what I'm doing. I have all the information I need in my bag. I will go where she lives, study her habits, hide in the shadows, and wait for my moment to strike. I must prepare myself to be unseen."

In the midst of his thoughts, a carriage came rattling down the street in front of him; this was what he had been waiting for. Kenrick pulled down his hood and whistled. The coachman brought his carriage to a stop. He casually walked over and motioned for the coachman, who leaned down so

Kenrick could whisper in his ear. The coachman listened intently and then nodded. The man only said one thing in response: "Kid, are you sure you want to go to a place like that?"

Kenrick resented being referred to as a child, so he intentionally ignored the man and entered the carriage. He leaned his head against the back of the seat; it had been a long time since he could afford being transformed by an alterations expert. *This should be fun,* he thought to himself.

~ Chapter Seven ~

The rocks were still crashing behind them, as they trekked up and down the forming stairs. Angeline hated the constant thundering rumble of the rocks, as they turned back into a solid wall behind them. She was in a state of perpetual fear that the rocks would rebel against them, and they would be encased in stone forever. Her shoulders were raised, as if someone was pouring cold water down her spine. The group had been traveling all night, and they were all feeling exhausted. If she hadn't been so scared, Angeline would have fallen asleep hours ago. To add to her frustration, Aristus was still walking at the same rate as when they had begun.

Just when she thought she couldn't take another step, Trinzic turned around. "Angeline, are you enjoying our little scenic adventure? I am always one for a light walk to stretch the old tendons."

She looked at Trinzic, as though he had just grown another head. "Maybe your tendons have been stretched," she said, once the shock had dissipated, "but mine have been going through the worst torture imaginable."

Trinzic ignored her gruff tone and chuckled, "Well then, you should be pleased to hear that in a few moments, this portion of our journey will be over. I believe that we are almost there."

This was welcome news to Angeline, and it gave her a burst of energy. She lurched forward, shoving past Trinzic. She didn't want to spend another second in this death trap! In passing him, she was able to catch sight of the wall opening up ahead of her. Light was streaming through the crack. Finally, they had arrived.

Once everyone had walked through the opening and had gathered together, Aristus addressed the group. "I know that we are all exhausted, but our journey is not quite over. We needed to come out in a quiet spot; I didn't want to draw any unwanted attention. We still have a little further to walk; please keep quiet, and follow me to the Wentworth's home."

Angeline glanced over the grotesque alleyway and quietly groaned. She had hoped the home they were going to would be far removed from this impoverished and dirty place, but she was wrong. When they arrived at the front door of the Wentworth's home, Angeline rudely interjected, "Are you all playing some kind of a sick joke on me? We can't possibly stay in a place like this! What kind of people would work with garbage for a living? I will not lower myself by associating with waste-walkers."

Aristus turned about sharply. "Of course you would say something like that. Do you ever think before you speak? Where would you have us stay?

Nevermind; it doesn't matter. Either you can stay here with the rest of us, or you can spend the night sleeping in the alley by yourself. If you choose to grace us with your presence, I never want to hear you refer to the Wentworth family as waste-walkers ever again! You have no idea what kind of people they are. They are priceless to me; not societal garbage meant for you to throw away."

Angeline was surprised to hear Aristus raise his voice at her; so surprised, in fact, that she even mumbled an apology. At her words, Aristus' face noticeably softened. "Angeline, I am sorry. I didn't mean lose my temper. I just wanted you to understand how highly I value the Wentworths. I owe them my life, and I guess I'm a little protective of them." There was a long pause, and then Aristus cleared his throat and turned to the door. "Well, I suppose we shouldn't stand out here all day, spending our time in fruitless arguments. Let's announce ourselves."

Aristus put his mouth around the welcome horn and blew lightly into it. The old horn almost sounded squeaky, as it musically announced their arrival. Not long after the welcome horn was blown, the sound of shuffling feet made its way slowly to the rusty metal door. The inner latch was released, and the door swung open to reveal a tiny little fellow standing at about half the size of Trinzic. The old man jumped comically in response to discovering Aristus behind the door and gave him a big hug. When the man released him, he opened his arms wide to receive a running Ellie.

"Simeon!"

As they embraced, Simeon Wentworth lost his footing, and the two of them fell to the ground laughing. Simeon had a long, full beard, accompanied by a dual spiraling mustache and numerous black smudges littering his face. Angeline glanced at his fingers and saw that they were tipped with black soot, which was transferring onto everyone he touched. She could feel her skin beginning to crawl, as she watched her companions touch Simeon affectionately. She wondered how they could let such a filthy man touch them. Not only was he dirty and short, but he was old as well. Then she remembered Melora, and how Honna had cared for that cripple like she was family.

"This family has disgusting habits," she whispered under her breath. Angeline remembered back to when she was a child and her last recollection of her grandparents. When they became old, and a burden to her parents, her father sold all of her grandparents' possessions and used half of the money to move them into a Home of Remembrance. These homes of remembrance were deceptively titled, because they were not a place to remember people but to forget about them. Once Angeline's family had placed her grandparents in this home, she never saw them again. She shuttered as she recalled her grandfather's tear-filled plea.

"I'm still useful! I'm still valuable! Please don't leave us in this horrible place. We just want to go home! Please." All the while, her grandmother just sat in a chair, quietly weeping with her head in her hands.

In revisiting this odd event from her childhood, something began to stir within her; something that caused her to wonder what ultimately happened to her grandparents. She wasn't sure if she was feeling more curiosity or concern for their possible suffering, but whatever the feeling, it was troubling her. Angeline's mind was so engrossed in attempting to process these foreign emotions and thoughts that she hardly noticed herself gliding past Simeon and patting him on the head.

Simeon, who had been holding the door, thought it strange that she had touched him; and though he desired to strike up a casual conversation, something inside him told him to remain quiet. He simply watched as she moved past him and carefully closed the door, so as not to disturb her thoughts.

Angeline was now standing in the main hallway. Her deep, inner reflection had brought her to somewhat of a conclusion; the realization that her family had always been saturated with betrayal. Aristus and Honna cared more for strangers than her whole family cared for one another. It was no wonder that her own sister was the one who had betrayed her. In her family, everyone lived for themselves, with only the Code of Glamour in common, authorizing every deceitful action. That code was still so much a part of her that she felt guilty questioning it; almost as if it were a living companion that would punish her for her unbelief. With this last thought, she set her bag down and slowly entered back into reality. Her eyes began to survey her new surroundings.

The home was essentially one large room, with wrought-iron railings set up to define the various spaces. There was one long hallway that ran the length of the home, and ended at the mouth of an enormous, glowing incinerator. She knew the waste-walkers used this method of burning to dispose of garbage. The whole back wall was covered with large, iron-pull boxes; each one labeled for its individual contents. The labels read: metal, glass, leather, silks, useful scraps, and burning. There were four open workstations that proceeded out from the furnace. One had pieces of leather and silk hanging on different stands. It contained a large table that had a partially sewn quilt lying flat across it, much like the one she had seen Melora wrapped in. The station adjoining the quilt shop contained furniture in various stages of completion. On the other side, there was a station packed full of reed crates containing a variety of items. Most crates were so full that many of them were overflowing.

The last station was the most remarkable; it was a glass shop. This station captured Angeline's complete attention. It was a unique space that was almost completely enclosed with two enormous stained-glass windows hanging on hooks from the ceiling, each suspended only a few inches above each metal railing. They were masterfully crafted and intricately detailed. Angeline felt compelled to get a closer look. Her eyes widened, as she made her way into the adjoining station and stepped right up to the stained glass wall. The colors took her breath away and her hands trembled, as she reached out to feel the color with her fingertips.

Angeline closed her eyes and whispered, "I wonder what historic tale you have captured within your glass. Your color is mesmerizing."

A small voice, filled with excitement, answered her question. "This is the story of our beginning; it explains how we arrived in the mountain. It is a sad story, but the story on the other side is my favorite." Ellie's arms were neatly positioned behind her, with her eyes inquisitively staring up at her.

It bothered Angeline that she had never heard of this story. She was very intrigued and would not allow her pride to keep her from finding out more. "I need to know who created this complex master-piece. I wish to speak to the artist, so that I may understand what kind of person, working in this kind of dismal trash heap, could accomplish this."

Ellie hopped giddily in response to Angeline's request. "Opella made this story window! I know she would be really excited to tell you about it. I could run to fetch her right now, if you would like."

Angeline flicked her wrist in Ellie's face. Ellie understood and ran off to find Opella. Angeline turned her attention back to the window, and her large, black eyes danced with the reflecting colors from the glass as she waited for Ellie to return.

The carriage jerked as it pulled to a halt. Kenrick's hand quivered, as he pulled back the silk curtain.

The left corner of his mouth curled steadily upward, revealing a half smile. The task of acquiring an alterations expert had proven to be easier than he had anticipated. The leather door swung easily open, as Kenrick made his soundless exit. He placed a solitary finger against his lips as he approached the coachman. Kenrick's hand moved steadily down to his satchel to retrieve five golden coins, which he carefully placed into the man's open hand. The coachman responded with a pleased nod, and then both men silently parted company.

Kenrick's feet shifted nervously, as he stood before a crumbling, nameless storefront. It appeared to be an old bookstore, but Kenrick knew from experience that he had reached the correct destination. He inhaled deeply as he moved through the old metal door. Once he was through it, he was greeted by a slender woman, painting her fingernails behind a large, marble desk.

She smiled flirtatiously as she addressed him. "Welcome, stranger. Are you here for a change of mind or a life change? Or, perhaps you've come for something else?"

Kenrick felt his cheeks burning beneath his dark, blue face paint. He quickly mumbled the code phrase: "Beauty by birth or beauty by distortion; all is the same."

"Well, aren't we formal? I could tell the moment you walked in the door that you weren't here for a mind change. Not that I thought you needed a life transformation; you look just fine to me," she said with a wink.

Kenrick was enjoying the advances of this woman, but he needed to get started on his alteration. This being the case, he changed the tone of the conversation. "Just show me where I get the alteration. I didn't come here to listen to your annoying little sales pitch; I'm ready to get this started."

The woman's smile vanished. She pushed in her chair sharply and motioned for him to follow her. Kenrick winced, as he heard the chair hit the marble desk; he was already beginning to regret his decision to speak harshly to this attractive desk attendant. He kept his distance while he followed her to a rusty door at the very back of the shop. Forcefully, she ushered Kenrick quickly into the room.

He turned reluctantly to face her as she mechanically addressed him. "Please sit here while the esteemed expert of alterations, Fenton Michaels, finishes with a client. He should be with you shortly. I'm sure you have heard this before, but since we are being so formal, I'll tell you anyway. Your visit here with Fenton will be kept in the utmost confidence. We promise you that any pain or discomfort you experience will be a small price to pay for perfection. Enjoy your wait, alone."

After finishing her speech, she walked out the door, leaving Kenrick alone in an unsettling room. A wide assortment of alteration devices hung upon the wall like trophies. Kenrick's eyes were having a difficult time adjusting to the extreme darkness. His hand reached out to feel the sharp, metal instruments that were dangling directly above his head. He surmised that the room was probably kept dark for secrecy; which was something he appreciated for his own purposes, but disliked for the uneasy feeling that was growing in the pit of his stomach. While he sat, his mind began to wander. *Why do they make these places so creepy? For being a place that makes people beautiful, it could sure use a dose of its own medicine.*

Kenrick's mental complaints were interrupted by the sound of a door creaking open and feet shuffling towards him. The door to the reception area pulled open and light streamed through, pouring over Kenrick's face. The man exiting through the door covered his face, obviously trying to hide his identity.

"Good," Kenrick mumbled. "I'm ready to get this whole thing over with." The door to the alterations room had been left wide open, and Kenrick felt as though it was beckoning him to enter. He cautiously got up from the cold bench and made his way to the open door. As he walked through, he found himself staring at a stone, operating table. Kenrick wasted no time; he quickly laid himself down and placed both of his arms casually behind his head. He began absentmindedly gazing up at the ceiling until the sound of light breathing reached his ears. His head turned toward the noise, and his dark eyes focused in on Fenton Michaels.

Fenton strolled right up to the operating table and peered down at him. His silver lips pleasantly transformed into a fixed smile, as he addressed his patient. "You need me to provide you with a transformation? What do you desire? What must be altered?"

"All I need is a simple dye job. The color I require is black, with a tinge of brown. My whole body must be colored. Basically, I am looking for camouflage; I want to be made invisible."

Fenton's voice was soaked with disappointment. "That simple, huh? Are you positive that is what you want? I could alter your face to make you appear taller, smarter, or even more intimidating. Perhaps you would be interested in a different body shape?"

Kenrick's face began to contort, as he shot back a reply. "I don't trust anyone with a knife near my face! Besides, I rather enjoy how my face currently looks. You can fool others into mutilating themselves, but I only need to be dyed. So, silver hair, can you do that for me or not?"

Fenton simply nodded. "The dying tub is this way. Follow me."

Kenrick followed Fenton up a few gradual stairs and behind a large, burgundy curtain. Once there, Kenrick lazily stripped down while Fenton filled a large, metal tub with black dye and hot water. After Fenton had finished setting everything up, he helped his client into the dark water, making sure to fold his wings carefully behind him.

When Kenrick was submerged up to his neck, Fenton began to explain the procedure. "In just a moment, I am going to give you this straw, which will allow you to breathe. Once you have practiced breathing through this tube, I will lower the large press hanging above your head onto your chest.

This will hold you under the water, and in place, for an exact hour. You will need these special eye lenses to prevent dye from entering your eyes, along with earplugs to protect your ears. At the end of the hour, several thousand needles will be injected into your flesh to complete the process. I think that's about everything; are you ready to begin?"

Kenrick quickly sat up in the tub and yelled, "What did you say? You are planning to plunge thousands of needles into me? Didn't I just explain how I dislike sharp things near my face? No! A simple dye job is what I want, none of your sick and twisted torture. Got that, you disturbed fool?"

Fenton compressed his lips and then let out a low chuckle. "I took you for a man who favored results over comfort. This procedure may cause some intense discomfort, but it will take at least three months for your body to work this dye out of your system. It is a particularly unique formula that I designed myself. It will enable you to blend into any shadow; imagine the advantage of being invisible to your prey. Have I convinced you now, assassin?"

Kenrick was scared, infuriated, and intrigued. He didn't understand how Fenton had figured out that he was an assassin. His mind debated over Fenton's words. He knew that above all else, he didn't want Fenton to think he was weak. "Sure, let's try it your way, but if I'm at all dissatisfied, I'll cut you and your fee in half."

Fenton grinned. "Oh, you won't be sorry. I guarantee you'll be more than satisfied."

Kenrick's eyes narrowed as Fenton walked towards him, handing over the straw. The young assassin practiced breathing a few times, and then allowed the expert to place the eye lenses, ear-plugs, and straw carefully in their correct locations. Fenton's face was expressionless while lowering the large press onto Kenrick's chest. Kenrick could feel the pressure, as he was forced under the water. His body instantly started to rebel by lightly spasming. Kenrick knew he needed to stop himself from pan-icking, or else he was about to swallow a deadly amount of dye. He took a controlled, deep breath through his straw. This allowed his mind to go blank, and his body to become comfortably numb. Rhythmic breaths became his only focus as time moved slowly by.

Fenton watched the last piece of sand fall into a nearby hourglass. He got up from his chair and pulled a long steel lever, causing the rectangular injection device to fall. This bed of needles locked into the press, then sprung immediately from the tub. Dark bloody water rolled over the tub's sides, as Kenrick sat up. Fenton moved behind him and placed a cold moss towel over his quivering shoul-ders. Kenrick felt immediate relief from the pul-sating pain that had enveloped him. Fenton carefully pulled him out of the water, then led him away from the tub and removed the towel. Cold water sprayed from a hose directly above him. The water washed down his body, removing the excess blood and dye; this whole ordeal left Kenrick feeling confused and disorientated. Fenton then covered Kenrick with a fresh moss towel and led him to an impressive, standing mirror. With trembling hands, Kenrick removed his protective eye lenses. The sight that greeted him almost caused him to topple over; he looked like a creature of darkness. From the top of his wings to the bottoms of his feet, he was black, completely covered. He felt invisible, strange, and powerful.

Then he turned to Fenton. "You have transformed me! Whatever your fee, it was worth all the pain and money to get these kind of results."

Fenton was beaming in response to Kenrick's praise. "Now that is what I love to hear. My attendant will receive your payment at the front desk and escort you out. It has been a pleasure altering you."

"Aren't you worried that I'll run out and not pay?"

Fenton smiled knowingly. "Remember, I told you that the dye would work its way out of your system in three months. Once someone has had a taste of my life changes, they always return. I'm the only one who has the power to change your life. You can't live without me. You'll pay."

Kenrick looked fearfully at Fenton through his natural black eyes, realizing that this man had power over him. He knew he would have to return for more alterations. It was strange how the same event could make him feel so powerful, and then so bound.

Kenrick dressed and walked through the door. Upon entering the waiting room, he saw a short, slightly round woman. She nervously looked toward the door he had just opened, but obviously couldn't see him in the darkness. He moved into a dark corner of the room and carefully observed the girl. He had become more than he bargained for, and his expectations had been surpassed; yet he hated how he envied this naive girl. If only she understood that she was throwing herself away. She was selling herself to Fenton, and she would gladly pay him to do it. Fenton would soon have a new pet; should he warn her?

Kenrick watched with disdain, as the girl slowly moved from the stone bench and walked through the beckoning door. He shivered and wondered again if the girl realized what she was doing. He shook his head; of course not. She was already gone; it was too late now. Why would he help her anyway? What was wrong with him?

Kenrick realized he was still wearing his earplugs. With a quivering hand, he yanked them from his head and threw them against the wall. He decided to blame his momentary compassion on his plugged ears. It wasn't logical, but it was enough to help Kenrick regain focus. He moved like a shadow, prepared to pay his price for alteration.

~ *Chapter Eight* ~

*E*llie found Opella busily working in the kitchen. Her little hand reached up and pulled lightly on Opella's patchwork dress to gain her attention.

Opella smiled lovingly down on her. "Hello, Ellie. How can I help you?"

"My friend Angeline wants to hear you tell the story of beginnings. Would you tell her now, Opella, please?"

Opella set her metal-mixing spoon down and looked into Ellie's eyes. "Dear child, nothing brings my heart more joy than telling that story, but I'm afraid that I have almost finished making a meal for everyone. And a good story is always better received on a full stomach. Please bring your friend to the table, so we can all eat together. Then, after everyone is too full to eat anymore, we will gather by the furnace for a story."

Ellie excitedly ran off to bring everyone to the table. The news of a story spread quickly to the rest of the company; dinner was soon over. Ellie shoved the last remaining roll into her mouth and pulled Angeline from the table. Within minutes, everyone was sitting comfortably in front of the incinerator.

Ellie passed out warm quilts and spiced tea, in preparation for the story. Opella politely asked Aristus and Trinzic to take down the stained glass window and chain it in front of the furnace. They both agreed and grabbed two long, receiving poles to help lower the window, which moved easily on the poles and hooked right into the ceiling.

It was a stunning sight. Angeline stared open-mouthed at the beauty of the artwork displayed before her. When the light from the furnace streamed through the window, the color shot through it like dancing fire; blanketing everything and causing the picture to come alive. Angeline looked at her gray hands and smiled, as they changed color in the light. Her gaze shifted gradually from her hands back to the window, the source of the streaming color.

Opella prepared herself to tell the story by reciting a simple prayer. "Please, Creator, be in this place and enable me to be true to your message. Open our ears and our hearts to the love you have for us."

Angeline examined Opella as she prayed. She had noticed that Opella was at least two inches taller than her husband. She was a thin wisp of a woman, with a light, delicate frame. She had the face of a youth, and her hair was white and curly, with soft, pink ribbons woven into it. Opella's voice was like a melodic song, as she began the mysterious tale of beginnings.

The Story of Beginnings

"In the beginning, the universe was blank, like an artist's canvas. The Creator waited in the still. Before time, He was there in the void. His voice resonated across the emptiness, creating the shell form of our world, spherical and magnificent. This empty shell He filled with water. His spirit moved purposefully over our now watery world, pushing the waters down to create a space between the water and the air. Then the universe exploded with light.

"His gaze focused lovingly down upon our now forgotten world. He made soil and rocks to divide the liquid depths. Then our blessed Maker hung a brilliant ball of light in the sky to govern the day. For the time of darkness, He blanketed the sky with countless shimmering lights, accompanied by a pale, glowing orb He named the moon; even in the darkness, there would always be a light. Now that there was light, He made creatures and colorful plants to inhabit this world. The last thing He created were beings that would reflect His glorious image. He called them the children of the sky; male and female, He created them. To the men, He gave strong, feathered wings to reflect the strength and protective nature of the Creator. To the women, He gave fragile, yet beautiful, fluttering wings to display the gentleness and beauty that also could be found in the Creator Himself.

"These children of the sky were intended to inhabit this perfect world, a place without even the knowledge of evil. He withheld this knowledge from them, so that they would be kept safe, and so the world could remain unblemished. This protection was only part of His love; He also gave them the free choice to love Him. The Creator knew, in His infinite wisdom, that unless love was freely given, it was not love at all. He never forced His creation to love or obey Him, but they did nonetheless. These children spent individual time each day with their Creator. They flew in the skies with Him, talking and exploring the world that had been created for them to enjoy and nurture.

"The love that the Creator had for His special creation was beyond comprehension. When the Creator formed the world, He trapped everything dark and evil into an onyx mountain. He placed it in the center of a clear lake to keep His children from lingering too close. Concerning this mountain, He gave the people of the sky only one rule: never enter the mountain gate. If anyone were to cross its threshold, they would be trapped inside, forever separated from the Creator. Apart from His presence, they would no longer be able to fly. They would be transformed by the evil, and become something different, something dark.

"Years of wonder and mystery passed beautifully by. Our world was peaceful and perfect, completely devoid of fear and pain. Until the day a stranger appeared from the mountain. His name was Apollyon, and he gathered everyone to the center of town. 'You fools! What are you doing on this side of the river? I have come to bring you to your true home in the mountain. Come with me and become your own creator. Your precious maker has lied to you. The only thing He fears is that you will become as powerful as He is. Come with me and taste true power.'

"The children of the sky glanced around to see if their Creator would respond, but all was quiet. The Creator, in His love, was allowing His children to decide whom they would listen to and trust.

"After a moment had passed, the first couple the Creator had made yelled from the crowd, 'How can you prove that we will become stronger than the Creator? Why should we trust you?'

"A sly smile spread like magic across Apollyon's face. 'I will give you no reason to trust me, but if you refuse to follow me, you will always wonder if you could have been better. Every day, you gaze at a mountain you know nothing about. Aren't you curious what the Creator has hidden from you?'

"The children of the sky agreed to place their trust in this outsider, and together they flew across the Crystal Lake. They followed Apollyon eagerly through the wide door and into the dark mountain. Once inside, the stone beneath their feet began to rumble. An enormous boulder fell: blocking the light, their escape, and all hope. As the Creator had warned, they were trapped! Instantly, the once children of the sky screamed out in anguish, as the darkness stole their color and turned their eyes black as coal. They felt their wings grow heavy and knew they had lost their ability to fly. Their selfish desires had deceived them into betraying the one who created and loved them.

"The Creator wept. His children had chosen to believe the words of Apollyon, the keeper of death, over the words of their loving Maker, who had always proven to be trustworthy. They had betrayed the one who had given them life.

"For all who hear this tale, you are not a child of the mountain; you are a child of the sky. This is was our story of betrayal. Each of us is born with this message stirring within us. He is calling to you, whispering always of His love and His desire for us to seek Him and find Him. Please answer the Creator's song, and return home."

The light still danced across Opella's gentle face as she finished the story. Angeline felt goose-bumps running along her forearm. She began rubbing her chilled arms as she surveyed the room. Almost everyone, excluding Trinzic, had tears rolling down their cheeks. Angeline noticed that her eyes were dry. She wasn't sad; she was scared. Her mind began to ask questions. What if the story was true? Was it possible that everything she had ever known could be wrong?

Simeon walked up to his wife and gave her a gentle kiss on the cheek. He placed his hand in hers and addressed the group. "The story of beginnings is so beautiful, and yet so tragic. I don't wish to take anything away from this amazing story. Therefore, let us pray and get some rest. 'Oh, faithful Creator, thank you for speaking to us tonight. Please allow your truth to transform us into your children of the sky and light. Bless us with your healing and rest, and prepare us for the work we have tomorrow. In the name of your sacrifice, we ask your help.'"

As the prayer ended, Trinzic and Aristus put the beautiful glass window back in its place. Angeline thought how wrong it seemed to use that gorgeous window as a wall; it was really meant to display light. Her thought was interrupted by Ellie, who was pulling lightly on her sleeve.

"What do you want?" Angeline harshly exclaimed.

Ellie's eyes were beaming. "What did you think?"

Angeline knew that Ellie was expecting some emotional, life-changing response from her, but Angeline couldn't stop staring at her sickeningly sweet smile. Angeline hated making other people happy. She forced an icy stare directly into Ellie's wide eyes. "I'm not sure what I thought of it. All I know is that my legs still hurt from walking, and I'm so tired my head is beginning to throb. You need to show me where I will be sleeping. Then you will sing for me. Yes, that is exactly what I need right now. Let's hurry, before I am overcome by my exhaustion, and I fall asleep in this filthy place."

Ellie's face dropped momentarily. Then she reached out for Angeline's hand and escorted her to the upper loft. The loft was filled with beds; Angeline tested each one carefully, until she found one she deemed suitable for sleep. Her body ached, as she crawled into bed, rolled onto her side, and carefully pulled the quilt up to her ear. Ellie sat upon the adjacent cot and began to sing. She watched Angeline's eyes begin to flutter. She sang the song two more times. When the last note hummed, she knelt at the side of her bed. There she quietly prayed for Angeline. Ellie fell fast asleep, with her last whispered words still on her lips. "Precious Creator, please help Angeline to see how much you love her."

~ *Chapter Nine* ~

*A*ngeline was awakened by two eager, little hands pressing persistently down on her shoulder; the pushing was followed by the sound of Ellie's voice excitedly repeating, "Wake up! Wake up! It's time for us to get going. You won't believe what we get to do today."

Angeline lazily pulled herself out of bed, feeling stiff and uncomfortable from sleeping in her clothes. She changed into something clean and followed Ellie down the spiral staircase, and into the kitchen. When she got there, everyone was already seated at the dining table, still full from the large breakfast Opella had prepared. Angeline sat in an open chair. Opella gently set a plate before her and poured a large glass of waterberry tea. Everyone stared at Angeline, as she ate her food. They had obviously been awake for hours, patiently waiting for her to grace them with her presence. Angeline ate her food slowly, enjoying every bite as well as their attention.

Once she had finished, Aristus cleared his throat. "Alright, today we will be dividing into two groups. Opella, Ellie, and Angeline will be going to Cheshire Street to rescue those being led away to death, while

85

Trinzic, Simeon, and I will be going to the rice fields to harvest." Aristus focused his attention on Angeline, and his voice became understanding as he addressed her. "Angeline, before we leave, you must understand that you are not obligated to join us. You can choose to stay here, or even leave, if you so desire. We would love for you to come, but I want to warn you that it is going to be dangerous, especially for you. Whatever you decide, we will support you."

Angeline was still tired and wasn't completely sure she understood what Aristus was inviting her to do. She wondered why he would be sending an old woman and a child to save lives, while the men went to do a little manual labor. A few days ago, she would have packed her few possessions and left: but after yesterday's story, Angeline knew she wanted to study this family more, to better understand why they behaved the way they did. It would be nice to not be confused by their odd behavior all the time. Angeline looked at Aristus and calmly replied, "Actually, I would love to go."

Aristus and Trinzic looked at Angeline with stunned expressions; it took a few moments for Aristus to respond. "Well, good. Let's get our things together and get moving." Ellie helped Angeline get ready. Quickly, the two small groups set out to leave, ready to begin their specific assignments.

Cheshire Street was damp and poorly lit. There was only one lamppost on the street, and it sporadically flickered on and off. The street was littered with a strange variety of broken-down shops.

A shady-looking tavern and a large, gray building appeared to be the only functioning establishments on the whole block.

While they walked down the stone sidewalk, Angeline felt unnerved as Ellie's small, chilled hand slipped into hers. Angeline felt vulnerable in this place, and something about this street made her skin crawl. She turned her head in the direction of Opella's ear and whispered, "Where, exactly, are we going?"

Opella's voice was matter-of-fact in her response: "The shop of an orb handler".

Angeline froze in place. Her hands and lips began to quiver. "An orb handler! Why would we be going there? No one goes there unless they have something to hide or dispose of."

Ellie was the one to answer. "Don't you remember? The Creator wants us to save lives."

Angeline snapped. "Yes, I understood that part! I am growing weary of your cryptic language. You should have mentioned we were going to an orb handler before we left. Why would anyone embark on such a pointless, disgraceful task? I have success-fully avoided ever having to deal with an orb han-dler. I would think people like you would especially avoid such places."

Ellie just pulled on Angeline, who continued to walk reluctantly with them until they stopped in front of a gray building. They stood there, in the eerie silence, for a moment. Then Opella reached her hand out to Angeline. "Dear one, we are doing what the Creator has designed us to do, which makes us more than merely happy. It satisfies our souls and brings us great joy, because we have a divine purpose. These lives that are being snuffed out are valued and loved by the Creator. He has a plan and purpose for each of them, just as He has a plan and purpose for you. We have been commissioned to love all those who provide us with an opportunity; this is an opportunity."

Angeline found Opella's answer unsatisfying; she pondered how joy could be different than happiness. She had been happy plenty of times, but she wasn't sure that she had ever experienced joy.

Opella spoke again, before Angeline could respond, with another question. "Before we begin, we must talk with the Creator. Ellie, love, would you speak on our behalf?"

"Yes, please." Ellie closed her eyes and tilted her head towards the cavern sky. "Dearest Creator, thank you for letting me come today. Please, be with us, and help your light to shine through us. Help us to save many little lives today. Love you, your child Ellie."

"Thank you, Ellie. That was perfect. It is almost time. Now, who is going to be the voice, and who wishes to be the strength?"

Angeline blurted out a quick response, "I am just here to watch; I want no part of this craziness."

Ellie pulled on Opella's sleeve. "Can I be the voice? I'm ready."

Opella knelt down, placing both hands gently on Ellie. Her eyes were glistening with awe. "Little one, you are fearless. Being the voice is still difficult for me." Opella took a slow, thoughtful breath and continued. "I think you will make a fine voice. Angeline and I will stand in the alley, and give you all the strength and support we can."

Opella handed Ellie a medium-sized leather pouch, accompanied by a small purse of coins. Then, she escorted Angeline to the alley. Once there, Opella started praying with her eyes tightly closed, while Angeline silently stared at Ellie; all alone on the dark street. Angeline's heart was racing. It was hard even for her to watch a child standing alone in a place like this. Ellie was pacing in front of the gray building, looking occasionally behind her.

Angeline was the first to see someone moving quickly through the darkness towards Ellie. It was a woman dressed in a sparkling, ruby cape. The woman was trembling, keeping her head turned, looking behind as she walked. The constant looking over her shoulder caused her to walk directly into Ellie. Ellie grabbed onto the woman's cape instinctively, trying to keep herself from toppling over. It worked, but the cape fell from the woman's shoulders, revealing a bright, glowing orb that was positioned right between her wings.

The woman looked down at Ellie, with tear-filled eyes. "I'm sorry. I guess I didn't see you there. Could I have my cloak back, please?"

Ellie's eyes stared right into the woman's moist eyes. "I know why you are here. You are going to sell your child to the orb handler. Please let me take care of it. I promise I will find someone who would make a good mother for your baby. If you go to the orb handler, you will always wonder, when you walk under a streetlight, whether or not that flickering light is that of your child's life leaving. Please, miss, have mercy."

The woman's tears were beginning to flow more steadily. "Why do you care so much for my orb? Strange child, why are you even here..." She paused and looked nervously around, "in this dangerous place, all by yourself?"

Ellie reached out to hold the woman's hand. She squeezed it firmly. "My name is Ellie. I'm here because the Creator loves you and your baby. He sent me to tell you that He knows how much you're hurting, how scared you are, and that He is the only one who can truly help you. Please give me the chance to show His love for you."

The woman frowned a little under her tears and lowered her voice into a desperate, teary whisper. "I can't have this thing growing on my back. I just can't! You are just a little girl; you can't possibly understand what I am going through!"

"I may be a little girl, but I know that you don't want to hurt your baby."

The woman turned away and began to sob. "You're right. I just didn't have anywhere else to go. Please, just get this thing off of me. I will not be bound to this mistake. If you don't take it, I'll have to sell it to him. I don't want to, but I will!"

Ellie turned her head towards the alley and signaled for Opella to join her. Angeline nudged Opella's arm to get her attention. Opella's face bore a determined frown, as she quickly ran to Ellie. Upon reaching them, Opella quickly set herself to the task before her. First, her hand soothingly rubbed the woman's shoulder. Her voice was gentle as she spoke. "Everything will be fine; just hold tightly onto Ellie's hand. Now, please kneel on your cape and look towards the ground."

Once the woman was in place, Opella rested her knee on the woman's spine. She then clutched the ball tightly in both hands. Her lips recited a silent prayer, and then she pulled hard. The orb made a popping sound, as it dislodged from its socket, causing Opella to stumble backwards. Angeline ran from the alley towards them, with her arms outstretched, prepared to catch her, but she had been too far away. Opella fell to the ground. Some fabric from her shoulder was torn, revealing a nasty bruise, but she had managed to protect the orb with her body. Opella handed the glowing sphere to Angeline, so that she could get up without risking it breaking.

Angeline felt awkward, holding the fragile orb in her hands; never in her life had she bothered to look at an orb before. She was surprised at how remarkable it was. Through the clear shell, she could see the tiny child moving, almost dancing, in the liquid light. Her eyes stayed focused on the orb, as it rolled out of her hands, disappearing silently into Ellie's leather bag.

Opella helped the woman stand up; then she placed a small piece of parchment into her cape pocket. "If you ever desire to know peace, remember this piece of parchment; it may help you find it. Hopefully, this will not be our last encounter. I pray that we will meet again."

The woman pulled her cape back over her shoulders; then pursed her lips as though she wanted to ask something. She wiped the last remaining tear from her eye, as she glanced at Ellie and the bag. She turned abruptly around and ran toward a carriage tucked away in the shadows.

At the end of a very long day, Ellie had seven orbs nestled safely in her bag. Angeline wrung her hands together; they were wet and sticky from the damp alley, and she was stiff from standing. Exhausted and ready to go home, Angeline began to complain verbally to Opella.

"Haven't we saved enough lives for today? I am hungry and tired. Have you forgotten that Ellie is supposed to be serving me?"

Opella smiled at Angeline. "Don't worry. The orb handler's shop will be closing soon. Then we can return home."

Angeline stopped her complaining and returned her attention to Ellie, who was speaking to a brightly painted orange woman. The woman began shrieking at Ellie in a high-pitched voice. Ellie's tone never changed; every word was calm and respectful. The orange woman grabbed Ellie's arm and spit into her face. The child appeared unshaken, as she continued pleading for the orb. Suddenly, the woman pushed Ellie, and, with arms flailing in anger, marched through the doors of the gray building.

Silence blanketed the dark street. Ellie was wiping the wet saliva from her cheek, when a large man stormed out of the shop. His square face was twisted with rage. He huffed and pointed his finger at the small girl. "You wretched thief; those orbs belong to me! You have dipped your grubby little hands into my profit and have cost me plenty. Hand me those orbs now, or else you will repay me with your blood!" The orb handler raised his hand, striking Ellie hard across her face. The force of the blow knocked her painfully to the ground.

She stayed down only a moment before rising to confront the man. Ellie stared him right in the eyes and spoke with courage. "I didn't steal these babies; they were given to me. I have promised to find them all new homes. They don't belong to you; they never belonged to you. If it is money you want, you can have mine."

Ellie handed the man her bag of coins, then turned and began walking towards Angeline and Opella. Angeline was stunned by Ellie's fearlessness. She even felt a little ashamed of complaining about her tiredness. Ellie had only taken a few steps when the orb handler reached into her bag. She quickly spun herself around, but it was too late.

With a twisted grin, he held one of the orbs high above his head. "These silly little things are what you care about? I thought you were trying to pass yourself off as an orb handler. You truly are a pathetic child. The only thing these orbs are any good for is to give people light. Once their light burns out, they go with rest of the garbage in the incinerator. I didn't realize this was the lesson you needed to learn."

He chuckled as he tossed the fragile orb into the air. It seemed to fall in slow motion, as it plummeted toward the ground. Ellie ran as fast as she could to catch the falling infant, but she wasn't quick enough. The orb brushed her fingertips and fell, bursting open with a loud crack.

Angeline saw the ball shatter, followed by the horrible sound of a little girl's scream. Ellie gently picked up the tiny form, and her hands shook as she began to sob. Angeline was enraged! She stormed out from the alley and walked right up to the orb handler. "You sick, disgusting man! How could you do something so cruel? How can you live with yourself? You are a filthy bottom-feeder, and you're the one who needs to be taught a lesson!" Angeline then kneed him in the crotch; while he was still bent over, she brought her knee up to meet his face. The orb handler fell to the ground, moaning.

Now that he was incapacitated, Angeline turned on Opella. "How could you just stand there and let this happen? Why didn't you grab the bag? Why didn't your Creator protect Ellie?"

Opella had tears running down her cheeks as she answered. "The Creator never intended the world to look this way. We are the ones who made it this horrible. He has a grand purpose for everything, and we don't always know why He chooses to not intervene. I chose not to act because it was Ellie's job to be the speaker. She did better on her own than I could have imagined. I am so proud of the love she showed. You shouldn't be angry with me; you should be wondering how such a little girl could display such strength. Now let's stop arguing, and do what we should be doing, comforting Ellie."

Angeline had been so angry that she had forgotten about Ellie; Ellie was crying all alone at the end of the street. Both women hurried over to comfort her.

"I promised that I would take care of her," Ellie said, through tear-filled eyes. "Those women trusted me to care for their babies. I lied to them; I failed them. This baby's precious light is gone."

Opella knelt down and hugged her. "Dear, sweet child, you did everything right. You didn't lie to them. You did your best to protect their babies; I am so proud of you, and I can't think of anything you could have done differently."

Ellie looked up at Opella. "But I couldn't catch her, and now her light is gone." Ellie held up the small body that was curled up in her hands. In those hands, a tiny infant with torn wings laid perfectly still.

Opella looked down with dampening eyes at the now colorless baby. "Ellie, you have more conviction and heart than anyone I've ever known. Watching you today made my faith stronger. I know these words won't make the pain go away, but hopefully they will lighten it. It is going to be hard to even think of moving on right now, but we need to leave this place. Our work here is finished."

Ellie ripped some cloth from her sleeve and carefully wrapped it around the baby. Opella took a ribbon from her silvery hair and tied the little shroud closed. Her voice shook as she fastened it. "Since you have done such amazing work today, I would love for you to personally deliver these children to their new homes. After you've finished, we will do right by this child and take the best care of her we can."

Ellie was still crying, but she managed to smile a little at the thought of seeing the faces of the awaiting mothers. She got up with the help of Angeline and Opella, and together they left the darkness of the alley. Six tiny babies, nestled in their orbs, rode safely in Ellie's leather bag, blissfully unaware of how close they had been to death.

~ *Chapter Ten* ~

*L*ady Celestra Penteon walked into an ornately decorated paint shop with three of her closest friends. A short distance behind, two armed guards walked in step with the women. Celestra was easily distinguishable from the group. She walked ahead, while the other three trailed slightly behind. She wore a pale pink, silk dress that was elegant and tasteful. Her face was painted a cream color, while her hair and eyes matched her dress.

Celestra played with an opal necklace, as she chatted with her friends. "It feels so good to be away from my home and out shopping in the city. I am so sick and tired of my father's paranoid whims. I can't believe he forced me to bring these watchers here; I am tired of being treated like a child."

One of her friends nodded. "Your father has been more paranoid these past few weeks. Tell me again, why you think he's being so overly protective?"

"He told me that he just wants me to be careful until the joining ceremony with Denham is over," Celestra said, after a lady-like whine. "I think he actually likes the attention our family receives, while I parade around with two bodyguards constantly following me. I'm positive he thinks it makes our family look important, but what it actually does is make me look ridiculous."

Celestra picked up a metal container of royal blue face paint to examine as her friends scattered about the store, talking and discussing colors. While she stood alone, looking at the blue paint, her friend Karmell became troubled by her uncharacteristic solemnity. Acting upon this concern, Karmell walked up beside her. "Celestra, are you feeling alright? You've seemed awfully distracted lately."

Celestra set the container of paint down and began to tap her fingertips against her lips. "I suppose I feel alright, but I haven't been getting the same enjoyment out of the things I used to. The ceremony with Denham has been on my mind a lot lately. I feel like all my time has been spent planning and organizing our union ceremony. I feel lost, like nothing really matters anymore. Do you know what I mean?"

Karmell nodded, but she couldn't identify with anything her friend had said. She casually left Celestra to join her more chatty friends. Celestra hardly noticed Karmell walk away, and as the others grew tired of standing around, they decided to go to the shop across the street. They told Celestra she could meet them over there when she was through looking at paint.

Celestra was glad to see her friends leave; she really needed some alone time. Her heart danced at the thought, and she turned to the watchers standing behind her. "Would you be willing to wait for me outside? I just need a few minutes to myself."

The watcher in charge, Bereck, responded with a firm, yet annoyed tone. "Missy, we aren't getting paid to protect the shop; we were hired to watch you. That means we're staying right here."

Celestra batted her eyes at him. "Oh, Bereck, you are so strong and wise. I am certain that you could still protect me from the shop entrance. I know that you're getting paid to watch me, but what if I paid you to watch the shop? I'm sure it can't be any fun watching a girl stare at paint all day. What I'm offering you is a break." Celestra held up her pink coin purse, proving that she was serious about paying.

Bereck gave her a disgusted look. "Fine, have it your way, but don't take too long. Come on Crypt, let's give the little princess some space."

The two watchers departed immediately, leaving Celestra still holding her coin purse out in the air. As she watched the pair disappear from sight, she could feel adrenaline surging through her body; she felt free. Celestra had always been a little impulsive, and having no one watching her triggered an impish thought. What if she snuck out the back door? Then she could really be free. She could do whatever she wanted, without anyone bothering her about her safety.

She decided to go with her impulse. She was ready to try almost anything, if it would make her feel more alive. She moved quietly to the back of the shop and pretended to examine some older paints.

She waited for the shopkeeper to glance away, before quickly slipping out the back door.

Celestra stepped out of the shop and into a damp alleyway. She was worried that Bereck would suspect something and come looking in this direction, so she moved quickly to the other end of the alley. Once there, she began sprinting behind long rows of buildings. She kicked off her shoes, and the more she ran, the more free she felt. Celestra ran until her feet were too sore to continue. As her pace slowed, she decided to lean against the nearest building to catch her breath. While she rested against the structure, she noticed how good the cold stone felt against her skin. Her eyes closed, while she basked in the glory of her newfound freedom.

Without warning, the door next to her swung open, and a hand slipped over her mouth. There was no time to react, and before she could even think, she was being pulled backwards. Quickly and quietly, she disappeared behind the locked door.

The door swung open, as Angeline entered the Wentworth's home. She was drained from the events at the orb handler's shop and was ready to climb into bed. Opella and Ellie had invited her to go with them to deliver the orbs to their new homes, but Angeline was not at all interested. While she eased into a kitchen chair, she began to wonder what kind of woman would care for an orb that wasn't her own. She started to nibble on some bread that was left on the table, but exhaustion overtook her need for nourishment, and she quickly fell asleep at the table.

Hours passed, and it was well into the early morning when a loud crash at the front door awakened Angeline. The sound caused her to jump straight up and out of her chair. She eyed a group of four men rushing down the hallway in her direction. She could identify Trinzic and Simeon out of the group, but not the other two men. They were having difficulty coming down the hallway, because of something they were carrying. As they drew closer, she realized they were holding Aristus. His right leg was covered in blood, and the rest of his body was soaking wet. His eyes were opening and closing, as his body twitched violently. The men hurried in and dropped Aristus on the kitchen table in front of her.

Simeon began yelling out instructions. "Trinzic, I need you to cut all the remaining clothing away from the bite. Then, clean it as best you can. You two; try to keep him still; we don't want him to shake himself off the table. I am going to grab some reeds and a hot iron. I'll be right back." Simeon rushed off to gather the tools he needed.

Angeline watched, as Trinzic tore bloodied material from Aristus's pants up to his thigh. Trinzic's face was the most serious Angeline had ever seen it. As he pulled his knife out to cut the final piece of cloth, Trinzic looked over at her. "Beautiful treasure, I need a sponge. Could you fetch it for me?" Trinzic gave her a half smile, but his eyes looked hollow.

Angeline shivered, as she hustled to grab a sponge off the shelf, along with a small bowl, before returning to Trinzic. He took the sponge and started wiping the wound clean. Angeline was now standing above Aristus, and the position gave her a much better view of his injury. His right leg had a deep, spiral burn that ascended all the way to his thigh. At the base of the spiral, two large holes penetrated his flesh. The holes appeared to be growing larger, while a hissing noise and light smoke were escaping from them.

Angeline turned her attention back to Trinzic. "What did this to him?"

"An acid serpent." Trinzic's voice seemed distant as he answered. Angeline linked arms with Trinzic, as she thought about the acid serpent and watched Aristus convulse on the table.

Simeon returned promptly with a hot iron rod that he had taken from the incinerator and a handful of reeds. As he neared the table, he called out instructions. "You two; keep holding his arms down. Trinzic, I'll need you to help me suck the acid out. Angeline, I'll need you to poke the tip of this rod into the holes. We are going to use these reeds to extract the acid, which will cause the reeds to smoke. When all the acid has been removed, we will spit out the blood. When you see red, that's when Angeline will cauterize the wound with the iron."

Angeline looked at Simeon in disbelief, as he handed her the rod. "I can't. I won't," she sputtered. "I don't know what I'm doing. I'm not a healer."

"Dear child, we don't have time to discuss this. He is dying. The acid is burning its way to his heart. We have to suck it out to heal the wound, and we need your help."

Angeline was terrified. All she could do was nod. She was scared, but she didn't want to be the reason that Aristus died. Trinzic and Simeon put their reeds into the holes and began siphoning out the poison. As the acid traveled up the reeds, they began to smoke. When the smoke was within inches of their mouths, they spit the reeds onto the floor and replaced them with new ones. Aristus was now not only twitching, but screaming out in pain. The two men who were trying to hold him down were having extreme difficulty.

Finally, they were both on their second-to-last reed. Trinzic's was no longer smoking, and he spit Aristus's blood out of his mouth and onto the floor. He jerked the reed out, and Angeline tentatively poked the hole with the hot iron. Simeon took only a few moments longer, but as soon as he spit red, she jabbed the iron into the second hole.

Aristus instantly stopped shaking; but as the shaking ceased, so did every other sign of life. An uncomfortable silence filled the room; Simeon placed his hands on Aristus's chest and began praying silently. Angeline could see Simeon's lips moving, and he was whispering something. Then Aristus started moaning, and his eyes began to flicker.

Simeon leaned his head back in relief and said, "The worst is over. He's going to live."

Everyone present sighed heavily; thankful Aristus was alive. Angeline felt dizzy; she clutched the nearest chair and collapsed into it. Her heart was still racing. She couldn't believe what she had just done. Simeon glanced over all those standing around the table. Once he had taken stock of everyone, he began giving out more orders.

"Aristus is going to need a comfortable place to recover; one that would not require us to carry him all the way up the stairs to the loft. I will search for a suitable room down here on the main floor. Drimus, I would like you and your brother Benjamin to acquire clean bedding and clothing for him. They can be found next to his cot in the loft. Trinzic, if you could finish the dressings for the burns and remove all of his wet clothing, that would be splendid. Now let's move quickly so that Aristus doesn't have to spend all night lying on the dinner table."

Simeon, Drimus, and Benjamin all ran off quickly, leaving Angeline and Trinzic alone. Trinzic paused for a moment to look upon Angeline, with his staple, roguish grin. "So, pretty, would you fetch me clean dressings for this poor soul? I could also use a new sponge and a nice, tall glass of waterberry tea."

Angeline ran off to find the items Trinzic said he needed. The kitchen was unfamiliar territory to her. The dressings and the sponge were easy to find; it was the silly glass she was wasting time searching for. When she finally located one, the surge that filled her heart, and the excitement over finding it, made her think about how things were so different at the House of Envy. She had never had to do anything that could be considered work. She merely had to look beautiful, so that others would buy the paint, clothing, or jewelry she was modeling. Now she had no possessions, no wealth, and none of the things she had valued before.

She looked long and hard at the glass, as she poured tea into it. What was wrong with her? She was willingly doing the work of a servant, and even worse, she was doing it honestly. She had no intention of getting something out of it for herself; she was being selfless. Something in her was changing. Why was she doing this? Perhaps she was beginning to care for these people. She didn't want any of them to be hurt. Maybe it was because she loved them? She had never loved anyone before.

Trinzic took the sponge, dressings, and glass from Angeline's hands. He took a quick gulp of tea and repaid Angeline with a flirtatious wink. "I thought you might bring me the waterberry tea. My charm must have been too much for you to resist. Either that, or these light people are starting to rub off on you."

Trinzic expertly finished dressing the burns. Angeline chose not to respond until he was completely done. It was definitely a temptation to defend herself to Trinzic, but his playful comment had raised a question that she wanted answered. "What did you mean when you said I was becoming like the light people? I thought they were called the people of the sky?"

His voice sounded remorseful, as he replied to her question. "They do call themselves the people of the sky, but everyone else calls them light people. Some call them that because they're always trying to bring people into the light. Others have labeled them that because they would consider them a disposable people. Anything around here that gives light is used up and then thrown away. Thus, they are called light people, or people of the light. I don't think of them as disposable; it's just an old habit to call them that."

Angeline thought it was strange that she had never heard of the people of the light before. She wanted to ask Trinzic more questions, but Simeon and the two brothers returned to the table.

Simeon looked tired as he spoke. "Everything is ready. Help me carry him to his room; then we can all get a good night's rest."

As the four men carried Aristus to a nearby room, Angeline realized that she wouldn't be able to ask any more of her questions tonight. The only thing left for her to do was to get some sleep. She quietly disappeared into the loft.

~ Chapter Eleven ~

*K*enrick was enraged. He had watched as Celestra disappeared behind a locked door, mere seconds before he had reached her. The perfect opportunity had eluded him, and he was not pleased. He reached out to touch the door to determine its strength. The door was made of heavy steel, which meant there would be no way for him to break into it without someone noticing. He pounded his fists on the door in anger; then disappeared into a corner to think.

"That foolish girl is probably dead already. I will not waste my time or talent attempting to complete a job that is already done. I need a drink. After a good, long swig, I will return to finish off whoever has stolen my kill. I need to destroy them, or Julia will probably send Adlar to murder me in my sleep." With this final thought, Kenrick decided to skip the drink; revenge would satisfy all his concerns nicely and protect him from Julia's wrath.

⌘

Celestra was being pulled down a long, dark hallway. The only sound was that of her own heartbeat, accompanied by her scattered thoughts, desperately attempting to be heard over the loud thumping. How could she have been so careless? She hoped her father's watchers would find her before it was too late. If she screamed, would they hear her? Would anyone hear her?

Celestra always had a strong spirit, and as the shock of being pulled through the door wore off, she began kicking and flailing her arms, trying frantically to break free. While kicking, she felt something sharp run across her leg, and she cried out in pain. Her hand instinctively grabbed the wound, where her fingers felt the warm, sticky sensation of blood. Celestra's heart was now racing; her breathing became erratic and raspy. Ever since she was a little girl, she panicked at the sight of blood. She heard a door smash violently against a wall, and everything went dark.

~ Chapter Twelve ~

*E*llie reached for the welcome horn and blew hard into it. This house was their final stop, and Ellie was nervous. Delivering the babies to their new homes was invigorating. She loved seeing the faces of the new mothers. Her heart continued to soar with excitement, as she waited for the door to open. Bearing a sweet smile, Opella remained calm and poised as the door swung gently open.

An angelic-looking woman stood before them. Her beauty was so intriguing; it immediately grabbed Ellie's attention. Her eyes were soft blue; so soft that at first glance, Ellie thought her eyes were solid white. Her natural blond hair sparkled under the light from a nearby lantern. She continued to examine the beautiful woman until Opella nudged her lightly with her wings. Ellie instantly came back to reality. Her cheeks burned red with embarrassment over her rude staring.

"Greetings, Contessa," said Opella. "We have come from the orb handler and have brought this blessing to your home. May we come in, so that we can share in this time of joy?"

Contessa's mouth formed delicately into a radiant smile. "Of course. I have been waiting all night for you. I knew you would be here, but when one is expecting something this special, any amount of waiting feels too long. Please come in." She eagerly ushered them through the door, and two towering adolescents quickly came to greet them. "These are my two sons, Ambrose and Uriah. Opella, of course, needs no introduction; but who is this sweet child you brought with you?"

"This is Ellie. She is the one who is responsible for us being here. Her faith, love, and strength moved mountains today."

Contessa's eyes filled with tears. "Thank you, little one. You have given our family the most incredible gift. If there is anything you desire, just ask, and if it is in our power, we will give it to you."

Ellie looked over at Opella and then down at the floor. "There is one thing that I desperately want. I have one more baby who needs a home. I promised the mother that I would take care of her child. Even though it's a little late for that, would you be willing to claim this little girl as your own?" Ellie held up the still, lifeless baby in front of Contessa.

Contessa gasped, and tears began to fall from her eyes. "May I hold her?"

Ellie handed the baby over. Contessa began to sob, as she cradled the small infant in her arms, and looked up at Ellie through a veil of tears. "Even though this child now lives with the Creator, I will joyfully claim this beautiful baby as my own."

Ellie felt a weight lift from her heart; her task was finished. Contessa handed the little child to her oldest son, Ambrose, who began the process of preparing the body. While Ambrose carried the baby to another room, Opella pulled the last orb out of the sack and presented Contessa with her other child.

Contessa looked lovingly down upon her new, growing child. "It's a strange thing to gain and lose a child all in the same day."

Opella placed her hand on Contessa's shoulder to comfort her. "Joy and sorrow visit those who love, as well as the wicked. The only difference is that we have hope and a profound purpose."

Contessa gently handed the orb back to Opella and knelt down to have the orb placed. Opella bent over Contessa and skillfully placed the orb in its socket. Contessa winced, as the orb clicked and moved securely into place. Opella called the brothers to come back into the room when it was finished. The two muscular youths were smiling from ear to ear. The boys hugged and kissed their mother; each taking turns looking at the new addition to their family.

Contessa was now glowing from the light that was coming from the orb. She turned her attention to Ellie and Opella. "You both must stay the night. It is far too late to be traveling. Please let us honor you both with a bit of hospitality."

Opella seemed uncertain, but when she looked into Ellie's pleading eyes, she soon agreed. Contessa was pleased that they had decided to stay and thanked them with a welcome cup of warm tea.

Together, the three women sat, chatting in whispers, as they finished their drinks.

Suddenly, Contessa stopped talking mid-sentence. She closed her eyes, as her wings began to flutter violently, and her hair whirled wildly around her. This strange change in behavior sent Ellie into action, and her arms reached out in an attempt to grab Contessa, but Opella stopped her. "My child, she's fine. Contessa has been given the gift of foresight by the Creator. Now, we must remain silent, because something important is being revealed to her, and we mustn't distract her from receiving the message."

Ellie carefully sat back down and tried to remain patient, as they waited for the vision to end. Soon Contessa's wings began to slow, and her eyes shot open. Her hand gracefully lifted to her forehead, as she slid to the floor. Her eyes made contact with Opella as she spoke. "I am sorry to have frightened you. When the Creator has something important to show me, He gives me very little warning."

"So what did He show you?" asked Opella.

"He gave me specific instructions that directly involve the two of you. I need you to listen carefully as I relate the vision. It started with me waiting anxiously for your arrival in my sitting chair. The horn bellowed, then I opened the door to usher you in. Opella handed me my two babies, and said, 'These babies are a blessing from the Creator, but they are not the only reason we were sent to you. We came to rescue a lost girl. I have been called by the Creator to use my gift of storytelling, and Ellie her gift of empathy, to assist you in carrying out this important mission.'

"Then you both vanished and the Creator stood before me. 'Hello, my beautiful child. I am about to tell you something very important. A girl will arrive at your back door tomorrow. She will not knock, yet she will be there. Place one of your sons at the door to wait for her. This girl is in danger. Your son must act quickly, or the girl will perish. My child, I love you. Always keep your ears open to my words. They are my protection and my unique gift for you. Always listen, my child. Always listen.'

"That was the end of the message. I hope you won't think me rude, but I must tell my sons this vision so that they can prepare for tomorrow."

Both Opella and Ellie sat in shock, trying to process what they had just heard. Opella was the first to break the silence. "We have both had a long day, and it looks like we have another adventure waiting for us tomorrow. Therefore, to be more than just functional, we had better get some rest."

Even with the new events unfolding, Opella and Ellie quickly fell into a deep slumber; both hoping sleep would be enough to prepare them for the task that awaited them.

The aroma of roasting fish and steamed eggs tickled Ellie's nostrils, and her feet hit the floor with a thump, as she responded by swinging gingerly out of bed. She easily found her way to the kitchen and sat comfortably at the table. Contessa planted a warm plate in front of her, which was accompanied by a cool glass of water. Ellie eagerly ate the fish and drank her glass of water. She thought about all the possibilities this new day would bring, as she watched the light coming from their beautiful, expecting hostess. Opella soon joined them, and together they enjoyed their meal in a pleasant silence; each was preparing herself for the task ahead. Opella prayed silently as she ate. Ellie seemed to be in her own little world, and Contessa busied herself with several daily chores. Her sons were taking turns waiting by the back door. Each youth enthusiastically opened it to see if the person they were waiting for had arrived. Breakfast passed uneventfully, as well as lunch.

By then, Ellie had grown impatient with all the waiting, so she decided to start up a conversation. "Opella, what do you think the others are doing right now?"

Opella sat straight up in her chair. "Oh my! We forgot to inform the others where we are! Simeon must be so worried." She paused to take a controlled breath. "No, most likely Angeline told them that we had a large number of orbs to deliver, so they probably assumed we stopped at one of the mother's homes to rest. Even still, we need to inform them of our whereabouts." Opella called Uriah over and asked him if he would be willing to deliver a message to Simeon for her. He politely agreed, and, without any hesitation, he ran out the front door.

That's when the women heard something that made their heads spin; their eyes focused on the back entryway, nestled in the far corner of the house. They could hear the faint sound of a door slamming and being locked. Ellie's breathing slowed, as she heard the heavy footsteps of Ambrose moving down the long hallway. The sound was accompanied by the swooshing and banging of something being dragged across the floor. Then the bolt to the back door clicked loudly and swung open with a crash.

Ellie's heart sank, as she watched Ambrose picking up the lifeless body of a young girl with flowing, pink hair. Her face and one of her legs were streaked with blood.

"Oh no," Ellie mournfully cried. "Is she dead? Not again, not another person hurt. Please, Creator, I loved that baby; don't let this lady die, too!" Ellie turned her head away, and let the tears fall freely down her soft cheeks.

~ Chapter Thirteen ~

*A*ngeline was resting peacefully; her body had finally relaxed, content in her deep sleep. The events of the previous day had been exhausting. She felt a faint, tickling sensation at the tips of her wings, and she lazily rolled over to find Trinzic standing by her bed.

Trinzic was, as always, handsomely painted in radiant shades of silver and white, his hair shining golden in the light. His clothing was flashy, but somehow seemed to suit him. She was a little irritated over being awakened, but it didn't carry over into her voice. "Trinzic, how is it that you manage to stay painted? I've never seen you work, or do anything that would lead me to believe you're independently wealthy."

Trinzic held his heart as though she had wounded him. "It pains me to think that my treasured lady would think me a thief, or worse, poorly bred. Tisk, tisk. I thought you, of all people, would have a better understanding of common courtesy. Don't worry; all is forgiven. I came to escort you to breakfast."

Angeline was amused by his comical act, but she was more interested in acquiring some of his paint. "Trinzic, if I allow you the privilege of escorting me downstairs, would you give me some of your paint?"

He answered her request quickly and smoothly, almost as though he'd been waiting for it. "If you promise to cook me breakfast, I'll gladly give you a nice supply of my paint."

At his words, Angeline's face crinkled. *That little charlatan; he was just biding his time, waiting for me to ask.* For whatever reason, Trinzic wanted her to cook for him. His plan was perfect, because she would have done anything to get some paint. She missed being beautiful. Her perspective was shifting, and she knew it. It was making her uneasy that she had changed this much so fast. She felt that if she could look the way she used to, she might gain a better understanding of everything.

She grinned and turned back towards him. "Sounds like a fair arrangement, but I expect to be escorted down the stairs with some elegance. I am rather weary, and I would like for you to carry me."

Trinzic bowed. "Why certainly, my lady. One should expect nothing less from an experienced gentleman like myself." Trinzic lifted her easily, making her feel weightless in his arms. She was surprised by his strength and noticed that his muscles were toned, though not noticeably large. They moved fluidly down the stairs, and when they were near the bottom, Trinzic leapt off the staircase and landed with a dramatic spin. Angeline giggled girlishly, as they twirled together before being gently set down.

Angeline's giggling had faded by the time they reached the kitchen, where three hungry men huddled around the table. Together, they walked towards the group, and Trinzic announced his accomplishment. "See, gentlemen, I told you that this lovely lady would be more than willing to make us all breakfast."

Angeline's mouth dropped open, and she instinctively hit Trinzic hard on the shoulder. Trinzic flinched, but never lost his triumphant grin. She swallowed hard and was about to lash back, when a hand gently touched her shoulder. She turned to look into the compassionate gaze of Simeon.

"Angeline, I'm sorry to have to ask you this, but Ellie and Opella never made it home last night. These poor men are starving, and I have no experience in the kitchen. I have been trying my best to prepare a meal, but I really need your help to ensure that it's edible. Would you please be willing to help me?"

Angeline really wanted to defend herself, but she consented to help him. Simeon was a hard person to be angry with; besides, it would mean she could still get the paint she desired.

Simeon and Angeline struggled through making breakfast. Simeon had rarely ventured beyond warming rice porridge, but his skills were just enough for him to get by. Angeline's only experience in the kitchen had been acquired yesterday when she was helping find dishes and supplies. Although Simeon's hands shook, his voice was calm, as he issued instructions to her. Together, they decided to make a simple fried mushroom and egg dish.

With the two of them working together, time passed quickly; Angeline even found herself having a little fun. When the meal was finished, Angeline smiled proudly, as she placed portions onto each of the men's plates. While serving Trinzic, she couldn't resist dropping a few hot mushrooms onto his lap. Watching him jump from his seat, and swat the steaming mushrooms to the floor, an impish grin spread across Angeline's face.

"They must have heard your charming voice and couldn't help but fling themselves at you. Poor little things; they have fallen prey to your silver tongue, and now sadly lay rejected on the floor."

The group of men, especially the two brothers, started laughing hysterically. Benjamin, the more boisterous of the two, spoke through his laughter. "Ha! Trinzic, it sure looks like this little lady has you figured out." Drimus nodded enthusiastically, while they both continued laughing until their sides hurt. Simeon chuckled quietly, trying very hard to seem impartial.

Trinzic looked stunned, as well as embarrassed. He sat back down in his chair and began eating his breakfast, pretending he couldn't hear any of them. Benjamin ended his laughter by wiping tears of merriment from his eyes. "Ah. Poor little mushrooms. That was beautiful; I'll have to remember that one."

Due to the events of the previous night, and the awkwardness that followed teasing Trinzic, the conversation moved gradually to lighter topics.

The two brothers discussed humorous work-related events, while Simeon and Angeline demonstrated their newfound kitchen abilities by clearing the table. They cleaned all the dishes and managed to put them all in their correct locations. After breakfast, the brothers returned home, and Trinzic went to his cot to retrieve something.

When Angeline and Simeon finished cleaning the kitchen, they congratulated each other on their success, and Simeon left to check on Aristus. Angeline turned and noticed Trinzic standing at the head of the table, holding a decorative, jeweled box. Her eyes quickly narrowed in on the tantalizing object; realization over its probable contents caused her heart to skip a beat. She moved hastily to Trinzic's side. He took her hand to escort her to a nearby room.

The room they entered was filled with Simeon's completed furniture restoration projects. Trinzic steered her carefully through the maze of furniture, into the room's center, where Simeon had placed at least a thousand small silk pillows. "I am pleased to welcome you to the most luxuriously comfortable room in the house. Please take a seat."

Angeline had some difficulty maneuvering her way across the pillows; being silk made them very slippery. She eventually slid into a comfortable position, and then looked back to see how Trinzic was managing the pillows. He hadn't moved and was fashioning a large grin. Angeline felt embarrassed. He had probably chosen this room, so that he could watch her look foolish. Angeline taunted him; "I doubt that you could walk over here without making a fool of yourself. I can't wait to watch you fall."

Trinzic smiled his sneaky, sweet grin, as words poured like honey from his lips. "If you're hoping to see me land on my face, I'm sorry, but I may have to disappoint you." He jumped high into the air, throwing the box above his head. In mid-air, he completed two somersaults and landed directly at Angeline's feet. Trinzic then placed his arm behind his back, gracefully catching the box in his right hand; and, in one fluid motion, he handed her the box. "I suppose if it strikes your fancy, you could fairly label that a fall if you like."

Angeline was disgusted by his antics; he was such a showoff. She would have said something, but her whole attention was being monopolized by that box. Her heart raced with anticipation, as she lifted the lid. The box opened to reveal a baffling amount of crystal containers. Angeline found herself nearly drooling, as she stared down at the expensive treasures set before her eyes. "Trinzic, where did you acquire these? These paints were made by Tranquil. Even as Madam of the House of Envy, I could hardly afford these."

Trinzic was obviously pleased by her question; his face beamed with pride. "A man of mystery never reveals his sources. Let's just say I'm fairly skilled at finding what I want." He gave her a wink, followed by a brief smirk.

Angeline cocked her head; then lowered her eyebrows. "Why would you be willing to give me such expensive paint for just a little cooking? Are you sure I can have as much as I want?"

Trinzic was enjoying this conversation immensely; his face was smug and beaming. "Well, if it makes you feel any better, I could just turn my head for a moment, and that way you can take what you want. Then you wouldn't have to worry your pretty little head about my feelings."

Angeline let out an exasperated sigh. "I wasn't thinking about your silly feelings. Oh, never mind! You're impossible."

Trinzic was amused by her frustration; he was trying hard not to laugh at her mild outburst. He attempted to watch her patiently, as she rummaged gracefully through the paints, but Trinzic had never been much for silence. Angeline's quiet searching was causing his ears to ring, and his patience had reached its limits. He flicked the top of the box to grab her attention. Her head shot up from behind the box.

"While you're selecting your perfect palate," he proclaimed, "I would love to tickle your ears with the details of Aristus' recent brush with death."

Angeline momentarily diverted her attention from the box. "I can't imagine anything else that I would like to hear about. I have been curious over what kind of creature could have done something so horrific to him." Angeline stopped shifting through the paint, giving Trinzic her full attention.

He rose to the occasion, launching up from his seat. Angeline couldn't help but laugh at his enthusiasm.

Her laughter stopped abruptly, as Trinzic began to sing a haunting melody.

> *My child, beware the acid serpent,*
> *which beckons from the deep.*
> *You must avoid her close embrace,*
> *for you will never be released.*
> *Once her kiss has found you,*
> *your time will be no more.*
> *Goodnight, goodnight, my child,*
> *for death is at your door.*

Contessa ran to her son's side to determine the injured girl's condition; then, she quickly cleared off a spot on a large chair to set her down. The girl slumped lifelessly into the awaiting chair, so Ambrose tried to prop her up with pillows.

Now that the shock had worn off, Ellie began to move towards the girl. Once at her side, she placed her small hand over the girl's heart and began to feel hope, as it beat lightly against her palm. While Ellie was finding joy in a beating heart, Contessa and Opella were trying to locate the source of all the blood.

"Here it is!" Opella exclaimed. "The cut isn't deep, but it runs along most of her right leg. Thankfully, it's not anything life-threatening; even still, we should keep searching in case we overlooked a more serious injury."

The two women searched, but were unable to find anything else wrong with the girl. Contessa sighed in relief. "Oh, this poor child must have fainted from fear, because this injury is far too small. Most of the blood is from her touching the cut, and smearing it onto her clothing and face. Opella, if you'd be so kind as to dress the wound, I really need to pray and ask the Creator for more instructions. Ellie, you can help by keeping a cool, wet sponge on her forehead; that should be about all we can do for now."

Ellie and Opella hardly said a word; they just rushed to do as they had been instructed. Opella dressed the wound, while Ellie lovingly dabbed the girl's forehead with the cool sponge. As they worked, Ellie began to sing her favorite song. Singing made the time go by quickly, and soon Ellie was watching as the girl's eyes slowly fluttered open.

When Celestra's eyes finally opened, she was startled to find herself in an unfamiliar place with people she did not recognize. Sudden terror pumped adrenaline through her limp body; her instinct was ordering her to run.

Celestra stumbled out of her chair and fell onto the floor; her leg had collapsed. With her leg too sore to walk on, she proceeded to make a pitiful attempt to escape. Not knowing what to do, Opella and Ellie watched as Celestra slowly crawled, using all her remaining strength to pull herself across the floor. She looked up in desperation, hoping to find a door, but instead was greeted by the man who had attacked her.

His voice was deep and firm. "You can't leave! It's not safe for you to go. You can't even walk! How are you going to protect yourself? Please, allow us to help you."

Celestra was stunned by this request. No words came from her mouth; she just lay on the floor, unmoving and silent. The huge man's hands slipped under her body, gently lifting her off the ground. As soon she was back in the chair, Celestra realized she wasn't going to be leaving just yet, so she determined to sit and rest until an opportune time presented itself for her escape. Meanwhile, a beautiful little girl was staring at her, with a concerned furrow on her face.

"Hi, I am Ellie. I was really scared that you were dead. I'm very glad you're not. Please stay with us until your leg is better; then Ambrose will escort you safely home."

Celestra was confused. She didn't understand why these strangers would kidnap her, just to bandage her up and then escort her home. She immediately voiced her thoughts to Ellie. "Why should I stay here with you? You kidnapped me. I have no idea what your real intentions are, and I have no reason to trust you."

Ambrose walked up to her, with his head slumped down. "I need to ask forgiveness. I did a poor job of rescuing you. I was told that if I didn't grab you quickly, you would be killed. I was terrified for you; that is why I grabbed you, slammed the door behind me, and rushed to bring you here.

I did not mean to hurt you. Please forgive my clumsiness."

Celestra looked into Ambrose's honest eyes and felt herself relax. He looked far less scary now, more like a gentle giant. He was a young man, perhaps only a few years younger than her. She didn't know why, but she wanted to believe him. "I suppose it could have been an honest mistake. All right; I'll grant you my forgiveness . . . if you take me home immediately."

Ellie kept pleading with her to stay, but Celestra's mind was absolutely set on leaving. She grew impatient with Ellie's kind words and gruffly rebuked them. "Why is everyone so concerned about my safety? I'm fine! I am perfectly capable of taking care of myself. No one is trying to kill me. You are all just like my father; completely insane, and worried about nothing. I am not a child! I don't need anyone's protection. I just want to live my own life!"

In the wake of her outburst, the room became silent. Opella thoughtfully wrung her hands, knowing it would be wrong to force Celestra to stay. Reluctantly, they began preparing the girl's fragile body for travel, when Contessa entered the room. Celestra couldn't help staring, as Contessa glided effortlessly towards her. It looked as though she was emitting a faint glow, and the air seemed to be filled with the aroma of lilies. As she walked, words came out of her mouth, clear and musical; Celestra felt each one resonate deep within her.

"Celestra, the Creator has used His servant to rescue you from death. A man who earns his wages from stealing life was only seconds away from taking yours. You have been feeling the Creator's love song calling out to you in the darkness. The truth of His words has caused you to become dissatisfied with everything this world has to offer. We cannot force you to stay, but we have the answers you seek. Please remain here, so that you can find satisfaction that lasts not merely a moment, but for all eternity. This is your divine appointment."

Celestra was shaken to her core: *how could this woman know my name? How could she know the secret cries of my heart? What if all the things she said were true?* These questions plagued her mind; she needed to find answers. Celestra looked imploringly into Contessa's eyes. "I'll stay. I need answers. I have to know why my heart is so empty."

As Opella prepared to tell the story of beginnings and sacrifice, Contessa made Celestra more comfortable with pillows and gave her a warm cup of tea. They all sat before Opella, as she used her gift of storytelling to answer the distraught girl's questions.

Celestra was in awe of all that she had heard. She knew in her heart that these amazing stories must be true. Opella had spoken with such energy that she felt as though the stories had played out before her eyes; it was almost as if she was a part of them.

Celestra was quickly realizing something was different in her, and she gazed into the eyes of Opella for more. "What must I do to become a child of the sky? I don't think I can live with this empty void in my soul any longer. I have felt this way for far too long."

A warm smile spread across Opella's face, and words flowed out of her mouth, with tears of joy accompanying them. "My child, all you need to do is invite the Creator to be the lord of your life, and trust that the story of His sacrifice is true. If you believe in your heart, ask Him now, and you will experience the joy of new life."

Celestra looked up. "Creator, I declare that I am your child. I believe that all your promises are true. Thank you for your sacrifice and deliverance. Come dwell in my innermost being, and transform me into something new."

Faster than the blink of an eye, she was gone; vanishing without a trace into the world unseen. Ellie, Opella, Contessa, and Ambrose immediately started rejoicing. The four embraced, thanking the Creator for the new life that Celestra had begun. Contessa quickly prepared a marvelous waterberry cream dessert. She graciously thanked Ellie and Opella for delivering her two new babies, and for sharing in the exciting victory of a new creation. After enjoying the dessert, Ellie and Opella said goodbye to their new friends. Hugging one last time, Ambrose graciously offered to escort them home. They accepted, and the three of them departed.

~ Chapter Fourteen ~

Trinzic continued humming the strange, haunting melody; only this time, he accompanied it with some of his artistic acrobatics. Angeline was pleased that he performed stories in the same fashion as the players in the House of Envy. She watched as his body twisted into beautifully complex shapes; these moving designs enhanced the story he told. She was watching an entire play being performed by only one man.

"It all began with three men crazily volunteering to work in the rice fields," Trinzic spoke, with an empty and expressionless face. "When you first gaze upon the fields, they are truly a horrifying sight to behold. The waters are dark and still. They lie in wait; ready to swallow any man who lingers too near their shores.

"The shoreline is littered with huts, constructed from nearby reeds. These small huts shelter the gathering men and their families. Their homes are always damp from the thick mist that constantly drifts inland from the lake. Resting beside each house is at least one gathering boat. The only light in this area comes from the glowing moss that has made its home on the cavern ceiling, and the swaying lanterns stationed at the bow of each boat. Every day, the gathering men, and sometimes a few women, cast off to begin their day's work of harvesting. The lake is filled with rice stalks, more than anyone could ever count. Their work is always waiting for them; they never run out of rice to harvest.

"Now, there are some important facts you need to know about the harvesting boats, so please listen carefully. These boats are long and come to narrow points on each end. Their centers open wide and go down deep for storage. They are perfectly designed to transport the rice, not to carry people. Only one man can ride in each boat; otherwise, these medium-sized vessels lean and take on water. Gathering men are trained as children to straddle their boats and balance carefully in the water. They use their wings, along with rounded paddles, to propel and steer.

"Every time a gathering man leaves the shore, he places himself in grave danger. Before the boats are filled with rice, they are unstable and prone to tip. In those cloudy, still waters are all sorts of monstrous creatures; but none is more well known, or deadly, than the acid serpent. This poisonous serpent can range from two to eight feet in length. It has dazzling crystal skin; when seen from above, they look like dancing lights. From that safe vantage point, one could almost call the serpent beautiful, but up close, it is a nightmarish manifestation.

"It has dull, diamond-shaped eyes that stare back at you like an empty corpse. Directly under these eyes is a set of teardrop-shaped nostrils that open and close at will. Where their nostrils end, their hanging crystalline fangs begin. These two razor-sharp teeth draw your attention to the jaw, which hangs below, crooked and toothless. Blubbery, long flaps of skin dangle from either side of its face. When the serpent is in the water, these flaps wrap around its mouth, keeping the jaw tightly in place. Once the creature attacks, the flaps wrap tightly around the victim, making an escape almost impossible.

"These creatures are only able to survive in the water. When their skin is exposed to air, their pores open up, causing their acid to run out. This leads a man to wonder; how does an acid serpent catch a gathering man? Imagine a long day of gathering rice. In your tired and distracted state, you allow one solitary leg to fall beneath the waterline. Under the water, the sound of a beating heart echoes, calling out to the acid serpents. They feel the unique thumping of your blood, as it courses through your body. A serpent follows these vibrations and punctures your flesh, with its long, poisonous fangs. You scream from the pain, and your vision begins to fade. You lose your balance and fall into the water. For most normal souls, that would be the end, but not for a man like Aristus.

"Now, I will introduce the hero of our story. Here is a man who chose to stare death in the eyes and has lived to tell the tale; a man who willingly put his life on the line for no monetary gain. He gives every coin he earns to those too sick or too old to provide for their families. He risks his life so others won't go hungry. Most would call him crazy, and perhaps he is, but many find his unique courage to be invigorating. Lend me your pretty ear, and you will hear a tale of impossible rarity. You must decide for yourself whether our hero is a madman, or a man of true courage.

"The three men arrived at the rice fields, just as the day's work had begun. Simeon, the tiny wonder, quickly departed from the group to offer his healing skills to the sick, while our adventurous hero set out in a boat alongside all the other gatherers. Aristus moved with ease through the calm, misty waters. His boat sliced like a knife through the fog, until he discovered a good spot to harvest rice. Aristus began hitting the stalks with his paddles and noticed a boy struggling to break the rice free from the stalks. Aristus, being a kindhearted gentleman, offered to help the boy gather rice, but the foolish youth was proud and told our champion to leave him alone.

"Our hero felt uncomfortable leaving the struggling boy, so he remained close. The boy mimicked Aristus' movements as he beat the stalks. The rice fell like feathers, landing perfectly into his boat. The youth quickly grew jealous of his neighbor's skills and attempted to show off his own abilities. He stood up on the rims of his boat and called out to Aristus. In gaining our hero's attention, the boy leaned over, reaching for some nearby stalks. Aristus yelled to tell him to sit back down, but the boy only mocked him. He leaned even farther to one side; and that's when the boat followed his lead and dumped him into the water.

"With no thought for his own safety, Aristus jumped into the water after the boy. Below the surface, the stunned boy descended motionless, staring at the glittering lights speeding towards him. The acid serpents had felt their prey hit the water, and a particularly large one headed straight for the boy. Our hero quickly struck the monster directly on the nose, halting it just long enough to perform the most beautiful rescue ever imagined. He grabbed the lad firmly with both hands and used his wings to propel himself high out of the water. He glided over the boy's boat, dropping him into its deep center. Aristus continued past the boy, landing flat across his own boat, with his legs dangling unprotected in the water.

"Rescuing that boy had taken nearly all the strength Aristus had, and at this point, he was having difficulty pulling himself out of the water. With his feet submerged, a small acid serpent swam up his leg. He could feel the creature coiling itself around his thigh, which compelled him to scramble the rest of the way into the boat. The moment the serpent left the water, its pores opened up and began to release acid. The creature inserted its crystal fangs into flesh, injecting poison straight into our hero's veins. Aristus' scream resonated over the lake and onto the shore.

"By this time, the boy and several gatherers had come to his aid. Two men came alongside Aristus and tied their boats to his. When his boat was secure, they moved quickly back to shore. Once on land, they pulled Aristus from the boat and placed him carefully on the beach. One of the men slashed open Aristus's pant leg, revealing the dead acid serpent, still latched on. The snake had burned into his skin, and its skin flaps had wrapped themselves completely around his thigh.

"That is when Trinzic, the most handsome and absolutely best-dressed of the three, came to his friend's aid. He had found a healer who held in his hands an intercessor; the only way to remove those deadly serpents. The healer clamped the device tightly at the base of the creature's neck, and an upper lever reached over its head, gripping securely between the two fangs. He grasped the intercessor firmly in his hands and then twisted it violently to remove the dead serpent. The intercessor had successfully ripped the creature from Aristus's leg; but once the snake was removed, there was still the problem of the acid working its way to his heart.

"No one really knew what to do. People rarely survive an attack by an acid serpent, and most never make it out of the water. Simeon proposed an idea on how to save him, but everyone listening was confused by his request to not allow the healer to use his typical healing method of injecting rice milk into the puncture sites. Simeon almost looked angry, if you could even call it that; I would say he strongly disagreed with the healer. 'You know that rice injections are rarely effective,' Simeon argued. 'They also have horrific side effects. I appreciate your help, but I really think there is a better way.'

"In the end, it was decided that Aristus would be treated at Simeon's house. Two gathering men had prepared a carriage and accompanied the three others home. The four men feared for Aristus as they listened to his screams, knowing he would likely die; but as you already know, death was not the outcome.

"Simeon had a simple, albeit genius, plan waiting, although it was nothing short of a miracle that Aristus survived the trip. So, whether crazy, amazing, or, perhaps, even a true child of the sky, that man survived something un-survivable. In my humble opinion, if that doesn't make a person a hero, I'm not sure what one would have to do to qualify. So, please allow me the good pleasure of bowing in honor of a job well done to Aristus; a man who always keeps me on my toes, and brings forth mighty tales of true adventure."

Trinzic bowed and smiled his boyish grin, in response to Angeline's enthusiastic clapping. She was amazed. Angeline had thought that Aristus sent the women out to do the hard work, while the men took the easy job; she now realized how wrong she had been. When she finished clapping, she thanked Trinzic for his dazzling performance.

Trinzic, in turn, thanked her for her generous compliment. He then offered to help her select colors. "Remember that I am a seeker of all things beautiful and wondrous. I have an artist's discerning eye and would love to give my advice concerning you."

Angeline laughed, and then told him she would be glad for his help. Together, they looked over the colors, until Trinzic pulled out a dark blue container. "This color seems to suit you."

Angeline thought back to the House of Envy, as she gazed down at the paint now resting in her palm. She looked up at Trinzic and remembered the story he had just recited. "Trinzic, you and I are much alike. I guess you could say I trust your dishonesty, and I know you understand what I mean by that. I have a question for you that requires a truthful answer. Do you believe that there is another world, and a Creator?"

Trinzic looked seriously at Angeline. "Madam, when you've been around light people for as long as I have, you can't help but wonder. I have seen so many wondrous things that it's becoming almost impossible to explain them away. I guess I believe in many different truths; I'm not ready to put all my trust in their Creator. Becoming something new is not something that I desire." Then Trinzic winked. "Why would I want to become something else when I'm already so charming and uncommonly dashing?"

Angeline seemed satisfied with his answer. Then the two of them spent the remaining time in meaningless small talk, as they browsed through Trinzic's paints.

~ Chapter Fifteen ~

Celestra's watchers, Bereck and Crypt, had grown suspicious when she didn't come out of the paint shop. They had grown tired of waiting and decided to go back in to retrieve her. Both watches searched the shop thoroughly, only to find that Celestra was gone. Bereck was infuriated with himself for choosing to listen to the girl. He knew the only way she could have slipped by him was through the back exit. Bereck voiced his deduction to Crypt, who nodded in agreement. They both left the shop through the back door, and as soon as their feet touched the cold stone of the alley, they began frantically searching for clues to Celestra's whereabouts.

For hours, the two men sought after any hint as to where she had gone, but in that time, all they found was her shoes. Both watchers hung their heads in defeat, until finally Bereck grabbed Crypt's shoulder. "Hey, Crypt! Slow down for a second. I think I know where she may have gone. We both know she wasn't forcibly taken from the shop. Otherwise, the shopkeeper would have heard something; that means she left on her own. The fact that she asked us to leave only proves I am right."

Crypt looked blankly at Bereck. "Why should that matter?"

"I am saying that I'm pretty sure no one kidnapped her. I think our little escape artist is back at the paint shop right now, having a big laugh at our expense. She probably did this to prove to her father she's capable of protecting herself. What really upsets me is how I fell for her pathetic needing-time-alone story. I guess I really must be getting rusty. We're going back to the shop to see if I'm right."

Together they rushed towards the shop, but before they had made it all the way back, they spotted something that made them pause. There was a girl, drenched from head to toe, spinning in the alley with her arms outstretched. She was singing, seemingly oblivious of their approach. What caught their attention was not her strange behavior, but the fact that she was wearing Celestra's clothes; that simple observation launched Bereck into action.

He ran to the girl, lifting her up by the throat, as his voice rattled with rage. "Where did you get this dress, you little thief? You listen carefully. I really don't care about the clothes, but you will tell me what happened to the woman they belong to. Where did she go?" Bereck set the girl down, still keeping a firm grip on her.

The girl coughed, as he released his hold on her throat. Then her face turned from shock to a friendly smile. "Bereck, it's me, Celestra! I have been changed! There really is a beautiful world of light. I was just there. I met the Creator personally! I knew it! I'm so glad I believed!"

Bereck and Crypt exchanged bewildered glances; neither was sure what was going on. The girl only vaguely resembled Celestra. As they carefully examined her, the pair noted her once cream-colored face was now a soft gold, with a little more rosy color resting on her cheeks. Her hair was no longer pink but honey-colored. A few curls dangled around her face, and the rest ran down the back of her long, dripping, wet hair. The eyes that were staring back at them were no longer pink, but could best be described as opal. They were almost white, with sparkling colors flashing throughout them. The only things that were similar were her voice and her body shape.

The more Bereck looked at her, however, the more he became convinced she was Celestra; it was her face that convinced him. Bereck thought her face was the same, only a different color. He quickly thought of a logical explanation for her drastic change in appearance. *Someone must have been waiting for her when she exited the shop. They took her to a secluded place and altered her appearance, by using twisted and unthinkable means, which has caused her to suppress the truth by speaking nonsense. Somehow, they let her go, or she escaped. The water I can't explain, but I'll figure that out later.*

Bereck pulled Crypt aside. "We have found Celestra, but someone has altered her mind and body. We must get her home immediately! Hopefully, once she is home, she will recover quickly, and we can keep our jobs. Now run ahead and get the carriage ready."

Celestra was neither concerned nor worried. She was still completely focused on the place she had just been. Her mind was busily processing all that had happened. She wanted to remember everything the Creator had said and done. The world she had just seen was so bright and beautiful; it was going to be hard adjusting back to this world of darkness. *It's no wonder I never really felt at home in this dreary place,* she thought to herself. *It was because this world of darkness and selfishness was never meant to be my home in the first place. We all have been living in our mistakes for far too long. I am so glad to be free from all this!*

Her thoughts slowed when Bereck picked her up and took her to the carriage. Once there, he placed her beside Crypt. Immediately, the carriage was on its way.

"Bereck, thank you for carrying me. That was very kind of you, but really, I truly am feeling fine. Actually, I'm feeling better than that! I'm not empty anymore. I don't feel fake anymore. I finally know who I am. Do you want to hear what happened to me?"

Bereck looked exhausted and annoyed. "The only story I have any interest in hearing is the one where you tell me where you really went, who did this to you, and how I can find them."

Celestra smiled. "I'd be glad to tell you. Actually, I came back to tell you." The carriage continued on, while Celestra spoke excitedly about all she had experienced.

⌘

Angeline and Trinzic had long since finished with their selection of paints. Presently, they were sitting at the dinner table, being informed by a youth named Uriah of the reason for Ellie and Opella's delay.

"No one can know the future!" exclaimed Angeline. "I know there are plenty of future reorganizers who can show you how to control your future, but no one can actually tell you the specifics of what is to come. Therefore, your mother is either insane or a con artist, and she will keep Ellie and Opella occupied for weeks listening to her nonsense."

Uriah was slightly taken aback by the harshness in Angeline's voice, and his own voice shook a little as he gave his answer. "It will be no longer than today. Otherwise, the Creator would have told us so. Concerning what you said about no one knowing the future, you are correct, except for the Creator. He knows everything past, present, and future. Therefore, since He knows the future, He sometimes informs us about the part we are supposed to play in it; He has a special purpose for each of His children. All gifts are designed for one goal: to bring people into the world of light. My mother has the gift of foresight; I have faith that her gift is genuine. Just wait, and you'll see that the Creator never lies, for He can only speak truth. He is truth."

Angeline was not satisfied by his answer. She thought seriously about arguing with him, but a small voice inside told her to hold back. *Don't say anything. Be still, and the outcome will reveal itself soon. Remember, you have seen them move solid rock. Patience.*

Angeline decided to listen to the voice, and wait until the day was done before she posed any more questions. She sat, listening carefully, as Simeon busily chatted with Uriah about the boy's family. Simeon smiled as the messenger conveyed the news about Opella and Ellie. It felt good to know that they were safe, and currently engaging in a special assignment from the Creator. That relief, mingled with anticipation, brought about a pleasant and friendly conversation between the young and old men.

Angeline sat, losing herself in their mindless conversation for quite some time, until the welcome horn sounded. Simeon politely halted his conversation with Uriah so that he could answer the door. As she watched with anticipation, the door revealed two people Angeline had not expected: a red-headed woman, and her white-haired little boy. It was Honna and Bowen. Honna's face was uncharacteristically pale, while Bowen was anxiously moving his head, obviously in search of something. Suddenly, his little head stopped, and his eyes focused right on Trinzic. He ran past Simeon and climbed easily into Trinzic's lap. Bowen then placed two pudgy toddler hands on Trinzic's cheeks and pressed. "'Ello, Trinzic. Missed you too much. Where's Daddy? Wanna 'ug him, too."

Trinzic now had two little handprints on his cheeks, because of the impression Bowen's hands had left on his painted face. Trinzic, though, appeared not to care, as he playfully messed up Bowen's fluffy hair. His reply to the toddler was jovial. "Well, my little tumbling wonder, your dad is tired from a grand adventure; but I will gladly take you to your father later. Why don't we take a gander at all the treasures Simeon has stashed away?"

Bowen's grin filled his rounded face, as he quickly jumped from Trinzic's lap. "I'll finden the bestest treasure first. You're pokey . . . me's the fastest . . . buh-bye."

Trinzic gave a face of mock concern as he yelled after Bowen, "Hey, you! I am not a man who has ever been called pokey. I don't think it is I who is pokey, but it is you who are a little cheater; a little cheater who may need to be taught a lesson. Perhaps I may just skip the treasure and tickle your little cheating toes instead. Here I come to get you, little rascal." Trinzic ran down the hallway after the toddling thuds against the floor. Little Bowen was giggling loudly, as he ran toward the incinerator.

As the two troublemakers played, the rest discussed the reason for Honna's arrival. She spoke to Simeon, and the others politely listened to the conversation. "When the Creator informed me that Aristus had been hurt, I came as fast as I could. This day has been so hard, Simeon. Just yesterday, when I went to get Melora for breakfast, I found that she had passed away in her sleep. Feeling heartbroken from losing her, I sought the Creator's comfort; it was then that He told me I was needed elsewhere. Please tell me Aristus is going to be all right; I have been sick with worry. "

Simeon chose his words carefully as he described Aristus's current state of recovery. "My dear, he's doing exceptionally well; when you take into consideration everything his body has been through. He is in good spirits and is talkative when awake. He sleeps most of the time, which his body needs in order to heal properly. Aristus is unable to walk, and it could be a long time before he can stand without assistance. Please come with me, and we'll check on him together. You are welcome to stay with him as long as you like. Bowen is being entertained by Trinzic, so there is no need to rush. Aristus needs your reassuring smile; it will give him hope."

Relief visibly washed over Honna's face. "I felt so helpless when I heard Aristus was hurt. I know he understands how much I love him, but it would feel good to show him by physically caring for him. I'm ready; please take me to my husband."

Angeline was now alone at the kitchen table. She watched as Simeon and Uriah left to join Trinzic's and Bowen's treasure hunt, now that things had calmed down. She, too, shifted her attention to the boys. Bowen was holding out a beat-up copper pot that was shaped like a fish.

He called to Trinzic, "Ha, ha. I founded the treasure first! I said you is pokey. I win! I win!"

Trinzic gave the boy a playful slap on the back. "Well, of course you found the treasure first, you little cheater. Remember, you got that headstart.

How about another treasure hunt, only this time we will conduct ourselves as gentlemen, fairly. Whoever finds silver first, wins. How about that?"

Bowen smiled up at Trinzic and let out an excited shriek. "Let's finden silver treasure! Bowen will be playin' fair dis time, und still beatin' you." He gave Trinzic an impish smirk. "Cuz you so pokey!" Then he scampered off to find more treasure.

Angeline quietly giggled, as she watched the two boys playfully banter back and forth. Soon Uriah joined the game, and the hunt for treasure grew more animated. As she watched their search for worthless treasure, her mind drifted to her own personal treasure: her priceless paints tucked safely under her bed. Questions filtered through her mind. She wondered what made her paints any different than Bowen's copper fish pot. To him, that beat-up copper pot was an amazing treasure, but to her, it was only garbage. He would look at her paints and see no use for them. She wondered what gave something its value; what made something have worth? Then her mind came up with an answer that satisfied her. The object's, or person's, worth is determined by the power or authority of the individual that values them.

Angeline wanted to be valued and desired by important people; her paints were a step on the road to finding her own value. She thought on this, until a familiar noise cut in and tore her from her thoughts. The front door had opened. Ellie, Opella, and Ambrose had finally arrived. All three were excitedly chatting with one another.

Their arrival confirmed Contessa's vision had been fulfilled. She was a little disappointed, because now the question she placed earlier to Uriah seemed foolish. She was growing weary of being wrong. Nevertheless, she put her pride aside to welcome her friends. As soon as Ellie laid eyes on Angeline, she ran to her and began telling her everything that had transpired at Contessa's house. Angeline rested her head thoughtfully in her hands, while she listened to her second miraculous story of the day.

~ Chapter Sixteen ~

*C*elestra finished her exciting tale and was patiently drumming her fingers, waiting for someone to speak. Crypt was staring at her, with eyes filled with boyish intrigue and wonder. He began to whisper under his breath; then, all of a sudden, he vanished. Bereck, too, had been staring at Celestra. Therefore, it took some time before he noticed that his comrade was gone. When he finally saw the empty seat, he raised his fist to Celestra and punched the seat, hitting squarely between her wings and her head.

"Where is Crypt?" he growled.

"You know where he is. He has gone to be with the Creator."

Bereck howled in frustration. "When I have finished giving you back to your father, I am going to find the ones who did this. I am going to make them suffer! I don't know where Crypt has run off to, but perhaps he couldn't stand one more second of your yapping. As a matter of fact, I am finished with your crazy speeches. When I return you to your father, Lord Alistair, we will see what he thinks of your nonsense. We are going to walk together in silence. Do you understand? Silence!"

Celestra nodded. The carriage came to a gentle stop in front of the Penteon family estate. Once grand and full of life, the estate was now only a shell, shadowing its former splendor. Above the arched doorway, pressed into the stone, was the Penteon family crest; a shield which bore the essence of their pride. On the shield was the image of a hand holding an ornate mirror, with the Penteon name inscribed within it. The dusty words screamed from the mirror, mocking Lord Alistair, reminding him that he was the last Penteon, and that his family's legacy would die with him. His only hope was Celestra's union to a more powerful family.

Bereck knew how fragile Lord Alistair's ego was. His mind thought on these things as he picked Celestra up, carrying her easily out of the carriage and into the estate. Once inside, he grabbed the nearest servant and commanded him to fetch Lord Alistair. The servant gave a fearful glance towards Celestra, and then ran down the hallway, disappearing behind a door at the end of the hall. Shortly after, the corridor echoed with the sound of two large doors hitting the wall. Lord Alistair was walking briskly towards them. His rounded belly shook with anger, as he stopped inches from Bereck.

"I told you to watch her! What have you done to my child?"

Bereck told Lord Alistair everything, as Celestra watched in silence. When Bereck had finished, Alistair turned his attention to his daughter.

"Celestra, I told you over and over again that you were not safe; but you did not heed my warning. Now look at you; you are a mess. What were you trying to do, run away from me like your ungrateful mother? You realize that if the Lord Denham finds out you are damaged, he will never have you. How could you do this to me? I am the one who kept you and cared for you when your own mother would have nothing to do with you. That's it! Bereck, take her from my sight, and lock her in her room. She can stay there until the joining ceremony with Denham."

Celestra was wounded by her father's harsh words. Before she was ready to reply, Bereck grabbed her arm and began dragging her up to her room, but Celestra yelled out, "Father! I wasn't trying to leave you. I love you."

Lord Alistair's response was stern. "Bereck, make sure you find out who did this to her. Then bring their carcasses to me. If you fail, I will never forgive you."

It had not been difficult for Bereck to find the home of Contessa. He pounded his fist as he knocked on the door. The door responded by creaking steadily open, revealing someone he hadn't expected. His mouth fell open; then he took a dramatic step backwards. His voice quivered, "Crypt?"

A man who had Crypt's figure, but with brown skin, brown hair, and topaz eyes, stood directly before him. He reached out, as though he was trying to keep Bereck from falling over. "Bereck, it's me. I can't even begin to explain the things I've seen."

Bereck's eyes became hard. He pulled his sword from its sheath. "You traitor! You are the one who planned for Celestra to escape. You are the one who orchestrated my failure! This is all your doing!"

Bereck lifted his sword high above his head. It whistled through the air, as it came crashing down towards Crypt. Crypt yanked out his sword to block, but the momentum of Bereck's weapon nicked his ear before Bereck pulled it back, preparing for the next strike. Crypt staggered back a step and braced himself. Then the two watchers' weapons clashed again. Finally, a sword drew blood; it was Crypt's blade that cut across Bereck's hand, slicing into his fingers. When Bereck's sword fell to the ground, Crypt placed his own back in its sheath.

"I do not want to fight you, Bereck. What could I possibly gain from betraying you? Everything I have learned about being a watcher has been under your guidance."

In response, Bereck tore a piece of cloth from his sleeve and wrapped it around his wounded hand. He glared vengefully up at Crypt; quickly lunging at him with all the force he could muster. Both men fell hard to the ground, blood and feathers flying everywhere.

Then, a soothing voice resonated in their ears. "Stop! You're hurting one another!" Both men looked up to see Contessa standing in the open door.

As soon as Bereck gazed upon her, he was transfixed. She walked over to help the two men stand,

and all of Bereck's desire to fight had morphed into a strange curiosity. He found himself following Contessa into her home, not realizing that soon his entire world would change.

Chapter Seventeen

*B*ereck and Crypt stood before the Lord Alistair: his face red with anger, and his voice echoing throughout the hall. "Where are they? You were supposed to bring me their rotting carcasses! You have failed me yet again! I am sick of your mistakes."

Crypt stood nervously behind Bereck. His skin was no longer brown, but the light cream color it had previously been. Bereck's voice was strong as he answered. "It was my fault that Celestra left the paint shop unnoticed; Crypt was only following my orders. I will pack my bags and leave tonight; but your daughter still needs someone to look after her. Crypt has always been a better watcher than me, and he should take the position of head watcher."

Lord Alistair was shaking with rage. "You make me sick! You couldn't manage to watch a girl in a paint shop? You are a poor excuse for a man! Get out of my sight, before I decide you should pay for your stupidity with your life!"

Bereck turned and left the room, leaving Crypt and Lord Alistair to talk alone. Alistair let out a frustrated growl. "Crypt, you will have Bereck's position. All you have to do is watch a locked door. Any fool should be able to do that. Now leave me and try to do your job!"

Crypt immediately retreated and caught up with Bereck in the hallway. Together they slipped into a dark corner, where Bereck rested a firm hand on Crypt's shoulder. "It is now your job to protect Celestra. Crypt, you have proven what kind of man you are by deciding to come back; I know you will do well."

Crypt smiled. "I have never felt so alive. I know that, through the Creator, amazing things are about to happen. I can't wait to see what He has planned for us. The only thing I'm worried about is how long I can handle this paint; it really itches."

Bereck laughed. "I know; I can't wait to wash it off. Shh! Alistair is coming. We can't be seen together. Quick, get to your post!" Bereck slapped his new brother on the back, and Crypt headed for Celestra's room. The energized young man struggled to evade Lord Alistair unnoticed, but once out of sight, he skipped steps as he sprinted up to Celestra's room. Crypt then rested quietly outside her door, waiting until everyone had gone to sleep before quietly knocking.

He hoped Celestra had heard him, as he unlocked and opened the door. Celestra was sitting on a chair with her legs crossed. Crypt was surprised to find that she, too, had been waiting for him. Together, they excitedly discussed the miraculous changes they had both experienced; each detailing their part to play in the events to come.

The grand task the Creator had given them was to find Celestra's mother. After several hours, they developed a plan. Crypt would question the oldest servants, and then personally follow up on their stories. He felt as though one of them must know where Penelope was. Then they would find a way to escape from the house, grab a carriage, and bring Celestra to her mother. Once they outlined their quest, Crypt departed, eager to find the missing woman.

Over the next week of seeking out information, many lives were changed. News of Celestra's strange transformation had quickly spread throughout the manor. Curious servants lurked outside her door, begging to hear the mysterious story that had transformed her. Many who heard the story of sacrifice believed; though some thought the story merely to be the ramblings of a damaged girl. Celestra was thrilled to see so many of the people she'd grown up with come to life by choosing to be transformed. She was glad she had made the decision to obey the Creator and come back.

Resting on her lavish silk bed, Celestra thought about what it would be like to see her mother again. She had been distracted by all the visitors asking questions, Celestra had nearly forgotten the main reason for coming back was her mother. Deep in thought, she heard a knock on her door.

Crypt entered her room, walking slowly with his shoulders slumped. His face was filled with dismay, almost hopelessness, as he told of his findings. "Celestra, I have found your mother; but after you hear what I have to say, I am not sure you will want to see her. She now resides in a house for temporary unions. She bears the names of countless men from endless false unions; they are written on her face and arms. All of her exposed skin bares their names. My lady, Penelope has no light shining in her eyes. Looking into them, I could see that she had completely lost herself from joining to so many men. Perhaps we should ask the Creator to find us another assignment. Besides, you don't want to be seen going into a place like that; it could taint people's image of you. Even walking into that place, you can physically feel the hope drain from your body."

Celestra didn't answer right away. She walked briskly around her room, collecting her cloak and her most practical pair of shoes. Then she grabbed Crypt gently by his shoulders and looked him in the eyes. "We have been called to bring hope to those who are hopeless; those who have given up on living. We have been given life, and we must share it. We must! Crypt, I need you to help get me out of this house undetected. Now, let's go shine light into the darkness, shall we?"

Celestra's enthusiasm was contagious, and Crypt couldn't help but smile. "Your faith and courage are admirable. Perhaps by spending more time with you, I will become more of an optimist. You have convinced me. I'm ready; let's change this world!

Crypt quickly left the room to see if anyone in the house was still awake. He returned within a few minutes, having found the house to be completely still. Together, they crept quietly down the stairs and through the halls. Once outside, their pace quickened, as they made their way to the carriage house. A solitary lantern greeted them as they entered the brick building. Crypt walked over to the stalls, where two large, glowing salamanders slept huddled together for warmth. He placed a reassuring hand on their noses, rubbing them gently to wake them. He put golden harnesses on them and attached them to the front of the carriage. He gently assisted Celestra inside, then leapt into the driver's seat. His hands firmly grasped the reins, and, with a quick flick of his wrists, the salamanders led them toward the House of Temporary Unions.

In the shadows, a dark carriage sat parked a short distance from the estate. Its coachman sat tall, dressed in black, with his hood pulled over his head. He looked like death waiting to claim a living soul. He sat unmoving, as he stared in frustration at the Penteon home. For nearly a week, he had been waiting and watching, and he was angry.

"So this is what living in my own personal nightmare looks like," Kenrick whispered, with annoyance under his breath. He placed his index fingers on his temples and began to rub. He was frustrated that a seemingly simple assignment to kill one girl had turned into a complicated mess; he hated anything complicated. He just wanted to kill and not have to think about it. Thinking always left him with an annoying headache. His head throbbed, as he thought over the week's events and everything that had gone wrong.

He remembered the anger he felt over watching his prey disappear behind a locked door, and his frustration over discovering Celestra was still alive. He had waited hours for someone to leave that building, so he could kill him/her and claim his reward from Julia. He remembered his surprise upon seeing a little girl, an old woman, and a youth exit the shabby-looking front door. He almost killed them right away, but his instincts told him to be less hasty and gather more information. He followed closely behind them, trying to eavesdrop on their exciting and loud conversation. Kenrick had clearly heard the words of the little girl.

"I really liked Celestra. I am so glad we got to share the Creator with her. Opella, do you think she'll stay there, or do you think she'll come back?"

Then he heard the older woman reply, "It's her choice, but I believe she is one of those who will listen to the heart of the Creator and return."

Kenrick didn't understand the depth of their conversation, but he knew these people had not killed Celestra. It sounded like they kidnapped her, had a nice visit, let her go, and hoped they'd get to see her again. The only thing Kenrick really cared about was that Celestra was still alive and free, which meant she was probably making her way back to the paint shop.

He remembered running desperately to make it to the shop, only to watch his prey escape for the second time. He observed as her watchers placed her in a carriage and left. His whole body burned with embarrassment and smoldering rage over his misfortune.

Upon reliving his mistakes, Kenrick's gaze hardened on the sight of the Penteon estate. He couldn't stop thinking of how that elusive girl was ruining everything for him; that's when Kenrick's mood flipped from anger to excitement. Right before his eyes, Celestra Penteon walked toward her carriage house with only a single watcher. Within a few short moments, her carriage pulled out of the garage and rattled down the road in front of him.

Kenrick could not believe his luck; his entire being focused on the task ahead. He knew he had to follow them at a safe distance, so he lightly flicked the old translucent salamander into action. Together, they moved down the road in steady pursuit. His only thought was, *Little girl, your time has come. I will not miss you a third time.*

~ Chapter Eighteen ~

For the past week, Angeline had been dressing herself in her old, expensive, layered silk gown. Her new face paint had her looking and feeling a little more like her old self. Now that Opella was home, she no longer had to cook, or do any physical labor. In her fancy attire, Angeline looked rather comical, as she paraded around the Wentworth's home. If only she could have seen herself prancing about other people's waste, perhaps she would have been a little less full of herself. Part of the reason she was becoming more self-assured was because of the attention she was receiving. Throughout the week, anyone who dropped by to have their waste burned couldn't help but stop and stare at her. One youth even recognized her, which only helped to further inflate her growing ego.

Angeline was so engrossed with herself that she hardly noticed Ellie pulling on her sleeve to gain her attention. When she finally decided to acknowledge her, she merely looked down with an expression of mild annoyance. Ellie, however, was too excited to notice Angeline's condescending gaze. The only thing she was thinking about was finally acquiring Angeline's attention, so she quickly seized the moment. "Guess what?"

Angeline didn't answer; she just kept looking at Ellie, as though she couldn't be less interested.

"We have been given another assignment! We get to bring food and medical supplies to the women at the House of Temporary Unions. Once we get there, we'll wait outside the building, while Opella goes in to distribute food and share with them the story of transformation."

Angeline wrinkled her nose in disgust; she couldn't believe what Ellie was asking her to do. She threw her arms up in the air, and then rested them firmly on her hips. "How dare you mention a place that vile in my presence! Why do you people constantly find the most disgusting, dangerous, and reputation-damaging places in this city to visit? Why couldn't you just clean yourselves up, and let me teach you what normal people do for fun?"

Ellie's face dropped in disappointment. She looked down at her feet, shuffling them. "Please, Angeline, we aren't even going to go into the building. Opella wouldn't let me go in anyway; she said it's too dangerous. She wants our help to carry food and supplies. Besides, we haven't had a real assignment since my father got hurt. I am tired of waiting to see if they're going to take his leg or not."

Angeline raised her eyebrows. "His leg? Who told you he might lose his leg?"

Ellie's voice became serious. "I overheard Simeon talking to my father. He told him if he doesn't start moving his leg, he might lose it. If his leg dies, Simeon will cut it off. Please . . . I don't want to stay here. I want to do important work for the Creator. Who knows; we might get to see something amazing happen."

Angeline thought about arguing, but her guard had been dropped by Ellie's news concerning Aristus' leg. Her mind began to wander across all the things she'd done over her time here. She had served Trinzic breakfast, kneed an orb handler, and helped save Aristus by cauterizing his leg with a hot iron. She took a moment to think about all the new things she had experienced. *Well, I suppose it couldn't hurt. Besides, I've never seen a building of temporary unions before; it could be interesting. I am already living in a home full of waste-walkers and other people's garbage. It's not as though my being there could hurt my nonexistent reputation.*

"Alright, I'll go," Angeline decided. "But I want you to understand that I am not going to step foot in that disgusting building. The only reason I'm choosing to go is to see if this Creator of yours will do anything interesting."

Ellie hugged Angeline around her waist and scampered off to tell Opella they would be joining her for the assignment. Together, Ellie and Opella packed all the food they could find into five, large, leather bags. Ellie strained to carry two bags on her own, while Angeline carried the lighter bag, leaving Opella the remaining two. As the three women made their way to the front door, Opella realized she needed to check the bags before they departed. While scanning the sacks, she remembered something.

"Ellie, would you be so kind as to fetch six gold coins from your father for the carriage ride? Also, I believe you may have forgotten to ask his permission to go along with us."

Ellie gave Opella an expression of genuine surprise. "Oh no! I almost forgot to say goodbye. I'll be right back." Ellie pushed her bags off to the side, then ran to speak with her father. Ellie stopped in front of a curtain door, unsure of what to say. Her father spotted her little feet poking out from under the curtain and said, "Ellie, my sweet child, please come in."

Ellie brushed the curtain aside and entered. Aristus was sitting upright, propped up by a number of large pillows; in his hand was a book Honna had brought for him. He set it aside and smiled, as his daughter entered the room. Ellie hesitated only briefly before running to him for a hug. He laughed lightheartedly, and they embraced. Ellie kissed him on the cheek, released him, and asked her question.

"Father, I'm sorry I didn't come and ask you earlier, but may I ask your permission to accompany Opella on her mission to the House of Temporary Unions? She needs help carrying food and supplies to the women there. I can carry two light sacks of food myself; Angeline can only carry one. I really think. . ."

Aristus broke in before his daughter could finish. "My brave sweet child, you do not have to explain. If Opella needs you, that's all I need to know. I trust her judgment; but that does not give you permission to be careless. I want you to promise me that you'll listen closely to her instruction."

Ellie shrugged her little shoulders. "Oh, Father, you don't have to worry. I will listen to Opella; but above all else, I will obey the whispers of the Creator. I will keep my ears open and my heart teachable. I have one last favor to ask before we go. Opella wanted to know if you could provide six coins for the carriage ride."

Aristus raised his right eyebrow; he was still trying to decide if he was satisfied with her answer. While he thought, he leaned forward and pulled a small bag from behind his back. He opened it, pulled out six shiny coins, and held them tightly in his rough hands. He slowly relinquished his grasp on the coins and carefully dropped them into her hands. Aristus decided that the Creator, who had saved his life, would be more than able to keep watch over his precious daughter.

Ellie glanced back behind her, as she exited her father's room. "Thank you, Daddy, for believing in me. I love you!" She moved past the curtain and excitedly made her way down the hallway.

Now that everything was in order, the three women lifted their bags and departed. Outside, they awaited the carriage that would take them to the House of Temporary Unions.

~ Chapter Nineteen ~

Celestra gazed upon the House of Temporary Unions, as the carriage jerked to a stop. Crypt jumped down from his coachman's perch and opened the carriage door. He offered Celestra his hand. Her feet hit the cold stone street with a thud, and she looked around to see with her own eyes what she had gotten herself into.

Celestra took in a deep breath and noticed a strange aroma; it irritated her throat and tickled her nostrils. She recognized the exotic scent as the fabled perfume of ensnarement, used as a tool to draw men into false unions. The brick building seemed out of place in its surroundings. The square blocks were bright crimson, with numerous windows opening out into the street. The chanting voices of countless women echoed out from these windows.

"I will make you feel powerful!"

"I will help you feel attractive!"

"I will keep you feeling young!"

"I will make you forget!"

Crypt's face drained of color, as these false promises sickened his mind. He reached into his pocket to retrieve a pair of small sponges. Knowing the

164

true danger of the House of Temporary Unions, he pinched them with his fingers and placed them firmly in his ears. Crypt saw the concern radiating from Celestra's eyes and explained.

"I brought these earplugs because the last time I was here, I was overwhelmed by the sounds and scent of this place. Please pardon my weakness. With these sponges shielding my hearing, I will be protected from their calls; but, sadly, I won't be able to hear you. I will need you to follow me closely from here, and then I will lead you to your mother as planned. When we arrive at her room, I will safely escort you in, and then wait for you outside her door. Now, if you're ready, follow me."

Celestra mumbled a silent prayer under her breath and carefully took Crypt's hand. Together, they climbed the stairs and entered through the large double doors. The hallway seemed unnervingly empty. A smoky red haze spiraled through the open doors, and the sweet scent of ensnarement filled Celestra's nostrils. Instinctively, she breathed in the perfume, which quickly made its way to her brain, leaving Celestra feeling disoriented. She rested her palm on a nearby wall for support.

A gruff-looking man with a pointed, black beard appeared from behind one of the many brightly colored doorways. His hands felt like sandpaper, as they latched tightly onto her arm. Celestra's body grew ridged, and the man's grip tightened as he pulled her closer. The strong scent of fish escaped his mouth as he snarled, "Come closer, girl."

Crypt's sword swiftly punctured the air; its point pressed ever so slightly on the stranger's Adam's apple. Crypt's voice shook in controlled anger, as he muttered, "I am a watcher, and this girl is in my charge; you will let her go now!"

The man released Celestra's arm, took a tentative step back, and sprinted out the House of Temporary Unions. When her heart stopped racing, and the strong scent of fish had cleared Celestra's mind, she reached out for Crypt's hand. He squeezed hers and whispered, "We are almost there; you can do this."

Celestra followed closely behind, as he led her carefully forward and up a flight of stairs to the second floor. Side by side, they moved down another long hallway and stopped in front of the last door- -Penelope's room.

Celestra hesitated before going in, fearful that she wouldn't be able to speak. She was anxious about seeing the face of the mother she barely remembered. Celestra wondered how Penelope would react to seeing her. Unable to move, her mind drifted to thoughts of the Creator, and her fear slowly melted away. Now that she had regained her courage, she was able to enter the chamber.

She could hardly tell whether or not the creature sitting before her was her mother, but in her heart, she knew. The longer she looked at the woman, the more her heart filled with sorrow and compassion. Celestra began walking slowly over to her, knelt down, and tightly squeezed her mother's hand. Celestra brushed a tear from her cheek, as she pleaded with Penelope.

"Mother, it's me, Celestra, your little girl. Mother, I want you to know that I love you, and I forgive you for choosing this life over me. I realize now that you were ensnared by the lie that men would make you happy. I understand because I believed the lie that the world we see is all there is. I was wrong; there is so much more. Please listen to what the Light Giver wanted me to tell you."

Penelope's eyes were still fixed blankly on the back corner, but a single tear was slowly making its way down her cheek. Celestra stood up, moving close enough to monopolize her mother's line of sight. Then she bent down and looked Penelope directly in her lifeless eyes.

"I have come to tell you a story about a loving Creator who has a plan for your life; part of that plan involves erasing all those names from your skin and your soul. The only one who has the power to do that is the one who made you. I have come to tell you about the hope I have found so that you may be made new."

Celestra gently cupped her mother's face in her hands and began telling her how she could escape her self-made prison. She told her about her true home, outside the mountain. Then she explained, in detail, the story of sacrifice. The more Penelope heard her daughter talk, the more tears rolled down her thin face. They ran so freely that the lenses over her eyes released from their sockets and glided to the floor. Celestra was now looking into the solid black eyes of her mother. With the lenses removed, Penelope was now looking at her daughter for the first time since she had arrived. The tears continued to fall, and a slow, mournful sound made its way out of her throat before the first choked, raspy words escaped.

"How can you look at me? How can you touch me? Why would you want to save the selfish wretch who abandoned you? I have been joined to so many men that I don't even know who or what I am anymore. I have tried to cover and scratch off their names, but no matter how much paint I use, I can still see them. Everywhere I look, I am reminded of them. The only thing keeping me alive is that corner. I keep my eyes focused on that spot so that I don't have to look at myself. All I want is to stay numb; I don't want to feel anything anymore. Please leave me alone; I am not worth saving."

Celestra debated over what she should tell her mother next. She let the time pass until the words eventually came to her. "Mother, please listen to what I am about to tell you. I need you to understand that my days in this world are numbered. I don't know how much time I have, but I knew my time would be short the moment I decided to come back for you. I want you to hear what the Light Giver told me.

"He said, 'My child, my love for you is deeper and truer than you can imagine. I wanted you to know this before I present you with a world-changing request, a task that you are uniquely designed to perform. This assignment will be difficult and will ultimately lead to the end of your worldly life. What I am saying is that to those in the mountain, you will be dead. I will not make this decision for you; it is yours to decide, but I will lay before you your two paths.

'The first path is one that many of my children have chosen, but it is not my desire for you or them. Now that you are in my kingdom, you can choose to live here and never return to the dark mountain. If you decide to stay, you will be choosing personal comfort over listening to me. Your life will be much better than the one you previously had, but you will never be completely fulfilled, unless you live in my will. I will explain it to you like this: once you were a fish out of water, gasping for air. I placed you in a beautiful glass bowl filled with water; that is where you are now. You are breathing for the first time and are amazed by merely living; but, my desire is for you to live in my will, which will open your eyes to a sea of joy and amazement. I never intended for you to be happy in a bowl, because I created you for the ocean.

'The second path is for you to return to the dark mountain and find your mother. When you see her, you will be able to offer her forgiveness and explain the Story of Sacrifice. I want her to know that I have come to set her free from the men who haunt her dreams. This is a rescue mission for your mother's life. If you choose to go back, I will be with you always, even if you cannot see me. Through this choice, thousands will decide to leave the mountain. Generations will know me because of your decision to walk with me. Living in my will brings more joy, wholeness, and excitement than you can understand right now. Come with me to the land without hope, and witness my love poured out over all those lost in the darkness.'"

Celestra continued in a soft voice, "As you can see, I chose the second path. Mother, I couldn't leave you trapped and hurting in this false world. I had to return for you, even if it means my physical death. The Creator has taught me to no longer fear death; now I simply see it as the reward at the end of a tough battle. I want to live out my story; not just pass this life away, wondering what the adventure would have looked like."

Celestra fulfilled her promise to the Creator by telling Penelope the Story of Sacrifice. She completed the historical tale with these final words. "He constantly calls out to you, singing His song of change and hope. All that you have to do is surrender yourself to Him, and you will be transformed."

Penelope's mind was becoming clearer as she allowed herself to feel. Her heart was touched by these specific thoughts. *The daughter I rejected was willing to sacrifice herself to save me. What kind of being could cause someone to no longer fear death?* These words were plaguing her mind until a light came on deep inside her.

Penelope's raspy voice called out into the darkness, "Oh, blessed Creator, I believe my daughter's words are true. Thank you for finding me in this place and calling to me, even when I was only listening to the song of my own desires. I believe in your sacrifice. Transform me. Remove these wretched names from my flesh. Please pour your hope and love into me! I am ready to be held in your arms. Take me."

The ground rumbled, and like so many others before her, Penelope disappeared, entering into the world of light. Joy quickly washed over Celestra, as though she was being filled with cool water. Warm tears full of hope and love streamed down her golden face. She sat on the dilapidated bed and thanked the Creator for allowing her to be a part of this miracle. She had changed so much in only a week; her old life felt like a distant memory. It was as if she had been a corpse walking in the shadows, only pretending to be live, and now, through the Creator, she was finally alive!

At this thought, Celestra rose from the bed and spread her arms, as she twirled around. A joyful laugh escaped her lips amidst the spinning. Even in this horrible, stench-filled room, she felt light and free. She had accomplished what she had been sent to do. When she was too dizzy to continue spinning, she clung to the bed frame until she could walk without falling over. She then gracefully glided out of the room and reached out to grab Crypt by the arm.

He had almost dozed off when he felt her gentle touch, causing him to jump to attention. Realizing the room was empty, and that Celestra's work was finished, Crypt took hold of her hand. He led her safely from the House of Temporary Unions into the street. Once outside, Crypt pulled out his ear-plugs, enabling him to hear Celestra. Loudly and animatedly, Celestra detailed everything that had transpired with her mother.

She was almost finished when Crypt abruptly signaled for her to stop. His eyes were scanning the street as he spoke, "Have you noticed that the carriage is missing?"

Celestra shrugged her shoulders. "There is no need to be worried. The salamanders probably just wandered off, or perhaps someone stole it. It wouldn't have been difficult for someone to take the carriage while no one was standing guard. We will just need to find another way home. I'm sure we can easily find another carriage to take us home."

Crypt raised one eyebrow thoughtfully. "If it's all the same to you, I think we should at least look for it. Your father is already going to be angry when he finds out where you've been. We should at least try to bring back his carriage."

Celestra reluctantly agreed. Together, they began searching for the missing carriage. Crypt had marginal tracking skills, but they proved to be more than adequate in their search. His gut was telling him that the carriage was resting down the alley, adjoining a nearby abandoned building. His instincts were right.

They stood at the mouth of the deserted alley and silently stared at their missing carriage. It was resting near the back of the alley, but its doors were spread wide, beckoning them to peer inside. The light from the lantern poured out into the darkness, making its own path into the street. Crypt instructed Celestra to stay close behind him, as he pulled out his sword. The cool blade was brilliant silver and shone reflectively in the dimmed light. They moved slowly and cautiously until they reached the carriage. Side by side, they made their way to the open doors and peered in. There was no one inside; it was completely empty. Crypt rested his sword by his side and let out a heavy sigh of relief.

"It would appear as though the salamanders merely grew restless and wandered down this alley. We were gone a long time, and they probably just needed exercise. It's funny how it's so easy to assume the worst conclusion. We might as well get moving. If you could just wait here for a moment, I need to make sure the salamanders are still connected properly. If you see anyone coming, call for me, and I'll be here as soon as the first sound leaves your lips."

Celestra nodded, but she was not convinced. She didn't care what Crypt said; she was certain there was no way these trained salamanders decided to wander aimlessly down this alley to park. Something wasn't right; she could sense it.

Celestra's intuition was correct; something was very wrong. At that very moment, in a shadowed doorway, a pair of glaring, black eyes was following their every movement, watching and calculating the perfect opportunity to strike. They had walked right into his trap, and now it was only a question of time before that perfect moment would present itself.

~ Chapter Twenty ~

Kenrick's heart was racing with anticipation. He knew this was his last chance to make a name for himself. He could feel adrenaline surging through his body. Then, like a wave rising and falling, his adrenaline peaked, and he fell into a deadly still. Instead of his mind racing, everything became clear and focused. He watched as Celestra's back turned towards him, while her watcher bent over to check the reins. This was his moment. Like a shadow, Kenrick slithered under the carriage. The darkness covered him like a cloak. He lay completely still, breathing silently as he watched Crypt's every movement.

Kneeling in front of the carriage, the watcher was concentrating intently on making sure the leather straps were connected correctly. Whenever he was doing anything, it captured all of his attention. Just then, a cool breeze drifted out from under the carriage. Crypt's body shivered as a chill ran slowly, like trickling water down his spine. The brisk air called to him, luring him towards the underside of the carriage. His body shook visibly, feeding his curiosity; something didn't feel right. He crouched down on all fours and cautiously peered under the carriage, but in the darkness, he couldn't see anything. So he stretched his head farther underneath to get a better look. He thought he could faintly hear someone breathing. Instinctively, he reached slowly for his sword, until he could feel his fingertips touch the hilt.

That's when a hand sharply clamped down on his, and dark fingers slid over his mouth. He was now looking at two rows of white teeth smiling back at him. The grinning monster quickly caused the ground to run red, signaling the end and the beginning of Crypt. Pain enveloped the watcher, and then he was welcomed by a familiar, blinding light.

He heard a strong, reassuring voice call to him from somewhere in a shining new reality. "Well done, Crypt, my good and faithful servant."

Celestra heard a brief rustle come from somewhere near her feet. She looked down and saw that she was standing in something wet and red. With shaking hands, she reached down to touch the substance. She rolled it between her fingers and brought it closer to her eyes. Celestra's stomach twisted inside her; it was blood. She immediately felt faint. She didn't have time to think about where the blood was coming from. All she could process was that she needed to sit down, and that something had gone horribly wrong. She opened the door to the carriage and climbed inside, then turned around to lock the door. She held onto her dress with one hand and curled up in the corner of the cushioned seat. Just as she closed her eyes and began to pray, the floor of the carriage rattled and moved. In her confusion, she had neglected to latch the trap door.

Kenrick easily climbed up through the small opening and stood over Celestra, looking down at the girl he had been commissioned to kill. Celestra sat with her arms around her legs, and her head resting on her knees. As he glared at her, he wondered how such a weak girl could have evaded him for so long; how so much work and frustration was wasted hunting down such a worthless target. He decided to take his time and enjoy what he was about to do. Kenrick slowly advanced as he whispered, "The shadow serpent has come for you and will usher you into the cold arms of death."

Celestra's head shot up with confidence, as she stared Kenrick right back in the eye. "I am not afraid of you. You are wrong to think that death will destroy me. In killing me, you are giving me victory. I will receive the champion's prize, but your lifestyle of death has placed a price on your head. While victory awaits me, a painful journey to the Core awaits you. At your end, you will be ushered into a place where hopelessness and suffering never cease. Please hear my warning so that you may be spared. Please call out to the Creator; believe in His love and sacrifice. Then you will no longer have to be a slave to death."

Kenrick was momentarily thrown off guard by her bold words and obvious lack of fear. Something about what she said really bothered him. Was there really a price on his head? He wondered if there were other watchers waiting outside the carriage.

Then he laughed a little to himself and gave Celestra a mocking smirk, as he pulled his poisoned dagger from his boot.

"Did you really think that you could trick me with that pathetic excuse for a threat? You are just a girl who has given me far too much trouble. I'll give you a little credit . . . I had planned on having a little fun watching you bleed out, but your pathetic speech has taken too much of my time. I'll be forced to take care of you quickly." Without another word, Kenrick plunged the dagger deep into Celestra's heart.

She took in a sharp, shallow breath and winced in pain. Celestra placed her hands over the dagger, but kept her eyes fixed on his. "I wasn't concerned for my life; I was trying to save yours." With her last words still haunting the air, Celestra was free from the mountain forever and was receiving the prize for her unshakable faith.

Kenrick felt two emotions: one being relief over finishing his assignment, and the other, a strong feeling of dread. He watched Celestra crumple at his feet. He thought carefully on her last words and felt a growing remorse. It was as though he had been robbed of his kill; all the satisfaction he normally felt was absent. He hastily opted to finish his task and think about his frustration later.

Kenrick placed a card with a hazy black serpent in a visible pocket on Celestra's dress and began to drag her body out of the carriage. He wanted to make sure that Julia knew he had been the one to finish the job. On the back of the card, he had placed an address, which was to the home of the

Lord Denham; ensuring that whoever discovered Celestra's remains would deliver the body directly to Denham's residence.

As Kenrick glanced back at the card, his pride started to return. *Julia knew that I was the most qualified for this job! Ha, take that, Adlar. I always knew I'd replace you. Silly old fool thought he could tell me what to do. He is the one who should have been coming to me for advice.*

Kenrick was now standing outside the door. He pulled Celestra's body, letting it dangle halfway out of the carriage. He positioned her at the perfect angle to insure that someone would find her. That's when he heard the sound of someone breathing, and he knew he wasn't alone.

Ellie, Opella, and Angeline had finally arrived at the House of Temporary Unions. Angeline had dominated the conversation during their journey, making sure everyone present heard how ridiculous she thought this trip was. When the carriage finally stopped, Ellie quickly grabbed her two sacks and leapt from the door. Ellie held her sacks high off the ground, trying to show how useful she was. Opella smiled as she gazed down upon Ellie, taking pleasure in admiring her strong spirit.

With a loving countenance, Opella began giving instructions. "I am so thankful you both decided to accompany me. These sacks are heavy, so I'll need you two to carry them to the door. After that, I would like you both to stay close. Please don't wander off. There may be a silk vendor at the end of the street. If you get bored, you could spend some time there; but make sure to come back and wait for me at the bottom of the stairs. This shouldn't take very long if we move efficiently."

Opella began to make her way up the stairs. Angeline followed nervously, carrying her one small sack, leaving Ellie in the back to carry the remaining heavy bags. The large tower of supplies made Ellie invisible, as she swayed back and forth up the stairs. When her foot finally touched the last step, her little arms gave out, and the bags hit the cement with a crash. Opella ignored the noise and disappeared into the building. Angeline forcefully grabbed Ellie by the arm and pinched her.

Now that she had Ellie's full attention, Angeline whispered in her ear, "Your clumsiness is going to draw attention to us. You have done your part; now let's hurry to the silk vendor before someone recognizes me, or even worse, thinks that I work here." Angeline shivered visibly at the thought of being seen as a union woman.

Ellie, on the other hand, didn't appreciate being pinched and had been looking forward to doing something useful. Browsing for silk was not something she had any desire to do, but she recalled how the Creator had sent her to serve Angeline. Ellie whispered, "Angeline, look at all these lost people coming in and out of the House of Temporary Unions. I'm sure that they could use our help. Don't you think we should talk to one of them?"

A crooked old man brushed against Angeline's hip. The man apologized and smiled through a toothless, drool-filled mouth. Angeline looked at the man with disgust, then she grabbed Ellie's arm. "The only thing I have any desire to do is go to the silk vendor! We are going to avoid any risk-seeking activities. Today, we are finally going to do something blissfully normal. Don't ruin this for me."

Reluctantly, Ellie followed Angeline down the street. Since neither of them had ever been to this part of the city, they closely examined their surroundings. Ellie directed Angeline's attention to a nearby alley. "Can we go around this way? There will be less people, and I really feel that this is the way we should take."

Angeline rolled her eyes, making sure Ellie noticed. "Fine, but when we get to the silk vendor, I don't want you saying one word to me."

Ellie smiled in agreement. Angeline couldn't care less where Ellie wanted to go; she just didn't want it to take too long. Together, they walked down the alley. Ellie was the first to notice the lone carriage waiting motionless in the dim, flickering light. She turned to face Angeline. "Look at that! Angeline, maybe that's the reason why we were brought here. I am going to get a closer look."

Ellie ran down the alley before Angeline could say anything. Angeline was not excited about finding an abandoned carriage, and her thoughts screamed, *I don't want this kind of adventure; I didn't want any adventure! I just wanted a normal day. This horrible thing probably means robbers, murderers, and a secret correspondence transpiring between criminals. This all points to death!* Even though she was terrified, she didn't want to leave without Ellie and knew she had to run after her. Angeline ran as quickly as she could, but her large dress was slowing her down.

By the time she reached Ellie, she was winded and struggled to get her words out. "Ellie! We need to leave right now!" Angeline grabbed Ellie's shoulder, but the girl would not budge. Her head was turned down and staring wide-eyed. Angeline was scared and annoyed; she pushed Ellie out of the way. "Move aside! What are you looking at?" Angeline couldn't see at her height and was forced to bend down to look underneath the carriage. Her eyes immediately focused on what had frozen Ellie. She peered into the unfeeling eyes of an open-mouthed corpse, lying in a pool of blood. Angeline stood up and began shaking Ellie.

"See, this is why you shouldn't be interested in creepy alleyways and abandoned carriages. Now listen carefully. Run as fast . . ."

Before she could finish, they heard the carriage door creaking and watched as the handle began to turn. Angeline grabbed Ellie fiercely by her collar and pulled her to the nearest hiding place. There was a doorway nearby, with four large steps leading down to it. Angeline nearly dragged Ellie down the steps, then yanked her upright. Together they stood before the door while Angeline tried turning the brass handle. She pushed and pulled, but the door would not budge. She would have attempted kicking it down, but knew it would have made too much noise. Instead, she let out a frustrated moan.

Ellie, unfazed, gently patted Angeline. "Don't worry; the Creator knows what He's doing. I knew that we were meant to go with Opella. In my heart, I heard a whisper telling me to explore. We are here for a reason. I'll just peek around the corner, and see what we're supposed to do."

Angeline was taken aback by Ellie's excited tone. She was not sure she agreed with her, but one point from her speech did make sense. Observing the carriage from a distance sounded like a decent idea, as long as they only watched until it was safe to leave. Angeline did not want to get murdered in an alley.

Ellie did not wait for Angeline to answer; she pushed past her and headed back up the steps. She hunched close to the ground, peering quietly around the corner. Her eyes watched as a dark, winged figure pulled a woman's body partially from the carriage. Ellie was horrified when she realized it was Celestra! Her heart sank. Even though she knew Celestra had been transformed, and that it was only her body that had been destroyed, the shock of seeing her like that was heartbreaking. She was about to scream out in pain and shock when a hand pressed down over her mouth.

"Shh . . ." Angeline had to keep Ellie from blowing their cover. She, herself, was trying to fight the overwhelming urge to throw up or run. She was horrified, but not by the sight of Celestra; rather from seeing one of the two guards that had taken her from the House of Envy. Her blood ran cold. She was too scared to even begin thinking about what he might do to her. All she could think about was that poison-tipped dagger glittering in the lamplight.

~ Chapter Twenty-One ~

Kenrick turned immediately to see who was touching his shoulder. He unsheathed his sword as he spun around. Upon recognizing the face, he quickly returned his blade. A cocky grin spread egotistically across Kenrick's face. "So, Adlar, you have come just in time to help me clean up. How thoughtful of you."

Adlar's voice was calm and friendly as he spoke. "Looks like you weren't as incompetent as I thought. This is some beautiful work you've done here. I have been watching you since you started. You're beginning to show some potential."

Kenrick was ecstatic over the compliment. "Well, of course, I did an amazing job. It's easy to be good at something that comes naturally. I am a born killer, like a serpent moving easily in the shadows and surprising his prey. I have even made a name for myself: the shadow serpent. I think it suits me." Kenrick paused for effect. "I would love to talk to you more, but I need to finish up here. Then I will be leaving to claim my prize from Madam Julia." He waited to see Adlar's reaction to the news that Julia had chosen him.

Adlar's expression did not change, and he continued speaking in the same casual tone. "I can see that you are a natural killer, but sadly you have forgotten nearly every rule of an assassin. The first principle you violated was being invisible, knowing the art of blending into your surroundings. Your body may be camouflaged, but you killed someone dramatically in an open alley. The second is never killing someone who is innocent, like a child or widow, because there is too much guilt and remorse connected with them. The more despicable the person is, the easier it is for you to sleep at night. Also, likable people tend to have friends or family to avenge them. Whether or not you lose any sleep at night seems to matter little to you. You are quick to kill, and still slow to think. Lastly, there is a third rule: always know all you can about the person you're working for. Never trust anyone; make sure that you know them better than your target. You must always be protecting your own neck, because an assassin has no friends."

Kenrick was annoyed that Adlar was again scolding him like a little child. His voice bellowed, "Well, obviously you were wrong about the third one! I chose my job very carefully, and it turned out to be a very profitable decision. Julia even told me that you were unfit for this job. So, old man, you can keep your ridiculous code. I am a natural killer, moved only by my own keen instinct. Why don't you do yourself a favor and help me clean up? Maybe I'll be kind enough to let you have a few coins. I always knew someday you'd be working for me."

Adlar chuckled. He began talking lightheartedly, as though they were having a pleasant dinner conversation. "You remind me so much of how I used to be at your age."

Kenrick was puzzled by Adlar's pleasant demeanor, and it bothered him. "No wonder you don't have any work. You're too old and picky! You didn't even have the guts to kill that silly reject from the House of Envy. If she can classify as an innocent, what kind of people do you consider worthy of a kill?"

Adlar's face still looked agreeable, as he drifted closer to Kenrick. He smiled knowingly as he placed a friendly hand on Kenrick's shoulder; Adlar leaned in close as he whispered in his ear. His dry lips moved slowly. "Kenrick, my dear boy, I reserve my blade for people like you."

Kenrick's eyes widened as he felt the cold sword enter his belly. He fell to his knees in pain. The words of Celestra ran over and over again in his ears, as his life slowly left him. *Your lifestyle of death has placed a price on your head. While victory awaits me, a painful journey to the Core awaits you. At your end, you will be ushered into a place where hopelessness and suffering never cease.*

He felt as though something was pulling him downward, and his eyes grew hazy as he stared up in shock at Adlar. His mentor's voice rang clearly in his ears. "My boy, you had so much potential, but you failed to listen. You did a splendid job on this kill, but you trusted in all the wrong people. It's too bad that your instinct alone wasn't able to save you."

Adlar swung his sword skillfully to finish off what little life Kenrick had left. The young assassin died betrayed, without hope, and completely alone. His despair, like a wave, carried him crashing to the Core. If only he had paid more attention to the dying plea of the only person who had ever tried to save him.

⌘

Angeline and Ellie watched as Adlar swept his blade across Kenrick's throat. Angeline quickly whispered coarsely in Ellie's ear. "We can't be seen! We need to hide, or we will end up like that man!"

Ellie simply obeyed, and together they moved to the bottom of the stairs. Once there, they remained still, straining their ears to listen. An eerie silence had fallen over the alleyway. It was so quiet that both Angeline and Ellie's ears began to ring, until the sound of boots shuffling across loose gravel reached their ears. Both girls pushed themselves hard into the corner, hoping to avoid detection. The sound grew louder and louder, until it came to an abrupt stop right above their hiding place. Angeline was now digging her fingers into Ellie's shoulders. The pain from Angeline's nails had been steadily increasing, until Ellie let out a tiny whimper. Angeline and Ellie both felt a rush of panic over the small noise.

The man Angeline knew as Adlar smiled at her from the top of the stairs. She frantically pulled at the door behind her, but the door wouldn't budge. Angeline and Ellie reluctantly turned to witness Adlar casually making his way down the steps; Angeline knew this was the end. He was so close! She closed her eyes, and kneeled cowering on the ground. Ellie laid her body over Angeline's. Adlar stopped, towering right above them, and released a loud chuckle.

"I never thought I'd ever run into you again. You have an amazing will to survive . . . although this child has definitely surpassed you in the area of bravery. What an amazing person who is willing to lay down her life for someone else. Well, that's probably enough for idle chatter. I just need to ask you ladies one simple question: what did you see?"

Angeline gave a frantic, muffled reply. "We saw nothing! Not anything! We were just taking a stroll and fell down these stairs!"

Ellie stood up and put her hands on her hips. She raised one hand, so she could point a finger boldly at Adlar. "That's a lie! We saw everything. I know that shadow man killed Celestra; and we watched you kill him. Then Angeline hid from you, because she is afraid that you will murder her. Are you a life-taker? Do you steal people's lives?"

Adlar's eyebrows rose in surprise. He sat down on the steps and looked right at Ellie. "Yes, I am a taker of lives. Funny how you are not afraid . . . perhaps you should be. Are you positive that is what you saw happen?"

Angeline screamed. "We didn't see anything! Ellie, shut your mouth!"

Ellie looked back at Adlar. "I'm sorry, sir. I don't think Angeline knows that it is wrong to tell lies. We both saw you kill that man, and we witnessed him pulling Celestra's body from the carriage before that."

A pleased smile spread across Adlar's face. Then he stood up to address them. His voice became firm as he spoke. "Lady Angeline, if you and the child will relate this account, perhaps a position at the House of Envy may again be provided for you. The two of you will come with me to give your testimony to the Lord Denham Fontaine. If you tell him this story, I will make sure you will both be rewarded; but if you lie, you will meet the same, sad fate as that man in the alley. Do you understand?"

Angeline's nervousness was evaporating into relief. She nodded enthusiastically, while Ellie turned to her and whispered, "I knew that the Creator had a purpose for us here." Angeline shoved Ellie behind her, as they followed Adlar up the stairs and into the alley.

When they arrived at the carriage, Adlar collected the three bodies and tossed them into the vehicle. He turned his attention to the salamanders, making sure they were fastened properly. When he was ready, he gave orders. "Lady Angeline will ride in the carriage while you, little girl, will ride in the front with me."

Angeline was mortified by the thought of riding in a carriage with three dead bodies. She immediately began to protest, but Adlar shot her a look that made her blood run cold. Angeline shut her mouth. Without another objection, the old assassin escorted her into the carriage and closed the door.

"Angeline, it will be alright!" Ellie yelled. "Just ask the Creator to be with you, and you won't be afraid." Ellie hoped her friend had heard her through the closed door, as she followed Adlar. He gently lifted her, placing her on the seat, and sat down beside her. She looked up at him from her seat. "Is it alright if I drive the carriage?"

Adlar chuckled. "Child, you are a gutsy little spitfire. I like that, but no! Just be thankful I'm letting you ride with me, instead of with all the corpses in the back." He turned from Ellie and snapped the reins. The carriage lunged forward, leaving the alley and a long trail of blood behind.

~ Chapter Twenty-Two ~

*O*pella wiped her brow as she left the House of Temporary Unions. She was tired and ready to go home. Her sleeves hung ragged from having to tear off some of the material to make bandages; she scolded herself for not bringing enough medical supplies. Opella went there often enough that nearly all the union girls knew her by name. This trip turned out to be a discouraging day. It was hard to see so many broken people unwilling to believe in the Creator; most of them had given up hope. She prayed from the depths of her heart that those poor girls would remember her words and transform out of that horrible life. She took a deep breath and headed down the steps.

Upon reaching the bottom of the stairs, she looked around to see if Angeline and Ellie were waiting nearby. She drummed her fingers thoughtfully on the stone railing. "Where are those two?" Opella loved words and tended to think out loud. "I was gone at least an hour. Is it possible they've been at the silk vendor this whole time? I suppose Angeline is enjoying getting to browse the shops; I bet it's relaxing for her."

For as old as Opella was, she looked quite youthful as she stepped onto the stone street. She had decided to meet up with them at the vendors. She glided down the street, casually making her way to the few street vendors that occupied the end of the block.

The shops looked rather shady and unimpressive, except for two: a silk vendor with multiple carts filled with flowing silks, and a shoemaker. Opella figured that those two carts would be the only ones that would have interested Angeline. She visited both stands, and began to feel nervous when she saw no sign of her friends. She walked over to the silk vendor, hoping that the woman there would know something.

Before she could ask, the woman spoke up. "You are in need of a new dress! For a fair price, I can sell you one that will cause men to take a second look."

Opella shook her head. "No, I'm sorry. I'm not searching for any silk today; I am looking for a little girl with pale blue wings and a yellow dress. She is with an overly dressed female, who tends to think very highly of herself. Have you seen them?"

The vendor pondered her question, as she pulled a pre-made dress out from behind her. It was a beautiful green gown, with a glowing pink underlay. She held it up to Opella. "This dress will make you look simply regal. If you buy this dress from me, I will tell you what I know. This fine item will cost you a mere fifteen gold pieces."

Opella had no desire to buy the dress, but believed the woman knew where Angeline and

Ellie had gone. Strangely enough, while Opella had been in the House of Temporary Unions, a man had thrown some coins at her. She had tried to give him the money back, but was unable to find him. Her only problem now was not having enough money to get home. Opella pulled twelve coins out of her purse and handed them to the woman. She negotiated a trade for her clothes to lower the price. The woman reluctantly agreed, and Opella entered the woman's carriage to change into her new, unwanted dress.

The silk vendor smiled as Opella exited the carriage. "You look stunning! A dress that beautiful, fitting so perfectly, was definitely meant for you."

Opella was out of breath from rushing to get changed. "Thank you for your sweet words, but I need to know where my friends are. When and where did you see them?"

The woman looked annoyed that Opella wasn't more excited about her new dress. Her eyebrows furrowed, as she replied dismissively, "I saw a little girl ride by a short while ago. I never saw the woman you mentioned, but the little girl was sitting up front with the carriage driver."

Opella was a calm woman, rarely given to worry, but this news caused her great concern. She whispered her fears aloud. "Perhaps they got tired of waiting, and Angeline somehow managed to pay for the ride back home. However, it's unlike Ellie to run off without telling me. What if someone killed Angeline and stole Ellie? No . . . I told Ellie not to enter the House of Temporary Unions. She probably grew weary of arguing with Angeline and decided to give in to her desire to return home." Opella took a deep, calming breath; this explanation seemed to satisfy her. She decided to head back and hoped that her hunch was right.

⌘

Ellie enjoyed sitting next to Adlar in the coachman's seat. She was fascinated with this assassin's appreciation of honesty and his gentleness towards her. In the chilled, damp air, she cuddled up next to him for warmth. Adlar's body stiffened, but then relaxed. He looked down at her, his natural gray face softening. His normally hard eyes became gentle. He turned his attention back to the road and uncomfortably cleared his throat. "Child of the light?"

Ellie looked curiously up at him. "Yes, life-taker?"

Adlar let out a brief chuckle. "You remind me of Lily; she was the first person to ever show me the bravery that is found in kindness."

"Is she your daughter?" Ellie asked gently.

Adlar reluctantly shook his head. "No, Ellie. I took her life many years ago. She is the reason there is code that I live by, and why I will never again take the life of an innocent."

Adlar paused to see if Ellie would pull away, but instead she tightly wrapped her arms around him and said, "On that day, Lily passed her kindness to you. It is in you; I can see it. It will someday lead you to become a child of the sky. I am so glad to have you as a friend."

Adlar almost responded, but the carriage had arrived at its destination. He turned his attention to the gatekeeper, who nodded somberly, allowing them to pass. The gate swung open with ease. Ellie released Adlar and sat up, taking in every detail. The Fontaine estate was nestled into a looming rock face. Four tall fountains with sculptured warriors frozen in battle decorated the grounds. Lavender and green moss swirled in intricate patterns, creating a patchwork lawn.

The carriage pulled up in front of the chiseled manor, and Adlar spoke to Ellie. "Now wait here. When I get back, I will question you in regards to Celestra's murder. Do not speak to the Lord Denham unless spoken to. Remember, do not move from this spot." Adlar tied the reins onto the carriage and formally walked up to the entrance. He was ushered in and disappeared behind the large, iron doors.

Ellie started humming a simple tune to pass the time. She had just completed her first song when Adlar walked out the front door. He was accompanied by the Lord Denham Fontaine, whose aristocratically handsome features were livid with shock and rage. He stopped next to Ellie.

"Where is the other one?" demanded the Lord Denham.

Adlar quickly went to fetch Angeline from the carriage. He opened the door, causing her to roll tumbling out. She had been leaning against the door, trying to stay as far away from the corpses as possible. Still in shock from her fall, Angeline stayed on the ground until Adlar helped her up. He glared firmly at Angeline. "Tell him exactly what you saw; no embellishing, only the facts."

Angeline stood speechless, so Ellie decided broke the awkward silence. "Angeline and I saw an empty carriage just sitting in the alley. I wanted to check it out. When we got close, we saw a dead man lying underneath it. Angeline was scared, so we hid. We then watched as the shadow man came out of the carriage, with Celestra's empty body. Then Adlar came and killed the shadow man." Ellie paused a moment, and then quickly added, "You don't have to be sad. She did not go to the Core. She is with the Creator now; she is safe."

The Lord Denham ignored the last of Ellie's words, as he focused on the murder. "Show me Celestra," he said, with emptiness in his voice.

The carriage door was still open, and Adlar efficiently swung it the rest of the way. Denham leaned forward into the silent darkness. He gently tugged Celestra's body into the lantern light. He held her close to himself and let a few tears escape. His eyes burned.

"She was like a sister to me; this woman was to be my life companion. Now, she's gone! I wish that you would have brought the assassin to me alive. Then my family would have been able to get satisfaction out of killing the man who did this. Who are you, and why have you decided to meddle in my affairs?"

Adlar pulled out a letter from his breast pocket and handed it to the Lord Denham, who received the letter and read it aloud to himself.

Greetings to the Lord Denham Fontaine:

It has recently come to my attention that one of my palettes has become disgustingly obsessed with you. I felt compelled to assign one of my guards to keep a close watch over her. The information he gathered confirmed my greatest fears that she was plotting to exterminate her competition. She has hired an assassin to kill your beloved fiancée.

In response to this, I am sending my finest guard, Adlar, to resolve the matter. My hope is that he will be able to assist you in guarding your fiancée. Many happy wishes be with you and Celestra.

From the esteemed House of Envy,
Madam Julia Tattersall

Denham thoughtfully refolded the piece of paper and looked slowly up from it. "Words cannot express how disappointed I am that you were too late to save her; but I appreciate the fact that you brought the assassin here for me to see. You also returned Celestra's body, ensuring that we can honor her memory. I must at least thank you for that."

Adlar clicked his feet together and bowed officially. Denham produced a forced smile. "Adlar, tell Madam Julia that I appreciate all she has tried to do for my family. My desire is to show her my appreciation in person. When arrangements have been made for Celestra, I wish to visit with Madam Julia personally. I also desire to deal with the woman who is responsible for Celestra's death. For now, please deliver these two witnesses to my servant, who will be waiting for you at the door. He will provide you with a room for the night. Tomorrow, I will make arrangements for you to return to the House of Envy."

Adlar complied, but not before retrieving some items from Kenrick's pockets. He showed the Lord Denham the evidence he had collected to further prove Kenrick's guilt. He pulled the assassin's calling card from Celestra's gown and carefully handed it over.

Denham almost crumpled the card in his hands. "I believe you. You don't have to give me any more proof. Please leave me now . . . so that I may grieve in peace."

Adlar nodded somberly and ordered the girls to follow him. Angeline was still visibly shaken from the carriage ride and her fall. She held tightly onto Ellie's hand, as they entered the castle-like home. Angeline was glad to be reentering her world. The exquisitely decorated entryway contained spiraling columns, high looming archways, stained glass windows, and silk-spun rugs. The atmosphere of the house immediately settled her nerves. She pulled her hand from Ellie's, as she began mending her appearance.

Together, they followed the servant up a stone staircase to the second floor. At the end of the main hallway, they stopped at their rooms. Adlar was given his own room, while Ellie and Angeline were given a room to share. The girl's room boasted of a large, four-poster bed made of marble and covered with silk pillows. A large dresser was left open, revealing its many complimentary dresses. Angeline ran to the dresser and began looking through the gowns. Once she discovered a gown she liked, she turned her head to check on Ellie.

Ellie was gone. Angeline dropped the dress, and frantically looked around the room. From the corner of her eye, she detected movement and spun around. Something in the bed had moved. She cautiously walked up to its edge. When she got close, an uncharacteristic smile graced her face. Ellie was completely submerged under a mountain of pillows, fast asleep. A solitary foot dangled from the bed, wiggling just enough to give away her location.

Angeline carefully pulled back a pillow to get a better look at Ellie, and then bent down to whisper, "Maybe there is something to this Creator of yours. You are a strange and mysterious little girl. Sleep well, child of the light. Tomorrow, we shall see if your precious Creator has enough luck to help me regain power."

~ Chapter Twenty-Three ~

*O*pella could hardly move as she leaned against her front door; she had finally made her way home. She blew the welcome horn and waited. The door soon opened, revealing her husband.

Simeon's face shifted from excitement to confusion. He opened his mouth, and voiced what was troubling him. "Dearest love, where are Ellie and Angeline?"

Opella's eyes widened, and her hands began to shake. "They're not here? I thought maybe they had come home. I guess I have no idea where they are."

Simeon put a comforting arm around his wife and ushered her through the door. He led her to the kitchen table and poured her a large glass of water. Desiring to give her a moment to collect her thoughts, he left quickly to gather Trinzic and Aristus. Within a few moments, Trinzic and Simeon made their way into the kitchen, carefully carrying Aristus to a chair. Simeon walked over to Opella and placed a comforting hand on his wife's shoulder. "Everything will be alright. Tell us what happened."

Opella was a master storyteller, but this time she had difficulty finding the right words. Even though she had been given some time to think, she was still unable to articulate what had happened. She finally decided to walk them through her memory, hoping they would have insight into where Angeline and Ellie might have gone. As she related the tale, her eyes stayed focused on Aristus, who had beads of sweat running down his forehead. When she had finished explaining, he was the first to speak up.

"Opella, do you think that there is any hope of tracking Ellie from the House of Temporary Unions, or do you feel that you acquired all the information that there was to be gleaned?"

She frowned. "It is as if they vanished. I am sorry, Aristus, but there is no trail left to follow."

The table grew silent. Then, after a long while, Aristus spoke in a solemn voice. "There is only one thing that we can do. We need to make a petition to the Creator, and wait to receive an answer."

Trinzic's hands slapped dramatically down on the table. "All of you can wait around here and do nothing. As for me, finding lost treasures is what I do best. Don't worry; I have my own ways of getting information." He patted Aristus on the shoulder, and then swiftly paraded out the door.

Aristus shook his head, as he watched his friend's dramatic exit and said, "Trinzic can do what he likes, but time is short. Let's find out what we need to do, and where we need to go from here."

Simeon and Opella got up from the table, their hands tightly clasped. Aristus, who was unable to move, remained at the table. With silent tears, he bowed his head and began to speak to the Creator.

⌘

Ellie awoke to the sound of rocks crunching under a carriage wheel. The vehicle was bobbing from side to side, which caused her to feel disorientated. "Where are we? And where are we going?"

Angeline was sitting, with Ellie's head resting comfortably in her lap. She let out a relaxed sigh as she answered, "We are traveling to the House of Envy."

Ellie sat up and rubbed her stomach. She slowly repeated Angeline's words to herself. Ellie's lips began to move in silent prayer. She clutched her stomach tighter and tighter, and then looked up at Angeline though watery eyes. "Angeline, something evil lives there. Every time I hear you say its name, my stomach hurts. It is the Creator's way of warning me that we are heading towards evil." Ellie shook a little and began singing her song quietly to herself.

Angeline's excited mood changed into puzzled nervousness. In all the time she had known Ellie, she had never seen her afraid; Ellie was fearless. She stared, transfixed on the small girl, as her mind hovered over the child's puzzling words. *Evil? What could be evil?* She supposed one could say that her sister was evil, but she could handle Julia. She smiled at herself as her thoughts continued. She had plenty of time to plot how she was going to turn Julia to her way of thinking. Angeline relaxed again in her seat and began quietly contemplating her plan.

After a half-day's journey, the carriage came to a stop. Angeline's heart raced with excitement, and she reached over to touch Ellie's arm. "We are here! Look out your window. This is my home! I almost can't believe I'm back!" She noticed Ellie looking cautiously out the window.

Angeline's tone changed from excited to formal, as she gave instructions. "Ellie, you and your family have been good to me. I promise you that I will never forget that; but now we are in my world, and things will . . . must be different. You have willingly given yourself to me as a servant, and as such, you will not open your mouth unless you're instructed to. You belong to me. Obey me, and you will be safe."

Ellie said only one thing in response: "I will serve you so that you may be changed, and, in turn, you will learn to have the heart of a servant."

Angeline, as always, ignored the depth of Ellie's words and took them to mean a simple yes. Before leaving the carriage, she ordered Ellie to follow behind her at a graceful pace. Adlar opened the carriage door for them. Together, they walked in a line through the front door, making their way to the chamber of Madam Julia.

~ Chapter Twenty-Four ~

Aristus wiped his brow with his sleeve, as he spoke with the Creator. He had been talking for hours, but had failed to get any response. The silence was causing him to grow impatient and frustrated; he wanted to know where his little girl was. He stopped praying and yelled for Simeon.

Within a few minutes, Simeon was at the table. "Has the Creator answered you?" asked Aristus. Simeon shook his head. Aristus's fists slammed down on the table. "I feel so useless. I can't do anything to help find my daughter! I'm tired of sitting!"

Simeon frowned. "My dear boy, you are not useless, and you are right about one thing: we can't do anything right now. I know this must be extremely hard for you; but you need to remember all of the amazing things that the Creator has done. He loves Ellie even more than you do. We just have to wait and trust."

Aristus let out a frustrated sigh. "I know you're right. I'm just having a hard time seeing that right now."

Simeon nodded understandingly. "There is one thing that might lighten this burden. Opella and

I are like one person. When we are together, it is easier to confront any trial that comes our way. You are missing your partner; it is not good for you to be alone in this. I will go and fetch Honna and Bowen from the market."

Simeon patted Aristus on the shoulder, calling to him as he headed out the door.

"Don't worry, my friend; your wife will be here soon. Opella, my dear, I'm not as good with words. Would you be so kind as to accompany me to help fetch Honna?" Opella promptly grabbed her shawl, and together they went out the front door.

Only a few moments after the door had swung shut, the welcome horn sounded. Aristus looked around and realized he was alone. *Maybe it's them. Perhaps it's my Ellie.* Aristus threw himself on the floor. He grabbed hold of furniture, walls, and anything else he could use to pull himself forward. He yelled and grunted, as he made his way painfully to the front door. His leg throbbed, as it bumped into countless objects on his way. Tears rolled to the floor as he reached for the doorknob. He pulled the door partially open and peered through the crack. His heart raced with anticipation, desperately hoping his daughter would be on the other side.

Aristus' heart sank as soon as he identified who was behind the door. He saw a beautiful woman with light, shimmering hair; she was standing with two youths and a muscular-looking man. Once he remember Opella's story, he was able to recall the women's name. Aristus welcomed them. "Hello, you must be Contessa. Please come in."

Bereck pushed the door open the rest of the way. "Would you mind if I helped you?"

Aristus face grew pale. "I would love to say that I could make it to the kitchen by myself, but obviously I am in need of some assistance. Thank you."

Bereck helped Aristus up and placed him carefully in one of the kitchen chairs. Aristus looked down at his leg, which was still throbbing from the abuse it had just received. He recoiled a little at the sight of blood seeping through his tightly wound bandage. He moved his leg casually under the table, in the hope that no one would notice. "Please sit with me. I am Aristus. Simeon and Opella have gone to the market to retrieve my wife and son. They should return shortly."

When they had seated themselves, Contessa was the first to break the silence. "We have come bearing some worrisome news, along with some insightful revelation. Shall we wait for Simeon and Opella to return, or should I tell you now?"

Aristus was too concerned for his child to wait. "Please, if you have any news concerning my daughter, I'd like to know now. We can tell the others when they get back."

Contessa leaned forward awkwardly, which enabled Aristus to see the large, glowing orb on her back. The baby she was carrying was glowing rather brightly. He was fairly certain that at any moment, the child would cocoon and then, in a month, be released into the world. He knew then that the news she was bringing must be very important, because mothers almost never leave their homes when their orbs are about to cocoon.

Contessa was perspiring, as the glowing heat radiated from her back. With a silver cloth, she dabbed her forehead and then began to speak. "I have decided to begin with the difficult news, so I can close with what the Creator revealed to me concerning you." Her hair turned a noticeable shade of blue before she delicately cleared her throat.

"I have come to tell you that in the same place where Celestra's life was removed from this mountain, Angeline and Ellie bore witness to her murder. As it happened, the Creator gave me His eyes to watch the terrible event. Angeline and Ellie were obtained by a guard to bear witness to what they saw. At this moment, they are being taken to a place called the House of Envy, which is a place wrought with evil. Its foundation is selfishness, deceit, and all manner of murderous thoughts and deeds.

"Aristus, the Creator wanted me to deliver this specific message to you. He said these words: 'Celestra was carrying out my will for her life. She re-entered the mountain to rescue her mother, and she succeeded. Just like Celestra, Ellie is at this moment living out my will for her life. I need you to deliver this message to Aristus, Ellie's father. Tell him that Trinzic, Honna, Ambrose, Uriah, and Bereck are all to go to the House of Envy. Honna carries my light within her, and my desire is for her to bring my hope into that dark and evil place. A small light shines even more brightly in a darkened room. Right now, Ellie is shining brilliantly for me. Tell Aristus that my desire is for him to see his daughter again, but that he must wait a full week before sending the group to find her. I am not going to give him the reasons behind waiting, but I can promise him it will all be revealed in time. For now, I am asking him to trust in the one who formed him; the one who called him out of the darkness. Remember that I am the truth, and that I am always faithful. "

At Contessa's last words, Aristus bowed his head and silently whispered, *My Creator, I am sorry that I doubted you. I should have known that you would answer. I will trust you, even though I may not understand your plan. I trust you.*

Aristus looked back up at Contessa. "Thank you for coming. I know that this is not officially my home, but I would like to ask all of you to stay. Simeon and Opella would be horribly offended if I didn't offer their home to you."

Contessa's face produced a warm smile. "I had hoped we could stay here. Since my sons and new husband," She glanced with love at Bereck, placing her hand on his arm, "will accompany you to the House of Envy, it would wonderful if I could be with friends. Also, I'm fairly certain that my little one is about to cocoon, and I have heard that Opella is gifted in such areas."

Aristus turned to Bereck. "So, you are the new husband? I'm sorry; I don't remember Ellie mentioning you."

Bereck smiled wide as he answered, "I just recently became a child of the sky. Celestra was the one who sent me to Contessa, who, in turn, provided me with the opportunity to be changed. When I was made new, the Creator revealed to me that Contessa was to be a part of His plan for my life, and that this child needed a father. Just yesterday, we went through a simple uniting ceremony."

Aristus returned a jovial grin. "Oh, so you are a very new couple." He was about to continue when the door burst wide open. Everyone looked to see who it was.

It was Trinzic, with a bold announcement on his lips. "Oh, marvelous, a crowd! I'm so glad that you all could be here to witness my breathtaking ability to acquire information. Aristus, while you sat here waiting for the news of Ellie's disappearance to fall into your lap, through that mysterious Creator of yours, I used my superior skills and cunning to track down the facts. Are you ready to be amazed?"

No one answered him. They were all too busy looking around at each other, trying to contain their laughter.

⌘

Ellie was trying hard to follow Angeline's instructions as carefully as she could. She was walking a fair distance behind her, though she couldn't seem to keep her head bowed. There were just too many things for her to look at. She smiled and waved at passing servants, who, in turn, gave her only puzzled or annoyed glances. She didn't appear to notice, and continued to wave in the hopes that one of them would wave back.

Ellie was soon standing in front of the entrance to Madam Julia's chamber. Upon reaching the long, silvery blue door, Angeline whispered in Adlar's ear. He responded to her words with a serious nod.

Then Angeline turned to Ellie. "I am going to need to speak to my sister alone, which means that you will sit here quietly. Do not move or speak to anyone. I will be with her for a long time, so be prepared to wait. Did you hear me?"

Ellie nodded. "It's alright; I won't be alone. The Creator is always with me. I need to spend some time talking to Him anyway. See you later. Have a nice time with your sister."

Angeline's head turned downward, as she muttered, "This should be interesting." Angeline straightened her shoulders, lifted her head high, and followed Adlar into her sister's lair. The old assassin pulled one of Julia's servants aside. "Tell Madam Julia that her guest has arrived."

The servant gave Angeline an obvious scowl, before darting out to fetch her mistress. Angeline and Adlar stood in silence until Julia came running from her room, with a noticeable tear gliding down her cheek. She ran up to them and wrapped her arms around Angeline, holding her in a tight embrace. Then she turned her head towards Adlar. "Leave us. My sister has returned, and I am overcome with emotion. I would like to spend some time alone with her."

Adlar looked as though he was going to be sick. He cleared his throat. "I can see your family means much to you. I will gladly leave you two alone. Good day to both of you." Adlar cringed as he briskly exited the chamber door.

Julia carefully watched until Adlar had completely vanished through the silk doorway, then she turned to her sister. "Angeline, I have missed you. I am glad to see you have returned. Please come and sit with me, so that we may dine together."

Julia clapped her hands high above her head, and two elaborately dressed servants came from behind one of the many large curtains. Each serving girl carried a large saucer filled with luxurious food. Julia grabbed Angeline's hand and pulled her to a long banquet table. Angeline placed her face against the cold marble table; this table had been hers. All these things had once been hers. She was fighting back tears, as she turned her head up to look at her sister.

"How could you?" Angeline blurted out. "I am the one who brought you into the House of Envy. I thought we could rule here together. Why did you try to destroy me?"

Julia's face was emotionless, but her voice sounded sorrowful. She lifted a silk handkerchief to her nose, and a few tears began to fall. "You have earned an apology, dear sister. My intention was to become supreme high madam, but not to have you destroyed. I was never interested in sharing your position with you. You know the words of Glamour . . . you helped me memorize them when we were children. Become the best, no matter the cost to others; I was only thinking of myself. I never intended for you to be hurt.

"In fact, I have no interest in staying Madam at the House of Envy for very long. In time, I plan to move into a better position. As fate would have it, Lady Ember has committed a crime against the Lord Denham Fontaine. She is the palette currently in charge of the Chamber of Crimson. After we have finished eating, we will go and take care that situation; and then I will hand over her position to you. How does that sound?"

Angeline was shocked. She didn't know whether she should believe Julia's offer, or be afraid that she was walking into some kind of trap. Then she realized she had no other choice but to believe her sister. She had nowhere else to go. "That is very generous of you, sister. Apology accepted."

A cat-like grin spread slowly across Julia's face. "Think nothing of it. I'm honestly impressed that you survived the ceremony of burden. I can't say that I have heard of anyone making it through that horror with his/her dignity intact. You have not only kept your sanity, but I hear that you managed to acquire a servant, albeit a rather pitiful one. When we have finished with dinner, I can either send you a more suitable and appropriate replacement, or just clean up that poor waif that is waiting for you outside."

Angeline was offended; she couldn't imagine giving up Ellie. In listening to her sister's insulting words, she realized Ellie was the reason for her survival. She would never have kept her sanity if it hadn't been for the little 'waif'. Angeline replied sharply, "I wouldn't have selected just anyone to serve me. She will do just fine. Clean her up if you wish, but she belongs to me."

The corner of Julia's mouth twitched. "The girl means nothing to me; you can have her. I was only offering you one of my most talented servants as an apology for everything that happened. Never mind, we have more important things to take care of. Krenna will get you cleaned up and into a stunning crimson dress. Then we will have our date with Lady Ember."

Angeline said a quiet goodbye to her sister and followed Krenna to be decorated. Julia remained at the table, her hands clenched into fists. As she squeezed tighter, one of her long nails punctured her skin, and a drop of blood splashed on the table. In her clenched hand, she held a blue handkerchief.

"Thesbian, come here this instant!" she snarled. A cowering wisp of a man nervously crept up to the table and stood quivering before her. She lifted the handkerchief and pitched it at the man. "I told you to put an excessive amount of terrance powder on this. Look, does that appear to be an excessive amount to you?"

"No, Madam Julia. Please forgive me."

"I was hardly able to come up with a single tear! If you want to keep your pathetic little job, I suggest you run down and visit the cook. Ask him to put an excessive amount of terrance powder in your eyes, and we will find out if he has the ability to follow instructions! Now leave before your presence makes me ill!"

The man ran quickly from her sight. Julia slowly moved from the table to her armchair. She took a long breath and whispered, "Apollyon, do not let my sister ruin my plans. Don't allow her to become greater than me."

~ Chapter Twenty-Five ~

*E*llie sat leaning against the wall in front of Lady Julia's chamber. She held her knees up to her chest and wrapped her arms comfortably around them. Her lips moved to the rhythm of whispered prayers, as she passed the time by talking to the Creator. After half an hour of speaking, she spent the remainder of her time singing. She was almost asleep when she felt a rough tap on her shoulder. She looked up into the crystal blue eyes of a servant girl. Her skin was light beige, and she wore a sparkling blue dress.

Ellie jumped to her feet and stuck one hand out. "Hi, I'm Ellie. Who are you?"

The servant took a step back, and cocked her head inquisitively to one side. "My name is Rosalyn. I have come to make sure that you are presentable for service. Your lady wishes that you come with me immediately. Please follow me."

Ellie obediently followed her through the main corridor. She was led up a hidden staircase that blended perfectly into the wall. Rosalyn quickly explained that this floor had been designed for two purposes: production and pampering. One side was for creating new fashions and paints: while the other was for dressing, bathing, painting, and dying. She quickly rushed Ellie to the area for pampering. Rosalyn took her to the bathing room, where three servants immediately set to work scrubbing Ellie from head to toe.

"It won't come off," one of the servants grumbled. "She must have had her skin dyed."

Ellie's skin hurt from all the rough scrubbing, so she politely spoke up. "Excuse me. I haven't been dyed. My color is permanent; it can never be washed away with soap and water. The Creator made me this way. Please stop scrubbing me."

The servant in charge of the washing station spoke. "She's right; it is not going to come off. They will just have to paint over it. No one will know the difference."

The other servants agreed and then dried Ellie off, and shoved her to the next room. This room was for skin painting. Ellie was given clean undergarments and told to stand straighter. She was then instructed to spin. An older woman, who was ornately colored and very large, grabbed Ellie's face, pinching her cheeks harshly. "Who did this pitiful paint job? It is disgraceful. Don't worry, child. Mama Poley will fix what was done."

Ellie's skin was throbbing, and now her heart felt like it was breaking. Tears began rolling down her cheeks. "My color is not disgraceful: it's beautiful; it's perfect. It is a love letter painted on me by the Creator. Please do not call Him mean names. It hurts me."

The lady laughed cruelly. "Sensitive little thing, aren't you? You look atrocious, and that's the final word on the matter. Now be a good little girl, and don't say another word while I fix you."

Ellie placed her quivering lower lip in her mouth and bit it to keep herself from saying anything more. Her chest began to ache, as Mama Poley painted her skin a pale pink and her lips a dark crimson. Then she was sprinkled with gold dust. A single tear rolled down Ellie's cheek, and Mama Poley scolded her to stop ruining her masterpiece. Ellie lowered her head and began praying to keep herself from crying. The woman continued, adding red face paint that she made into spiraling flowers that spread from the corners of her eyes to her temples.

When she had finally finished covering Ellie with paint, she slid a sparkling silk dress of crimson and pink over Ellie's shoulders. Now that Ellie was dressed, Mama Poley moved her to another room to have her hair and eyes done. The woman inside this new room greeted Ellie and was, by Angeline's standards, beautiful. Her name was Luanda: and she was small and thin, with long, curly, green hair and matching attire. Ellie sat in a chair, while the woman carefully inspected her.

Once she decided on Ellie's beauty treatments, Luanda spoke in a sweet voice. "Now child, I will start with your hair. I am going to dye it crimson with pink streaks. Then we'll move on to your eyes, alright?"

Ellie wanted to scream, "No!" but the words did not come out. She found herself merely nodding.

Luanda quickly went to work dying Ellie's curls. When her hair had dried, Luanda pulled it neatly back into large buns stationed neatly on either side of her head. Her fingers drew two strips of hair down to hang in front of Ellie's ears and curled them.

Luanda took a step back and smiled. "You look adorable, like a doll. Now it's time for your eyes." After closely examining Ellie's eyes to determine the right shape for the lenses, she left for a few minutes and returned with a small, black marble box in her hands. She opened it and peered down at two shining, pink lenses. Luanda then instructed Ellie to remove her eye lenses, so she could replace them with the new ones.

Ellie was now frightened, and her voice cracked. "I am a child of the light; these are my real eyes. Please don't take them out."

Luanda walked up to Ellie and told her to hold still. She reached out with a quivering finger and touched Ellie's eye. Ellie recoiled, and so did Luanda. "How is this possible?" she wondered. She placed two fingers on each of her temples and started thoughtfully tapping. "Hmm . . ." Then, all at once, she stopped the tapping, leaned down, and whispered to the girl. "Just put these in, and no one else will have to know you are damaged. Don't worry, child; I won't tell anyone."

Ellie's heart sank a little more. When she didn't respond, Luanda simply walked up to her, lifted Ellie's eyelids, and placed the lenses. With that completed, it was time for the last room, where they sprayed painted red and gold dust onto Ellie's wings. Finally, she was finished, and they brought Ellie before a mirrored wall.

Rosalyn, who was waiting for her in the room, saw Ellie and gasped, "Oh my, you are stunning! You look very presentable."

Ellie's reaction to her reflection, however, was far from happy. Ellie gazed into the large, full-length mirror and started to whimper. "They've changed me. I look like the people of the mountain. I don't look like myself; I feel broken."

Rosalyn snapped at Ellie. "Stop crying this instant! We can't have you ruining all the work that was put into fixing you! I am here to take you back to Lady Angeline of the Chamber of Crimson. First, I will touch up your paint. Then we will go."

⌘

Opella and Simeon had returned and were sitting at the dinner table, discussing what happened to Angeline and Ellie. Trinzic was sitting at the end of the table, with his arms crossed and his feet up, reclining in his chair. He was sulking over having his entrance ruined while Aristus lead the conversation.

"Thankfully, we know where Ellie is; we need to talk with the Creator and ask how we are going to retrieve her. My wife and Bowen should be here shortly. Honna is a wise and sensible woman; I would like to save some of the finer details for her. We will discuss the information we have gathered, and discern what is important and what should be ignored. Does anyone know if Ellie being a witness will affect our ability to rescue her?"

Bereck nodded his head. He waited until all eyes were on him before speaking. "A witness is anyone who sees or hears anything considered to be a crime, by the standards set by the ruling council. To be a witness is a dangerous thing, so they are protected under the law. This law roughly states that the wronged individual, or someone belonging to the wronged individual's family, is entrusted with the care of the witness. The witness must stay with the family until they can confess to the ruling council what crime they observed."

Aristus listened carefully to Bereck's words, pausing to consider all the information. Once he had arranged his thoughts, Aristus said, "Thank you, Bereck, for clarifying that for us. Now we know the problem we are facing with their laws, but there is still another problem from our side. Ellie was given to Angeline by the Creator to take care of and serve. If Angeline wishes for her to stay in the House of Envy, should we still take her?"

At this question, Simeon nodded his head to show he was ready to answer. "The Creator never forces us on a path. Ultimately, Ellie has to decide for herself if she is willing to continue serving Angeline. However, we also need to consider that the Creator told us to go and rescue her. This leads me to believe that her time with Angeline will be over soon. If her work was left unfinished, I doubt He would have instructed us to bring her home."

Aristus nodded his head in agreement and said, "Simeon, you are a wise man. I believe that what you have shared with us is true. We need to put our faith in the Creator; we know He would not send us on meaningless errands. I have one last question for which I would like your input. Should we march in and ask for Ellie, or should we try to talk with her first?"

Trinzic, who had not really been paying attention until this point, jumped to life to answer. "Well, Aristus, my old chum, I believe that I have the expertise to answer this question. This is what should happen; I will sneak into the House of Envy. I will go alone and speak with Ellie. I promise I won't remove her. I'm quite sure that within four days, I could travel there, meet with Ellie, and be back to give you my report. Your sweet child should be able to tell me whether or not she is free to leave. Aristus, the House of Envy is filled with mystery and beautiful women; who else could be more qualified?"

Aristus's mouth turned up in an amused smile. He laughed a little, despite the somber mood that had characterized most of the conversation. "Trinzic, I do feel that you are the only one who could manage to pull off a feat like that. Sending you with the intent of solely gathering information would not go against the Creator's instructions. You are a good friend, and I am honored that you would place your life at risk to aid in the safe return of my daughter."

Trinzic's eyes began to water, as he looked at his faithful friend. "Aristus, your family is the only one

I have ever known. I would give my life to save you, Honna, Bowen, or Ellie, because I know that all of you would do the same for me." Trinzic cleared his throat a little, and then gave Aristus a wink. "Well, just to be fair, my friend, women and mystery are what I live for. The House of Envy is the kind of place that I would simply break into for a holiday. No need to brand me a hero just yet."

Everyone laughed a little. Aristus motioned for Trinzic to walk over to him and gave him a playful slap on the shoulder. "So, when are you planning on leaving?"

Trinzic smiled. "Hadn't you noticed? I've already left."

Aristus felt a tap on his shoulder and quickly spun his head around, but no one was there. He turned his head back to look at Trinzic. A large smile spread across his face, as he looked around the empty space. Trinzic had vanished.

~ Chapter Twenty-Six ~

A low-ranking guard was holding tightly onto Lady Ember of the Chamber of Crimson. Paint-stained tears were running in steady streams down her face, as the guard pulled back on her hair. She tried to look Julia in the eyes as she screamed, "Why have you accused me of such a horrible thing? I don't believe that I have ever even met the Lord Denham Fontaine! Let me go; I have done nothing!" Then her tone changed into a flat, defeated wail, as she began to articulate the answer to her own question. "My color crimson has been selling equal to yours. I am a rising palette. I am the only one who is a threat to you."

Julia's evil grin spread slowly across her face, as she answered Lady Ember's declaration. "You were never a genuine threat to my position. The real reason that this whole thing is happening to you is that you were too slow in realizing that my eyes see everything. I knew what you were up to before your little brain even came up with this despicable plan. My spies are everywhere, and I knew you were planning some treachery, but I would never have suspected murder, or else I'd have had my guard move faster."

Lady Ember screamed again. She lunged forward, almost breaking free from the guard. Her arms were outstretched, grabbing desperately to tear Julia apart. "Liar! Treacherous lies! You evil, detestable monster!" she screamed.

Julia didn't move. Her gaze became hard, and a quiet rage was almost emanating from her skin. Lady Ember caught a glance of her eyes and froze for only a moment, giving the guard enough time to regain his hold on her. As soon as Ember was secure, Julia hissed her response. "Take her to the cages! In five days, the Lord Denham will be coming for you. There will be no trial. I know that his family will take good care of you. My sister will be taking your place in the Chamber of Crimson. Think on that, as you await your end."

Angeline had been standing next to her sister, watching in silence. Julia turned towards her, and her voice changed into a melodic song. "My dear sister, this hall is now yours. I will walk with you to inform the servants of their new mistress. You will do well here, Lady Angeline."

At her sister's words, Angeline was filled with a mixture of excitement and repulsion. It felt good to be able to taste real power again, but watching her sister deal with Lady Ember had left her skin crawling. She tried to hide her uneasiness, as Julia educated the servants on her return and Lady Ember's dismissal. The Chamber of Crimson was now hers, and Madam Julia quietly excused herself to take care of other matters.

Angeline desired to find a mirror; she needed to look at herself. Upon locating a golden, floor-length mirror, she carefully began examining her appearance. Angeline sighed, "I am back. Everything will soon be mine again. I will be worshiped and desired just as before. In time, I will have it all."

Angeline called for a servant to come and lead her to her private chamber. She had decided it necessary to take an inventory of all her new possessions, because that is what she truly missed: her wealth and power.

In a bedchamber filled with silks, Angeline lay sprawled out on her extravagant new bed. She was daydreaming, thinking about how magnificent she must be for surviving the ceremony of burden. Not only had she survived it, but she had made it back into the House of Envy as a lady. She imagined how impressed people would be with her, and how she had done something no one else ever had.

Amidst her fantasizing, she heard the sound of a servant playing the flute, and she recognized the tune's message. It meant someone was waiting for her to grant him/her entry. She slowly sat up and clapped her hands loudly. Rosalyn walked in with her head slightly turned down; she was waiting for Angeline to address her.

"Why have you disturbed me?" Angeline asked, with an intentional harshness in her voice.

"Your child servant has been made fit for service. Would you like to see her, my lady?"

Angeline had forgotten about Ellie; she had been too focused on herself. "Oh, Ellie . . . I mean . . . my head servant; show her in. I would love to see how you have modified her."

Rosalyn curtsied. "Child, you may enter. Your lady wishes to inspect you. Display yourself for her."

Ellie came out from behind a curtain wall. She was almost unrecognizable; only her shape and size were the same. She stumbled as she tried to walk in the long silk dress, and her eyes squinted as she strained to look through her pink lenses. With her poor vision, Ellie tripped and fell to the floor, which caused Rosalyn to involuntarily snap.

"Clumsy child, that is not how one presents oneself to a lady. Enter again, and this time, do it properly!"

Angeline jumped from the bed and stood to her feet. "How dare you speak . . ." She stopped herself mid-sentence. She knew Rosalyn was about to realize that Ellie was closer to her than a servant. "How dare you correct the child! She is mine. Leave us, so that I can train her more properly!"

Rosalyn gave a simple nod and glided quickly from the room. Ellie turned to see her leave, and fell pitifully to the floor again. Angeline didn't say anything; she just stared at the floor with a sick churning in her stomach. She walked over to Ellie, knelt down, and examined the little girl. She thought back to how Ellie had been the one to heal her mind. She looked at the paint, and it made her feel sick. If she had never known Ellie, the paint would have looked beautiful on her, but as she peered closer, she found herself hating it. *It doesn't look right. She looks different, as though she's trapped in there.*

She was now looking into Ellie's eyes, and she had to put a hand over her mouth to stop herself from screaming. The eyes were lifeless; they were the eyes of a stranger, and she didn't like them at all. She wanted them to look familiar, warm, and not so empty. Ellie looked like a muffled doll, and Angeline couldn't stand it. She broke the silence. "Oh, Ellie? Are you all right?"

Ellie began looking around, trying to find Angeline's voice in the near total darkness. Her hands reached out, grabbing empty air in front of her until she happened to brush a finger against Angeline's silk dress. Her hand pulled the dress closer to her, and then they hugged. "Angeline, I am so glad to have you here. Please take these things off me! I want to be real again."

Angeline didn't know exactly why, but she felt tears welling up in her eyes. She didn't want Ellie to hurt. Ellie was her sanctuary; she wanted her to be real. The idea of her being fake, a pretender, tore at her. She quietly whispered back, "Ellie, I'll wash it off. Just wait here one moment."

She grabbed a washbasin and returned, kneeling before Ellie. Carefully, she scrubbed off all the paint from the girl's face. Once clean, she helped Ellie take out her eye lenses. "Good, you're back," Angeline said, as she looked into Ellie's real eyes. "I need you to be this way. You are my good-luck charm; you can't change. I was afraid you might lose your magic." Then she started scrubbing the paint off

Ellie's arms. Unconsciously, she began humming Ellie's tune.

"I am not magic," said Ellie. "I did not like the paint because it covered up the Creator's work. I am His masterpiece, not theirs. Everything I have must shine for Him. I don't want to be made to look like the darkness instead of the light."

Angeline half heard what Ellie was saying, and she chose to interpret it in her own way. "All I know is that wherever you go, life gets better for me. You calm me with your songs. You have vowed to serve me, and I need you to not change. Whatever you believe is fine. I plan on using that belief to grow in the House of Envy. With you serving me, I know that everything is going to go my way."

Ellie wanted to correct her, but a voice inside her head held her back: *My child, be patient. All is not lost on her. Look at your face and your arms. Look through your eyes. She is learning how to serve; all she needs is a little more time.*

Ellie gave Angeline another hug. "Thank you, Angeline. You are my best friend. I know that you'll find the Creator for yourself. Please remember all that He has shown you. We'll never give up on you."

Angeline had grown accustomed to ignoring Ellie. She returned the hug, but then gently pushed her away. "I need to get some rest. I have made arrangements for you to sleep in my chamber. A small bed has been set aside for you. Before we rest, I would like for you to tell me one of your charming little stories. I think some entertainment would be nice to help me fall asleep. When you are done, then you may sing to me."

Ellie felt a rush of excitement, as she realized that this was indeed a divine opportunity, and her little voice squeaked with anticipation. "I will tell you the Story of Sacrifice; it is my favorite. Do you want me to tell you now?"

Angeline shook her head. "Not yet. First, we must prepare for bed. While my servants prepare me, I want you to remain out of sight. No one can see you without your paint. You may have the wash-room to yourself. Now go there and wait."

Ellie obeyed by quickly running to hide in the lavish bathing room. She waited there until Angeline called for her. Ellie then crawled onto Angeline's bed and stationed herself at the end. There she stayed, waiting for her friend to give her the signal to begin. Angeline fluffed the pillows and sank gently into them. Once she was completely relaxed, she waved her hand to signal that she was ready. Ellie stood up and began telling the Story of sacrifice.

The Story of Sacrifice

"The Creator wept, as He watched His beloved creation enter the mountain. He could hear their cries. They were begging Him to have mercy on them, to save them. In that moment, a plan of rescue was set in motion. The Creator began singing to the mountain, telling His people He would provide a way for them to escape.

"The years passed, and still no rescue. Many had given up hope. They felt like their Creator had abandoned them. So together, they decided to find their own way out. The years continued to roll by as they dug deep into the mountain; but no matter how long or hard they tried, they could not find a way of escape. Soon the people gave up all hope of returning to their beloved home. They knew that on their own, they could do nothing. They became resigned to their fate and began carving cities.

"At the depth of their hopelessness, the Creator fulfilled His promise. The perfect moment had arrived. The Creator gazed over the dark waters that had once been crystal, and He knew what He had to do. He began walking to the water's edge.

"Apollyon and his army of deceivers sat at the top of the mountain, watching and waiting to see what the Creator would do. They kept their distance, because they knew they had no real power. The only power they possessed was the ability to twist and distort the truth; that is why his servants were named deceivers, because that was their true nature.

"Long ago, the Creator had banished Apollyon to the mountain. Since the Creator's world was perfect, Apollyon, who is evil, had to be separated from it. Evil had to be kept away, because once any part of it entered one of his creation, they would die, destined for the Core. This wicked creature had become the master of death the moment the Creator's children had chosen to follow him; death had not existed until then. In exchange for their trust, Apollyon gave the people of the sky selfish, evil hearts bent towards destruction, and bodies destined to die.

"The Creator knew there was only one way to save His creation. He, Himself, being life, must be handed over to death. He stepped one foot into the dark acidic waters. Apollyon, along with his deceivers, called down from the mountain, mocking him, 'Wisdom himself has turned into a fool. Why didn't you just destroy the whole world and begin again? Your creation is mine now. They are my captives, destined to die, and I will keep them for an eternity in the Core, to be separated from you forever. Go ahead; destroy yourself. You have failed. Your creation no longer loves you. Die!'

"The Creator did not respond; He kept walking into death. As He entered the waters, they could not overpower Him. He raised His arms into the air and released all His power. As it left Him, the dark, shadowy waters began swirling around Him. The Creator cried out in agony, as the poisonous liquid began entering His pores. The deadly water burned Him from the inside out. The Creator, at any time, could have stopped His suffering, but He knew this was the only way to save His children. The dark water filtered through His body for hours, until the lake shone like crystal. The Creator had purified the water with His blood, and, in the process, His life was poured out. His empty body sunk to the bottom of the lake, dead. The whole planet shook in mourning.

"Apollyon laughed as the world trembled. He believed in his foolishness that everything now belonged to him. Throughout the night, he and his deceivers rejoiced. When the sun rose in the sky, Apollyon examined the crystal waters, but all was still. Every day he checked, until on the third day, he noticed something moving in the water. It began to bubble and swirl. Steam rose high into the air, and a blinding light shot from the water, forcing Apollyon and his deceivers to look away. Then, the Creator rose from the depths in a burst of light.

"The Creator spoke with authority, 'Death has been overcome. This lake shall now be called the Lake of Eternal Life. Anyone who is washed by these waters will not die, but will live eternally with me. In my dwelling place, hearts of shadow will become light. Listen to my voice, children, and return to me. I have provided a way for you to leave the mountain. If you believe in your heart that I am your Creator, and confess with your mouth that I have saved you, you will be set free. Return, my children, to the world of light.'

"Apollyon, realizing what had happened, ran in terror into the mountain, with his deceivers following him. Their only purpose now was to weave lies in the hearts of the people. They would teach the children of the mountain to only love themselves. The deceivers would help them fall so in love with their evil desires that they would ignore the sacrifice of the Creator.

"The Creator continued to sing His song, calling for His children to believe in His sacrifice and return to Him. Some heard and recognized His voice. They were removed from the mountain and granted new life. They were given back their color and fashioned with new hearts. Once they had been changed, many returned to rescue those still taken captive by Apollyon. Those who returned to the mountain did not go back alone, because their Creator promised He would be with them always.

"To this day, He has never stopped calling to the people of the mountain. If you listen, you can hear His voice echoing in your heart, singing to all of His children to return to Him and be set free. Please, listen to the words of the Creator; He is calling for you to escape from death. Cry out to Him, believe in His sacrifice, and you will be set free."

When the story ended, Ellie's voice turned to eloquent song.

> *The wind blows over the Crystal Lake*
> *A voice calls to all those who have ears to hear.*
> *It is the Creator. He calls to you. He sings . . .*
> *Let my healing waters restore.*
> *Let my love make a home in your heart.*
> *Let my truth open your blinded eyes.*
> *Return, my child, to your father's arms,*
> *Return . . . return . . . home.*
> *The place you dwell is dark and empty.*
> *Come to his world of light.*
> *Hear him sing his song of love*
> *And to you he sings . . .*
> *Let my healing waters restore.*
> *Let my love make a home in your heart.*
> *Let my truth open your blinded eyes.*
> *Return, my child, to your father's arms,*
> *Return . . . return . . . home.*

Angeline's eyes were wide with fear, as Ellie's song filled the chamber. She was scared because, in her heart, she knew the Creator had been calling to her. He had been speaking to her through Ellie. Her heart was racing; she didn't want to serve others. She wanted to be in control of her own life. Now that she had a taste of power again, how could she give it up?

Angeline closed her eyes, while Ellie was lost in her song. She decided to pretend to be sleeping, and hoped Ellie would leave her alone and go to sleep. She believed that by the time she awoke, the story would be forgotten and she could continue doing things her own way.

In time, Ellie finished singing. She looked lovingly at Angeline and patted her gently on the head. Ellie took one last look at Angeline before crawling into bed. As she fell asleep, she kept quietly humming. Unknowingly, Ellie left Angeline wide awake, mentally recalling every word of the song.

~ *Chapter Twenty-Seven* ~

Trinzic's cape flapped wildly, as the carriage moved towards Hawthorne City. It was almost a full day's journey to the House of Envy, and the trip was starting to wear on his muscles. He clung tightly to the underside of the carriage, and wrapped his feathered wings around himself to keep the dust from getting into his eyes. To take his mind off his sore body, he passed the time by embellishing stories about himself.

At the end of the long ride, Trinzic had finally arrived in Hawthorne City. He waited in the darkness for the perfect moment to release himself from beneath the carriage. An opportunity presented itself when the carriage stopped to allow a young woman to cross. He quickly unclenched his fists and dropped to the ground. The carriage continued on, passing easily above him. He jumped to his feet and began dusting himself off.

He examined his cape and saw that it had been shredded. With an annoyed sigh, Trinzic merely tossed it aside and tucked himself into a nearby alley. He changed his clothes, fixed his hair, put on some fresh paint, and replaced his eye lenses: everything matching his green-and-gold theme. When he was sure he was ready, Trinzic began walking with an air of confidence towards the House of Envy.

Once he arrived, he casually walked through the front gate and headed towards the famous palette stations. He was grateful he had arrived during business hours. He casually surveyed his surroundings, and immediately joined a large crowd moving towards the Chamber of Crimson. Trinzic easily tailored his movements to protect himself from being trampled. A warrior from the Coliseum of Power was purposefully pushing people to the ground. Trinzic watched as a young aristocrat was hit hard, falling mere feet in front of him. He immediately placed his arms under the youth, pulling him up and out of the crowd. The young gentleman was grateful for Trinzic's help and thanked him profusely. "You, my dear sir, are truly extraordinary! I would have been crushed, if not for your help. That giant buffoon nearly prevented me from seeing my favorite palette, Lady Angeline. Her beauty is simply legendary; even more so, with all the rumors concerning her return. I have always felt her beauty was unmatched. My only fear is that I will return home with an empty coin purse."

Trinzic's heart began to race upon hearing Angeline's name. Hearing the gentleman swooning over her led to a hasty goodbye and an immediate return to the crowd. Soon Trinzic was standing near Angeline's station. Trinzic carefully made his way up to the front to acquire a better view. His eyes locked in on her and remained transfixed. Her red hair flowed like silk, brushing softly across her golden cheeks. Her ruby eyes sparkled in the lamp-light. The dress she wore was elegant, with silk crimson and gold ribbons trailing downward. Two female servants, dressed to match, fanned her while she remained posed in place.

A burly man roughly pushed against Trinzic's shoulder, which forced him out of his daze. He lowered his eyes to examine the paints, which were nestled in amongst a countless assortment of other intriguing items. In his hand, he held a green silk bag, and as he brushed his hand casually across the table, several items silently disappeared into it. When he finished acquiring a few new things to wear, and a variety of different paints, he made his way to a female servant standing near Angeline's station.

He stood next to the quiet girl and leaned in to whisper. "You, my lady, possess a rare beauty, which surpasses Lady Angeline and any other lady I have seen thus far. Since you are such an exquisite work of art, I thought you might enjoy something equally as breathtaking." In his hands, he held a small, jeweled box. She opened it and gasped with gleeful shock; it was filled with real gold dust.

She began to giggle. "Well, mysterious stranger, how can I ever repay you?"

Trinzic winked, then handed her an envelope with an official-looking seal. "All I desire from you is one small repayment. Could you make sure that this finds its way to Lady Angeline? This letter contains my humble recommendation that you be elevated to something more fitting for someone of your beauty."

The girl fanned herself with the envelope, bowed her head, and curtsied. Trinzic kissed her hand and then disappeared into the crowd. He watched from a distance as she took the letter discreetly to one of the servants fanning Angeline. The letter fell from her fan, descending perfectly into Angeline's lap.

Trinzic stood watching as Angeline read the letter. Her lips bore a pleasant smirk as she read his letter. She began gently swaying her head from side to side, glancing over the audience in an attempt to find him. Unable to find him in the crowd, she whispered something to the fan girl, who immediately left to speak with the girl he had conned. The two servants chatted for a moment, and then Trinzic watched as the girl began searching for him. To amuse himself, Trinzic sprung up behind her and gave her wing a gentle tug.

She spun around and gasped with excitement, "There you are! You scared me! Lady Angeline must have enjoyed what you wrote, because she wants me to bring you to her private chamber."

The girl giggled playfully, as they chatted all the way to Angeline's room. Once there, he kissed her hands and waved at her as she departed. Trinzic immediately felt two tiny arms squeezing his legs. He looked down and saw Ellie staring up at him.

"Did my parents come with you?"

"Ellie!" He patted her fondly on the head. "No, sweet girl, your Creator told your family they are not to come for you for a week. I believe that was yesterday afternoon, which means that your family will be coming in six days."

Ellie gave Trinzic one more squeeze and then let go of him. "Then why have you come ahead of them?"

"I was sent to inquire whether or not you were bound here as a witness under the protection of the House of Envy."

Ellie cocked her head to one side, and then put one finger on her lip as she thought. "I haven't heard anyone mention a trial. I don't think that is the reason why I was brought here."

Trinzic smiled and clapped his hands. "What stupendous news! That makes things a whole lot easier. So then, in six days, your mother, three men, and I will be coming to bring you home."

Ellie's tone turned official. "Trinzic, I can't leave if Angeline wants me to stay. I have been chosen to serve her."

Trinzic picked Ellie up. "Well then, little troublemaker, if that is how you are going to be, then I only have one more question left to ask. Is your family allowed to visit you here, or do I need to sneak them in?"

Ellie answered with a question of her own. "Well, how did you get in here?"

Trinzic shrugged. "I just gave Angeline a note, and they escorted me in."

"I think they would be able to see me the same way," Ellie responded.

Trinzic wasn't sure, but nodded in agreement and carefully set Ellie back on her feet. They sat beside each other on the floor and began swapping tales of their adventures. Near the end of their discussion, Angeline glided in. She entered alone, with no servants accompanying her. Trinzic was the first to notice her quiet entrance.

He quickly jumped from the floor and greeted her with a dramatic bow. "Lady Angeline of the House of Crimson, it is a pleasure to gaze upon your exquisite beauty. No one has ever carried the color crimson so elegantly."

Angeline was amused. "Trinzic, I can say this about you; you are a charmer. It is nice seeing you in my world. With your skills and handsome features, I would surely find you a place of prominence in my house."

He bowed low and admitted, "Nothing would bring me more pleasure than to be given the opportunity to always be near you. Sadly, my cherished one, I am on an important quest to gather information, which Ellie has already provided. Therefore, my dear, all I need from you is a simple favor. Honna and some of the others want to see you and Ellie. My love, I will be back in six days, if you will have us."

Angeline's face was beaming with deep satisfaction. The right corner of her mouth turned up. "That is marvelous news. I would love to have them come. I gave my word that if they helped me, I would take care of them. Now it is my chance to offer them their reward; they can be my servants. I know it will be uncomfortable for them at first, but in time, I'm sure they will enjoy not having to live in the dirt."

Trinzic had been around Aristus for a long time, and was quite certain that he would never willingly work for Angeline. He knew this, but decided he would not voice his opinions out loud. Trinzic enjoyed causing mischief, so he simply agreed that they would be fortunate to have her as a mistress. His mind was already contemplating Aristus' reaction to her generous offer. It amused him so much that he allowed a small chuckle to escape. Angeline stared at him disapprovingly.

"Angeline, my dear, I must confess that it was quite the adventure traveling here. I would tell you all the details, but in my rush to see you, I did not obtain any rest. My treasure, I hate to impose on you, but is there a place that I may sleep until morning?"

She waved her hands and said it would be no trouble at all. She ordered Ellie to make up a bed for Trinzic. There was a long fainting couch with many silk pillows adorning it; Ellie easily converted it into a bed for him. Trinzic continued to entertain the girls for a while longer, and then quickly fell asleep on the fainting couch.

When Angeline and Ellie awoke in the morning, Trinzic was gone. The room looked as though he had never been there. The pillows and blankets he had slept with had all been put away. The only thing out of place was a singular missing item: a crimson ribbon stolen from Lady Angeline's hair.

Julia snapped at Krenna, "The Lord Denham will be coming tonight. Everything must be perfect for his arrival. Have these letters delivered to every palette, informing them they will be performing in the grand banquet hall in three days. We haven't time to spare. Now go, and begin preparations." Krenna curtsied and swiftly departed.

Julia opened her silk handbag, looked inside, and gently pulled out a shapely emerald vial; it rested weightlessly in her hands. She placed her fingers around the stopper, pulling up to remove it, and a red vapor rose from the bottle. Julia leaned in to smell its contents, and as soon as the aroma entered her nose, she let out a relaxed sigh and whispered, "Nothing smells as sweet as the scent of ensnarement." She then placed two fingers on the top of the bottle and tipped it. She dabbed her moist fingertips lightly around her hairline to spread the fragrance, without damaging her paint. When she had finished with her hairline, she placed a drop on her tongue. "Make my words sweet," she murmured deviously.

Julia had finished with the vial and returned it to her purse. She delicately got up from her seat and glided to a nearby mirror. She stared, mesmerized by her own reflection. Her fingers brushed the glass, as she darkly hissed her intentions. "All too easy; Denham is practically already won. No one, not even Angeline, could ruin this for me. I need to unravel the mystery of that servant child. How dense does she think I am? Angeline hates children. My sister can't keep the waif hidden from me forever; soon I will discover her secret."

Julia felt a slight twinge in her heart. A memory played through her mind, capturing her thoughts. *Father always gave Angeline the rarest of choice foods, like my favorite caramelized cheshernuts. He would make me watch, as she savored every bite in front of me. Angeline was always his favorite; I was his mistake; just an extra child that placed a burden on their finances. If only he had realized his error before I poisoned him. He never suspected that I would outsmart even him. Mother was wise to help me, and she was right in fearing me. Angeline, you may have wormed your way back into the House of Envy, but I promise you; never again will you take what is rightfully mine.*

Chapter Twenty-Eight

The Wentworth's home was bustling with all sorts of activity. Trinzic and Bowen were playing their treasure-finding game, along with their new friends Ambrose and Uriah. Contessa and Opella were working with the stained glass. Honna lay cozily next to her husband, while he casually ran his fingers through her hair.

Aristus took in a deep, relaxing breath. "It is so nice to have you back. You know me far better than I even know myself." He shifted slightly and ran his hand through his own hair. "It has been hard not being able to move or help with anything. I can't stand just waiting and doing nothing, while our sweet, little girl is facing untold danger all alone. Not only that, but you, my beloved, will soon be doing the job that I should be doing. I am the protector of this family, but at this moment, I feel as though I've failed."

Honna's eyes were watering. She turned to look at her husband, her voice quivering, "Aristus, you are a wonderful protector. Look at your leg. There is a boy who was saved because you cared more about him than your own safety! Would you rather

244

that boy was dead and suffering in the Core, so you could come with us? No, of course not. Please, stop hurting yourself with these damaging thoughts, these lies. The Creator knows what He's doing; we just need to trust Him."

Aristus' body stiffened, and then relaxed. "I know all that. It's merely the fact that I have to wait. I am a person of action." He hesitated, then continued, "I miss our Ellie, and I want to see her. If Ellie is going to be living with Angeline, who knows when I will see her again."

Honna squeezed her husband tightly and kissed the side of his face. She noticed his sunken eyes, and how they reflected the physical and emotional tolls of his trauma. As she snuggled into the nest of his large, feathered wing, her voice was soft and understanding. "I love you. It's been difficult watching you go through this. Hearing that you had been attacked by an acid serpent, I panicked, worried that I might lose you: but once I calmed down, I realized that even if your life was removed from your body, we would see each other again. It is comforting to know that you can never truly be lost. As long as we know the Creator, there will always be comfort in the knowledge that even when our purposes here are fulfilled, we will both live eternally with Him. We know our time in this dark world is only temporary." Honna looked up into her husband's stubbled face. "Let's keep our eyes focused on the truth. We were never designed to live forever in darkness."

"Sorry, my beloved. I know I have a tendency to ramble when I'm passionate about something. I love you, and I'm not as strong as you are. I would rather have you come with us; I feel weak and small when we are apart. Tomorrow, before I leave, please put something of yours in my bag. It will help me feel closer to you. Did I mention how much I need your strength?" Honna looked at her husband with still-watering eyes, squeezed him tight, and didn't say another word.

Aristus was the one who finished the conversation. "My beloved, the Creator has gifted you with wisdom. You are far braver than you realize. You tell me what I need to hear, not what I want you to tell me. Honna, you always encourage me. You start by telling me the good things I have done, and then point me to the Creator. Your words call me back to the truth of who I am. Thank you, my darling. You are truly my dearest friend."

Honna smiled warmly at her husband. Aristus soaked in her love, and together they fell asleep, with Honna curled up like a fall leaf in his strong right wing. The tranquility of the moment provided a temporary break from the unknown terrors that awaited them in the morning.

⌘

The Lord Denham Fontaine had finally arrived. It was officially the fifth day of Lady Ember's imprisonment, and the Lord Denham wanted to meet the instigator of Celestra's murder. He knew little about the House of Envy, as he had always sent his servants to purchase his paints. All he knew was that it housed women of fabled beauty.

As the coachman drove away, the Lord Denham felt angry and determined; but as he strolled through the main door, he gazed upon the sheer splendor of the House of Envy. Excitement and intrigue began to stir within him. Krenna bowed before him and escorted him to the grand banquet hall, which had been extravagantly decorated solely for his arrival.

Upon entering the room, the Lord Denham took a step back. The whole banquet hall was dimly lit by hundreds of glowing chandeliers. In the center of the room, Madam Julia was waiting at a large table, surrounded with couch-like chairs. Each table was covered with ornate carvings of beautiful women dancing with serpents. Even though the room was breathtakingly beautiful, the Lord Denham's attention was solely on the captivating presence of Madam Julia.

Her hair was long and blond, and it shone brightly from the gold dust sprinkled throughout it. He was mesmerized by the sight of her; and his eyes danced, as he watched her gliding effortlessly to greet him. The closer she came to him, the more he felt as though he was floating. Each time he took a breath, he felt more lost in her splendor.

Julia opened her rose-colored lips to speak. "Greetings, my Lord Denham. It is my great pleasure to welcome you to my humble home. Please sit and have a modest dinner with me."

As she spoke, Denham thought he had never in all his life heard such a beautiful voice. When she finished addressing him, she gently took his hand in hers and led him to the table. His eyes never left her. He thought her diamond dress made her a vision. He felt as though he was living in a fantastic dream.

Once they were seated, the conversation between them remained light and jovial. Soon, an elegant variety of foods were brought before them. Somewhere during the casual conversation, the Lord Denham completely forgot his reason for coming.

"My dear lord," inquired Julia, "how long will we have the pleasure of your company?"

His mind had become clouded, and he was having a difficult time responding, but Julia was patient as he formed his answer. "My dear madam, I had arranged to leave tomorrow morning with the murderess. I had planned on bringing her to my family and Celestra's father. I wanted them to bear witness to her destruction; however, plans can change. This may sound a bit strange, but after meeting you, it will be hard for me to leave your enchanting company. Forgive me if that is too forward of me. I am sure that a lady as famous as you grows tired of young men flattering and chasing after your affection."

Madam Julia's face looked as though she had just won something. She managed to produce a seemingly sweet smile. "Words of praise from a worthy man are never unappreciated. I am sure that I would be equally as distressed by your departure. Please do us both a favor and stay here as my personal guest. I have already planned a banquet in your honor that is set to be carried out in three days. Would you do me the pleasure of attending?"

The Lord Denham Fontaine felt as though his chest was constricting, and was experiencing shortness of breath; not from fear, but rather from excitement. He quickly agreed; all he could think about was winning her heart and doing whatever she asked.

Julia felt invincible; all her hard work had finally paid off. She smiled to herself, as she told him of her plans for the next day. "Tomorrow, I will personally give you a tour of the House of Envy, and then we shall dine in my private chamber. For now, my Lord Denham, the hour has grown late. I believe it is time for both of us to retire. Krenna can show you the room I have fixed for you." She blew him a kiss, the power of which nearly knocked him from his seat. Krenna was summoned and escorted the Lord Denham, as he stumbled out of the banquet hall.

Julia drew her fingernails across the table, as she watched him exit the room. "Thank you for the lovely evening, my Lord Denham," she whispered to herself. "If only you knew the power I have over you. You are already mine. I have bought you with the blood of your fiancé. Sleep well, my ignorant lord."

~ Chapter Twenty-Nine ~

Honna anxiously rubbed the glowing silk dress between her fingers; Opella had gifted her the gown before they departed. It unnerved her that they had been so late in leaving Simeon's house. Everyone had overslept, which meant they wouldn't be arriving at the House of Envy until far into the night. Honna began to question the Creator's reasoning for sending her as the only woman on a mission, with two adolescent boys and two immature men.

She looked up from her thoughts to survey the carriage. Ambrose and Uriah had fallen asleep, leaning against one another. It would have been quite comical if the situation wasn't so serious. Trinzic sat next to her, facing Bereck on the other side. Both men were having an animated discussion of who had, had the grandest of adventures. Honna felt out of place in this group. She wondered, *Creator, what good am I here? I don't understand . . . why me?*

A strong and kind voice resounded plainly in her ears. "My child, you carry with you the gift of my wisdom. You are also Ellie's mother, and you are needed to fulfill my plan in the House of Envy. Trust me; have faith that I always know what is best for you and all my children."

In hearing these words, Honna felt ashamed. Just hours before, she had challenged her husband to have faith in the Creator's judgment, and now here she was already doubting. She smiled to herself, as she thought of the irony of it all. Then she quietly thanked the Creator for His gentle reproach, and spent the remainder of the time listening to Trinzic and Bereck casually banter back and forth.

When a banquet was hosted at the House of Envy, all who were in the royal council were sent an invitation, along with anyone else who could afford to come. The feast to honor the Lord Denham was no exception. The enormous banquet hall was packed with excited guests: each sitting at their chosen dinner table, and awaiting the palettes' grand entrance. At the front of the room was an impressive platform decorated with blue and silver silks, large floral arrangements, and jewels dangling from thin, leather cords.

Music hummed quietly as the lights began to dim. Eight enchanting women sang a haunting, steady melody, with a reed flute as accompaniment, and their voices echoed through the hall. Suddenly, a large burst of green smoke billowed in waves from the stage. As the haze cleared, a woman dressed in green silk began to dance. Each hall was taught a unique dance, and Lady Sage of the Chamber of

Emerald was the first to perform for the introduction. She held in her hands two flowing streamers; and as she danced, she twisted and spun them into a variety of shapes. Her white-and-green-streaked hair was bound to her head in intricately woven braids. She gracefully lifted one leg high above her head and spun faster and faster. The steamers swirled around her like a cage.

As Lady Sage spun, the long ribbons wrapped themselves snugly around her body. The audience gasped, as she used her razor sharp nails to slice through the steamers. She threw the pieces high in the air, letting them spiral down into the audience. A puff of red smoke then enveloped the stage, and when it subsided, a large flame erupted from the platform. The audience gasped as the lingering smoke parted, revealing the next palette, Lady Angeline of the Chamber of Crimson.

Angeline was elated; her adrenaline surging. As the madam in the House of Envy, she had been required to master all of the palettes' traditional dances. Crimson was by far the most difficult, because that hall was known for its dance of fire. It was the most challenging because the silk could easily get pulled into the flames. Angeline knew this, but she had spent her whole life being fashioned to be a palette. Tonight, she knew what she was doing. Moving two torches fluidly in her hands, Angeline watched them twirl as she thought, *If only Trinzic could be here, then this night would be perfect. He would see that he is not the only one who can perform for an audience.* She spun and twisted her body to the music, and all eyes watched the flame dance in the darkened room.

With her heart racing as the culmination of her performance neared, she threw the torches high into the air and watched them spin in slow motion back down to her. At the same time, Angeline quickly inserted some oil into her mouth and held it there until she caught the torches. Clutching both torches firmly in her hands, the flames burned hot in front of her, as she lifted them high above her head and united them fluidly into one radiant blaze. Steadily, with her head tilted back, she lowered the flame to the level of her mouth and blew the oil into the fire. The flame burst into a brilliant yellow above her. Amber smoke erupted from both sides of the stage, signaling the next act. Angeline wiped her brow carefully, and her feet made no sound as she slid unnoticed into her seat.

After each of the eight palettes had completed their dances, the final performance had arrived. It was time for Madam Julia to take the stage. The flute music stopped and was replaced by a fast-beating drum. The smoke billowing from the platform shifted to dark blue, and then grew lighter and lighter until it turned white.

Suddenly, the drumbeat stopped; the smoke faded away, and Madam Julia appeared, crouching low. As she slowly stood, she revealed the presence of six golden serpents, wrapped strategically around her body. With her arms raised high above her head, she began the traditional dance of the House of Envy, the dance of the serpent. Her eyes closed, and a quiet hiss escaped from her throat into the air.

Angeline watched and remembered how her snakes would sleep with her at night. She smiled as she thought of all the times she had performed as the madam. Continuing to watch her sister, a shiver raced down her spine without warning. Julia was releasing the serpents slowly into the audience, as she weaved the air and smoke with her hands and body. The serpents maneuvered into the audience, each finding a victim's leg to slither up. Angeline clutched her throat, as a serpent rested like a necklace around the neck of a man sitting next to her. Julia then reached down to pick up the lone creature remaining on stage and, with one fluid motion, she spun and twirled the serpent around her neck. Instantly, a horn blew, causing the snake to bite into Julia's throat, along with all the other guests whom the snakes had chosen. Within moments, each of their eyes began to glow a brilliant blue. Julia continued her dance, moving from the platform to the audience; gliding by each person she had selected, and leading them personally to a seat next to hers at the head dining table.

Once they were all seated, the singers and musicians took their places on the stage, and the lights brightened slightly. It was now time for the meal to be served. Plates filled with cobalt crabs and crystal oysters on a bed of rice were brought to each table. A servant placed a dish before Angeline, and she could smell the powerful aroma of the curry-like sauce that had been drizzled over her meal. She reached out and snatched the pearl from the oyster, and placed it in a secret pocket in her dress.

Angeline's table was mostly devoid of conversation; each guest was too focused on his/her meal to say much. As she pushed her food around the plate with her knife, her brow furrowed, producing a troubled frown. From out of the table's silence, Angeline's mind was plagued with some disturbing questions. *Ellie spoke of evil being in this place,* she thought, *and Julia's performance sent chills down my spine. It felt eerie, perhaps even evil; but that doesn't make any sense. I have performed that same dance and felt nothing. What has changed? Why do I feel so different about everything?* That's when her brain locked in on the answer. *It's because of Ellie and her family. Being around them has changed me.*

Angeline began to ponder the Story of Sacrifice. As she shifted uneasily in her seat, others at her table began to notice her strange behavior, and one person in particular chose to speak up. She was an elderly aristocrat, whose high-pitched voice was saturated with arrogance. "Lady Angeline, whatever has come over you? Is this dreadful food making you ill?"

Angeline's expression was dazed, as she hesitantly pushed her chair back and stood up. She robotically answered the woman's question. "I'm still recovering from the ceremony of burden." The guests at the table gasped politely in renewed understanding. "I'm afraid that I may need to retire for the evening," Angeline continued. "It has been a pleasure dining with all of you, but I really need to rest."

The aristocrats all bore satisfied grins; each guest excited about this juicy morsel of gossip they had just received. The ceremony of burden was a very secretive and intriguing topic. With this at the forefront of their minds, they politely gave her their resounding approval for leaving, sending many phony acclamations of concern. Angeline moved away from her table and set out to speak with her sister.

Julia was laughing merrily with Lord Denham, who was mushily thanking her and showering her with compliments. Angeline tapped her sister on the shoulder and whispered in her ear. "Madam Julia, I have come down with a horrendous headache. I wish to retire for the evening?"

Julia waved her hand dismissively and daintily responded, "Of course you may go . . ." Then Julia stopped mid-sentence, realizing that she wanted something in return. She got up from her seat and stood uncomfortably close to Angeline. She leaned forward and said, "I have a small request to ask of you, and then you may leave. That little serving girl you fought so hard to keep; you didn't bring her with you tonight. There are rumors circulating because you never let her out. It is puzzling to me that hardly anyone has seen her. I will permit you to leave only if you let me see her alone. I want to know why you are keeping her from me."

Angeline's eye began to wander out of fear, and she immediately turned her head, hoping Julia wouldn't notice. The fear came from what her sister was implying, that Ellie was Angeline's child. In the House of Envy, palettes were forbidden from having children. Being childless made them more desirable to the men viewing them. She knew she needed to seem unbothered by her sister's request, so she relaxed her body and casually replied, "That should be fine".

Julia waved her hand. "I will see you later tonight; sweet dreams, my sister."

Angeline winced from the threatening tone behind her sister's words. She bowed in response and left. Angeline walked briskly to her room as her mind screamed. *Trinzic is coming tonight, Ellie is unpainted, and I am too confused to even think of a plan to fix all this!*

~ Chapter Thirty ~

$\mathcal{E}$llie squirmed as Angeline hurriedly painted her face and sporadically adjusted her clothes. Angeline was frantically spouting out instructions, as she adjusted the ribbons in Ellie's hair. "Ellie, I know that I said you wouldn't have to wear any of these things, but my sister Julia wants to meet you. Only speak when you're spoken to, and use only one word answers whenever possible."

Ellie looked up at Angeline with concern radiating from her eyes. "If I do a good job, would you talk with me about what you thought of the story I told you a couple days ago?" Ellie smiled pleadingly.

Angeline returned her smile, her obvious fondness for Ellie beaming through. "After all this is over, I would love to talk with you about that story. To be honest, it has been haunting my thoughts every day since you told it to me. I hate to admit it, but I'm beginning to think you may have been right about everything. I've been wondering if the world you live in may be better than this place. Everything looks different since I met you." She lifted the girl's face with her hand and smiled down at her. "Thank you, Ellie, for showing me how to love."

Ellie's eyes danced as she responded, "Angeline, you're my best friend, and you are easy to love and serve."

Angeline paused, as realization settled in. "And you are the only true friend that I have ever known."

Before they could discuss anything else, they heard the sound of footsteps entering Angeline's chamber. Without warning, Julia quickly brushed past Angeline to get a look at Ellie. "So this is the treasure you have been keeping all to yourself. She is cute for a child, but I can't imagine why you have chosen to hide her from the rest of us. You have piqued my curiosity. Now keep your promise; please leave us. I'd like to address the child alone. You can stand in the hallway. When we're finished, I'll call for you."

Angeline was scared. She had an uneasy feeling growing in her stomach over leaving Ellie alone with her sister, and her voice resonated with anxiety. "Julia, do whatever you want. The girl means nothing to me; other than the fact that she is an exceptional servant, and I don't want any more offers to trade her."

Julia returned a skeptical grimace. "Well, that may be true, but I would like to come to that conclusion on my own. Now leave us; you're beginning to try my patience, sister."

Angeline apologized for offending her and quickly glided into the hallway. When she had gone, Julia turned her full attention to Ellie. Ellie didn't know why, but her body began shaking as Julia approached her. Ellie couldn't stop looking into her glowing, blue eyes. It wasn't merely her eyes, but also the golden serpent that was slithering slowly around her body. Ellie did not like being alone with this woman.

Julia knelt down to look Ellie in the eye as she talked to her. "It is nice to finally see the child my sister has been attempting to hide from me. You look normal enough to me; why has she been hiding you here?"

Ellie's tone was polite and honest. "I don't like wearing this paint, and those fish eyes make it so I can't see."

Julia laughed a little in surprise. "You mean to say that my sister has become so weak that she is letting you sleep in her chamber, actually allowing you to be so bold as to assert your own preferences? Why in the name of Apollyon would she keep you then?"

Ellie cringed at the sound of Apollyon's name. It caught her off guard, but she still wanted to get her chance to talk to Angeline about the Creator, so she blurted out the answer. "She likes the songs I sing to her and the stories I tell her. They help her go to sleep; I'm also her friend."

Julia was now laughing even harder. "No wonder she didn't want any of her servants to see you. She was worried that none of them would respect her. The ceremony of burden has made her mad." Julia's shoulders shook as she laughed; but amidst her laughter, she paused as a new question entered her mind. "Child, what is wrong with your eyes? You said you don't wear eye lenses, but your eyes should be black, and they're not."

Ellie's demeanor changed; she was excited to have a chance to speak candidly about her Creator. "It's true; I'm not wearing lenses. The Creator made these eyes for me. He made me beautiful."

Julia pulled back in revulsion, and her snake hissed angrily at Ellie. "Don't say that disgusting name in my presence again, you twisted variation."

Now Ellie was offended. She looked Julia directly in her eyes and put her hands on her hips. "I love the Creator, and I will never stop saying His name. He saved me from being a cranky, mean woman like you."

Julia's voice screeched. "Stop saying that name!" Julia reached forward, placing both hands tightly on Ellie's cheeks, and then squeezed hard. "You are a foolish little insect, aren't you?" The snake was slowly slithering its way down Julia's arm, and she kept her hands firmly on Ellie's face. Ellie squirmed as the serpent traveled onto her shoulder, winding itself around her neck.

Then Julia removed her hand from Ellie's face. She leaned down and slapped her hand hard against the marble floor, simulating the sound of the horn from the banquet dance. The snake bit Ellie's neck as soon as it heard the slap. Julia took a step back to watch. She didn't want to kill Ellie; she just wanted to punish her. Ellie let out a small whimper at the onset of the bite, but instead of her eyes glowing, the snake fell off, dead.

When the serpent hit the floor, Ellie took a step back from Julia and pointed one tiny finger at her. "You are a life-taker. When you touched me, I could hear your heart speak the truth to me. You are a deceiver, you worship Apollyon, and Celestra's blood is on your hands. Call out to the Creator to make you into a new creation, or you will be punished for your evil."

Julia was now enraged, and her voice was crazed as she ran for Ellie. "You little monster! Now you will suffer! Come here!"

Ellie ran toward the place she knew Angeline was waiting. She made it halfway to her friend when Julia caught her. Ellie screamed, as Julia withdrew a knife and savagely sliced off one of her wing, sending blood down the girl's back and legs. The force of having her wing removed caused Ellie to trip, and she slid a few feet ahead of Julia, who hurried to Ellie's side and stomped hard on her back.

"All your kind would die like this if I had my way. For now, killing you will have to do. I hope this hurts you at least half as much as it pleases me to watch." She reached down with her knife and viciously removed Ellie's other wing. Ellie screamed out in pain. This time, it was so loud that Angeline heard and ran out from behind the wall. Julia kicked Ellie over, so she was now lying on her back. Tears flowed freely from Ellie's tightly closed eyes.

Julia saw her sister running towards them. She took her foot and smashed it forcefully on Ellie's throat. Now it was Angeline who was screaming. "No! Julia, stop!"

Julia stared hard at Angeline, her voice cold, "I'm doing you a favor. She's made you forget who you are." Julia stomped down again, and Ellie went limp. Angeline shoved her sister off of Ellie, knocking Julia forcefully to the floor, where she hit her head.

Angeline sobbed, "Ellie, I'm so sorry! I have been wrong my whole life about everything. Please be all right! I have so many questions to ask you. I want to change; I don't want to be like her." The child didn't move. Angeline knelt close to Ellie's chest and began rocking back and forth, tears pouring onto Ellie's arm. "Creator, I believe in your sacrifice. Change me into something new. Please don't make me stay here alone, trapped in this horrible place. Please rescue me."

The ground shook, and they were gone. Just as the tremors subsided, Honna, Trinzic, Bereck, Ambrose, and Uriah charged into the room. Julia had watched Angeline and Ellie disappear; now she was sitting in Ellie's blood and bleeding from her own wound. When she saw Honna and the men enter, she saw her opportunity to escape the mess she had gotten herself into. Julia quickly called out to them. Ambrose, the most tenderhearted, rushed to her aid. She clung to him, getting blood all over.

"They killed my sister and that serving girl," she blubbered. "I watched everything; it was horrible! They almost got me, and then you strong gentlemen were so kind to show up."

Honna spotted the two wings lying discarded on the marble floor. She put her hands over her mouth and cried, "Ellie! My sweet Ellie! No . . ." She ran over and picked up a wing, holding it close to her chest. Tears streamed from Honna's face. "Who did this? And where is my daughter?" she yelled.

Julia couldn't help but smirk. "Oh, I see Ellie was your offspring. Poor dear; well, the people who did this might still be in the building. You must all stay here while I gather some assistance." Julia broke free from Ambrose and ran into the darkness.

As soon as Julia disappeared, Honna knew something was wrong. She looked at Ambrose, stained with blood, and then at her own arms, holding onto the severed wing. *Oh, no! NO NO NO!* Adrenaline kicked in with Honna's realization, and she yelled imploring orders to the men. "Run! Now! That woman is the one who took their lives, and she's going to get others so she can blame us!"

The men looked at each other, not yet understanding. "Get out of here!" she screamed, waving one arm toward the door. "Leave this place! I will stay behind to bear witness! Ellie was my daughter! I have nothing to lose here! Go home! Go now!" She continued pointing to the door, as if to help them to understand the urgency.

Bereck caught on as Trinzic did, and they grabbed the arms of the twins, pulling at them to run. The four rushed for the exit; only Trinzic looked back momentarily, as they ran from the room.

Honna was suddenly alone, holding the torn and bloody wing of her little girl, and she immediately began to mourn. She barely managed to whisper, "Creator, help us!" as she sank to her knees in agony.

Honna was not alone long before Madam Julia, the Lord Denham, and a host of guards appeared in the room. Julia pointed to Honna and screamed, "She was with them! She was with the men that murdered my sister and her servant; they must have run off with the bodies. Quickly, we must make them pay!"

Honna yelled back in a tear-filled voice. "I am the serving girl's mother. I swear that I had nothing to do with harming my own child. That woman is the one you should question. Not all that blood is her own; my daughter's blood is on her hands!"

Julia screamed, "Quiet, witch! Take her to the cages. You can interrogate her later."

The guards looked confused, but they obeyed their master. They lifted Honna from the floor and led her to the cages, leaving the remaining guards to find Trinzic and the others. Adlar was with the guards, but had a suspicion he knew where the intruders had fled. He left the chase to find them on his own.

~ Chapter Thirty-One ~

Trinzic, Ambrose, Uriah, and Bereck had entered the House of Envy through a side entrance; but Trinzic thought he had seen a more private escape route and was leading the group there. He moved at such a hurried pace that the others were struggling to keep up with him. Trinzic weaved in and out of the columns as he ran ahead. Eventually, he led them to a grungy, black door.

When all four had passed the threshold, Trinzic whispered, "This is obviously the room that contains the old waste chute. For you two young ones, this is what was used before everyone started sending their waste to the incinerator. Now that we have had a history lesson, we are going to escape through this chute. Who's going first?"

Ambrose and Uriah were eager to volunteer. "We will!"

In response to their declaration, Trinzic smiled. "Here is my plan. I want you inexperienced youths to report back to Aristus. Bereck and I will stay behind to see if we can rescue Honna. I, for one, am not comfortable with a woman handling all this excitement and loss on her own. Bereck, in the carriage ride here, you challenged my sense of adventure. Let's see who can save the day first without getting caught."

Ambrose and Uriah were now wishing they hadn't been so quick to speak up. They both shrugged their shoulders in reluctant agreement. Ambrose went down the chute first, and then Uriah. At the bottom, they dusted off their clothes and hurried to the street to hail a carriage.

Bereck and Trinzic smiled knowingly at one another. The two men were about to leave when the door swung open and immediately closed. Before either man could see who had come in, there was a loud shattering sound, as the two dimly lit lights went out. Trinzic pulled Bereck back from the door, and together they laid flat on the floor. They peered into the darkness silently, listening for footsteps. They heard nothing, not even breathing. Then they heard the faint sound of a latch being released and of something falling from the ceiling.

Adlar had released a metal, four-inch beam that fell squarely on their backs. As he leaned forward and placed his boot on the iron beam, Trinzic and Bereck moaned under the pain and weight. Then Adlar gruffly whispered to them, "I don't know why you broke in here, but if you want to live, you will promptly tell me exactly what happened."

Bereck was the first to speak up. "We came to fetch Aristus' little girl, Ellie, and we had been granted an audience with Lady Angeline. One of her servants even waited for us in the kitchen entryway and ushered us into Angeline's personal chamber. It was then that we saw a woman covered in blood. She told us she had been attacked, and that Lady Angeline and Ellie had been killed. Then she ran off. Ellie's mother, Honna, knew not to trust that woman, and she instructed us to run. My friend and I were just about to rescue her when you stopped us."

Adlar's tone became emotionless. "Did you see their bodies?"

"No. We only saw that woman."

Adlar thought for a moment and then continued. "I believe that you're both innocent. I could tell as soon as I looked at Julia that she had done it, but I always confirm my suspicions before acting on them. Now, I want you both to listen carefully to my instructions. In a moment, I'm going to release this bar. If you try to fight me, I will kill you. As a rule, I don't kill innocents, but I will make an exception if you don't obey me. If you behave, I will leave you both to wait silently in the dark until I get back. When I return, I will have some guard uniforms. You will put them on and act as my new recruits. Once dressed, you will hide in my chamber until morning. This may keep you free from detection. Then we will find where Madam Julia has hidden the bodies. Do you understand?"

Neither of the two men knew what to think. Bereck was the only one to answer. "We have no choice. I guess we will see where this plan leads us."

Adlar released his foot from the beam, and then with a swirl of his cape, he was gone. Bereck turned to Trinzic. "Wasn't that humiliating? Looks like neither of us has proven anything of our skills. We just got bested by some burly old man."

Trinzic laughed nervously. "You were stuck, trapped under that rusty old thing? I certainty was not. I thought you were just waiting to hear the old man out. I, personally, could have escaped that little obstacle with no real effort on my part. I have been told it is really hard accepting defeat, but obviously I wouldn't know from experience, and it looks as though I may never know. How does it feel knowing that I have clearly taken the lead?"

Bereck's mouth was hanging open; Trinzic had completely thrown him off guard. His claim was so ridiculous that he couldn't even form the words to argue. In his silence, Bereck unwittingly allowed Trinzic to take the lead.

The time passed slowly, as they waited for the captain of the guard to return. Trinzic stretched and yawned just in time to be seen by Adlar, stepping through the door. He abruptly handed over two uniforms and ordered them to dress quickly, causing both men to jump to attention. Bereck's uniform went on easily, fitting him perfectly, while Trinzic's clothes looked as though they had been made for a child. He hopped on one foot and pulled hard, trying to force a leg into the tiny pants. Trinzic uttered non-stop complaints as he fought with his clothes. "What are these, children's clothes? They are far too tight."

Adlar responded promptly, "You whine like a little girl. Now I am certain that I made the perfect selection for you. No more speaking; we need to get moving." Adlar adjusted each man's uniform quickly and efficiently, before carefully inspecting them one last time. When he finished, his voice boomed, "You look like you should be on the street, begging for food. I think you just might pass for new recruits. Pull up your hoods, walk side-by-side, and follow me."

Together they made their way steadily down the hallway towards the guards' quarters, which were stationed near the cages. Trinzic quietly mumbled to himself, "Rudeness is not acceptable. Calling me, Trinzic, a girl? What utter nonsense. Can't he see my radiant superiority? He will learn."

⌘

The rocks that made up the mountain felt smooth as Angeline slid quickly past. She could feel air moving across her face, as she gained speed with every moment. Her hands grasped tightly onto Ellie's body; she was afraid she might lose her dearest friend along this terrifying slide. Her mind began to fill with fear. *Where am I going? What if the Creator doesn't want me? What if all those wonderful stories were just a lie? Am I falling to my death?* She squeezed Ellie. "You should have given up on me. My life being changed was not worth yours being lost."

Suddenly, she felt moisture sprinkle her face. Her head popped up to see why, and she saw the tunnel starting to shine and sparkle with light. Up ahead, she could see where the water was coming from: a glowing whirlpool. This slide she was on was nearing its end.

Whoosh! She hit the water hard, and the force of the blow was so great that she lost her grip on Ellie. Frantically, she grasped for Ellie under the water, ignoring her own need to breathe. Then a strong current grabbed hold of her and whirled her around violently. Time passed slowly as her head lightened. The water picked up speed and spun her around and around, making a cocoon about her. Angeline clutched her chest, as she felt her lungs careen toward bursting, and then she gasped. She was startled to find that she was able to breathe; her head was in a large air bubble, which she watched grow to encompass her whole body.

Then she heard a strong, commanding voice. "Angeline, my child, breathe! Calm yourself and listen to the sound of my voice." Angeline's heart stopped racing. She waited in anticipation for the voice to return. "Take a deep breath and hold it in. Trust me; you are about to be recreated. Breathe in now!"

Angeline inhaled deeply, shut her mouth tight, and watched as the bubble popped. The air from the bubble pushed her swiftly up through the water, which rubbed over her skin, peeling it off. She could feel her hair falling out as her head, facing skyward, approached a blinding light. She felt the last hair pull away, as her head broke the surface. Angeline screamed out into the blinding light, "Save me! I'm blind! I'm drowning! Somebody, help me!"

Two strong arms lifted her out of the water. Her heart raced as the Creator held her close; His steady, strong hands moving gently across her scalp. She could hear His voice explaining what she could not see. "The darkness has distorted you, my child. All of its lies have damaged your heart and mind. You have been washed in my life, and now, in my arms, I will re-create you as a child of light."

Angeline could feel her hair growing back, and the cool winds lightly tossing it about. She could hear the Creator take in a deep breath, then exhale, blowing warm air across her skin. Her body no longer shivered, but was saturated in a calming and engulfing warmth. She didn't understand why she couldn't see. So, in a voice barely above a whisper, she asked, "Creator, what about my eyes?"

A rumbling chuckle echoed from His throat. "Angeline, my beloved child; you have always been so impatient. It was only a short time ago that I asked you to trust me, and now you are already questioning. Be patient; your eyes will be renewed. You have lived in the darkness for so long that your eyes cannot yet gaze upon my world of light. Angeline, ready your heart to see for the first time."

The Creator placed both His hands over her eyes. She cried as He removed something sharp, and her tears pushed the last remaining scale from her eyes. She lifted her hands to rub her eyes; they were so soft. She blinked rapidly as she peered into the light, and slowly the world began to come into focus. She gasped in awe as she saw the real world for the first time; it was so big and full of color. Then the

Creator set her carefully down. She couldn't close her eyes; there were too many things she had never seen before. Above her head, there was no longer a plain, black rock face, but rather open, blue sky that seemed to go on forever. At her feet, she felt something tickling her toes, and she knelt down to pick some of it up. She clutched it tightly in her hands and, displaying it to the Creator, asked, "What are these silvery, green plants?"

The Creator smiled. "It is called grass."

Angeline tied some into a fold she had made in her dress and then asked another question, "What is that brilliant, shining sphere up there?"

The Creator answered, "I placed the ball of brightness in the sky to cast light over the whole world; I call it the sun. Angeline, these are all wonderful questions, but you still have not asked my favorite one."

Her face scrunched up in puzzled curiosity. "What question is that?"

The Creator smirked. "You haven't asked me why I gave you wings."

Angeline's mind traveled back to when Opella told her the story of beginnings. She remembered how her ancestors had been called the people of the sky. She looked up at the Creator and then asked, with her face upturned, "You created us to fly way up there?"

He held out His hand. "Remember to trust in me."

She grabbed the Creator's hand, and He threw her high up into the air. Angeline was terrified, as she soared higher and higher into the sky. She frantically beat her wings and closed her eyes, too afraid to open them. In her head, she kept repeating, *Trust, trust, trust.* With a rush of courage, she opened her eyes and gasped. "This is incredible!" she squealed. "I can't believe it! I'm actually flying!"

Then she heard the Creator's voice in her ear. "Of course you are. You were made for the sky. On the day of your creation, this surprise was waiting for you. It is the gift of freedom that awaits all those trapped in that mountain."

She fluttered slowly back down, and He put His hands on her shoulders. "There is still so much to see, and many things I need to share with you. One thing you need to learn is how to listen for the sound of my voice. All of my children know my voice; even my silent whisper they can hear. They have learned how to follow me. It is time for you to fly."

Her wings fluttered rapidly, and she soared high into the sky. When she could barely see Him, she heard His voice whisper in her ear, "Stop." She obeyed. "Now we will fly together. I will show you this world of light and share with you many truths. My presence and my voice will go with you. Listen carefully, and if you obey, my words will never be lost. Angeline, are you ready?"

Angeline's heart was filling up with so much love and excitement that she didn't even hesitate, "Yes, I am ready to go anywhere you lead."

The Creator whispered to her; Angeline followed His beautiful voice. Much like a father and daughter dancing, she moved with loving obedience to please the will of her maker.

~ *Chapter Thirty-Two* ~

*H*onna held tightly to the dark, iron bars that were her prison. She was trying hard not to panic, because any movement caused the cage to sway drastically back and forth. She knelt down, placing her hands over her heart. "Oh precious Creator, please protect my little Ellie. Give Aristus strength to wait, and show me your purpose for being in this horrible place." She carefully scooted to the center of her cage, held her knees close to her chest, and began humming.

From out of the darkness, a feminine voice yelled out to her, "Hello? Is someone there? Whoever you are, please answer."

Honna stopped humming so she could answer. "Hello friend. You are not alone. My name is Honna, and the Creator has sent me to you." Honna rose slowly and carefully from her seat, placing two hands on the bars. She peered into the darkness, trying to see the woman speaking to her.

The cages hung from the ceiling by thick chains, each about twenty feet apart. They were placed in a cavern hidden under the House of Envy. It was dark and damp; the only light came from Honna's gifted dress, along with a few glowing insects called drainals. These creatures were given this name because even the small ones could completely drain a person's blood in less than fifteen minutes. She watched as a particularly large one lazily fluttered past her cage.

The woman next to her called out. "Hello to you! Thank you for being a light in this darkness. My name is . . . well, was Lady Ember. Your dress is comfortingly beautiful. The only things I have been able to see and hear are the drainals. I've been terrified that one of them is going to squeeze through these bars while I'm sleeping and drain me. You have a kind voice; what have you done to earn yourself a cage?"

As quickly as she could, Honna told her story, filling her new friend in on the Creator, Ellie, and Madam Julia.

Ember burst into tears and slapped her hands against the floor. "Julia destroys people. She is the one who put me in here. She is evil, treacherous, and cruel! She is a monster! She should be made queen of the drainals!"

Honna spoke softly to calm her down. "Miss Ember, please take a deep breath and listen to my voice. This whole situation may look hopeless, but I was sent here to offer you hope; to show you that the Creator can turn what Julia meant for destruction into something good."

Ember stilled, her rage calming into silence, and she was quiet for a long time. Honna patiently waited for a response. Then Lady Ember cleared her throat. As she spoke, her voice sounded hollow and empty. "I have nothing left. I honestly don't believe that anything you could say will bring any hope into this pit I am sinking into. My beautiful life has been destroyed; I have no future."

Lady Ember felt a chill, and she thoughtfully began to wring her hands as she continued speaking. "First, I fell for a nobleman's flattery and ended up carrying an orb, which is a death sentence here at the House of Envy. So . . . it was either the child's life or mine; I chose mine. I went to an orb handler, and a strange little girl convinced me to give her my baby. I thought that, with the child gone, my problems would be over. If only I had known then that my fame in the House of Envy would cause Julia to become jealous enough to plan a horrible death for me. There is no hope for me; I am going to die. I'm so tired of waiting for death all alone; it is a welcome distraction to hear someone else's voice. Please talk as long as you want. Your ramblings have to be better than the humming of that horrible insect."

Honna smiled to herself. "Creator, you never cease to amaze me. Your plans are always perfect; thank you for letting me be a part of them." After her whispered prayer, Honna began to relate the story of beginnings. She spoke slowly and clearly so that Ember could hear every word. When she finished, the poor woman flooded her with many questions, and Honna answered each one with patience and love. With so many questions to answer, her voice soon became hoarse. Honna desperately needed a drink of water, so she broke into Ember's barrage of inquires to ask a simple one of her own.

"Miss Ember, I have been . . ." she began, and then halted abruptly to cough, "overjoyed to answer all your questions, but I don't think I can talk anymore tonight."

Ember's voice shouted back nervously, "No, please tell me another story. I know that even if you go really slowly, I will still be able to pay attention."

Honna felt compelled to continue, even though it was difficult for her to speak. Her next tale was the story of sacrifice. As Honna choked out each word, Ember was visibly captivated. Tears filled her eyes, as she visualized the Creator dying for her.

At the story's conclusion, Ember asked, "Is that all? I feel like there has to be more. Please, don't stop."

Honna hollered back to make sure that Ember heard every word. "The rest of the story is up to you. If you accept the Creator's call, then together you and He will begin your own unique story. He will not force you to leave your prison; you have to freely choose to turn your life over to Him."

"What must I do to be saved from this horrible cage?"

Honna explained everything that she would have to say and believe to be true, and Ember sat quietly, as she thought for a long time. "I'm not completely sure that I believe in these stories just yet. I want them to be true; I'm just having a hard time believing something that amazing could really be out there. Can I think about it a little more, and then tomorrow, would you be so kind as to tell them to me again?"

Honna touched her throbbing throat with her hands. Her body was screaming no, but her heart knew what she must do. "I would love to tell you the stories as many times as you need to hear them."

Ember thanked her, and both women fell asleep to the humming of the drainals; each one dreaming about what the next day would bring.

⌘

Angeline was smiling, but her head was spinning. She had just seen wonders that, in her wildest dreams, she never could have imagined. Her brain could hardly take in all the new sights. A cool, steady breeze blew through her dark purple hair, as she floated through the air. In her heart, she hoped this day would never end.

Then the Creator's voice told her to stop. She obeyed; before her was crystal blue water as far as her eyes could see. Angeline took in a deep breath and sighed, "It's so beautiful." Angeline was content to stare at the water and listen to the Creator's voice. After explaining a great many things to her, He said that it was time for her to return to the river of life. Angeline hesitated for a moment; she was afraid of what might happen next, that this dream might end, but again, she obeyed and carefully followed His directions home.

On the journey back, she realized what a great distance she had traveled. She reflected on her adventures so far, and all the things in her life that had brought her to this point. "Why was I so stubborn and selfish? If only I would have listened to Ellie sooner. If only I had known all this was waiting for me. Thank you so much, Creator, for sending her to me. She loved and served you well."

Angeline had made her way back, and in her careful descent toward the ground, she could see the Creator below her. As she neared Him, she saw that He was holding something. It didn't take long for her to realize that it was Ellie's limp body. At that moment, she didn't know what to feel or how to react. She continued her steady descent until she landed at the Creator's feet. She clung to Him and began to cry. "I am so sorry; it's all my fault! I did this to her with my stubbornness."

His face was kind, as He lovingly smiled upon her. The Creator's calm voice was filled with truth and compassion, as He addressed her. "My child; Ellie needs not to be pitied. She has a hero's heart. She was always eager to love others. She was a true servant. You need to know that this empty shell is not her. She is going to a place that is even more glorious than the world you have just seen. She is, at this moment, walking towards the crystal gates of the Celestial City. Do not weep for her, as though she were lost."

The Creator gently placed Ellie's body in the grass. He turned back to Angeline and looked into her eyes. Reaching His hand forward, He wiped the tears from her glistening, purple eyes. Angeline's heart warmed, as all her guilt melted away. Knowing that Ellie was safe comforted her heart. She embraced the Creator.

"I never want to leave this place. Can I stay with you here forever?"

The Creator appeared saddened by her words, and then He explained His will to her. "My child, you can stay here as long as you like, but I need you to understand that this is not my desire for you. I want you to remember how horrible it was being a slave to your own selfishness. I want you to think about Ellie, and how she gave up her life to save you. I want you to live an abundant life by following my plan for you. Will you trust me with your life?"

Angeline wanted to say no, only because she didn't want to ever go back to the mountain. She dropped her gaze and caught a glimpse of Ellie; that still, small body gave Angeline her answer. "My Creator, Ellie gave up her life in service to you. I know I should go back into the mountain, but I don't want to leave you. It scares me thinking of being alone in that evil place."

He smiled sweetly at her. "My child, you will never be alone in the mountain; I will always be with you."

"You will?"

The Creator laughed a little. "I am truth. I am the life. I cannot lie. I will go with you. My child, now that you know I will be with you, would you go back into the mountain to rescue those trapped within?"

Angeline nodded. "I will go anywhere, as long as I know you are coming with me."

The Creator then proceeded to tell her His plan for her life; particularly that He wanted her to return to the House of Envy to tell the truth about what happened to Ellie. Angeline was excited about carrying out this plan. After He gave her a few more instructions, He asked if she was ready to leave. She straightened a little and nodded.

The Creator reached out and placed both hands over her heart. A blinding light exploded from His fingers and shot right into her chest. Angeline arched her back, as the warm light exploded inside her. She placed her hands over her heart and inquisitively looked up at the Creator. "What did you do to me?"

"All my children that live within the mountain carry my spirit inside them. I placed my light into your heart. Now you will never be alone, because I am the light. My light will protect you from the darkness of the mountain; it cannot enter you as long as my light shines through you. Thus, you will be in the mountain, but not a part of it."

Her eyes welled up with tears. She wrapped her arms around the Creator and whispered back to Him, "Thank you . . . for everything."

The Creator patted her affectionately on the head. Then He asked again if she was ready; she nodded. The Creator picked her up and walked carefully into the water. Once He was up to His waist, He gently released her. The Creator said one last thing. "Angeline, tell Aristus and Honna that Ellie's work is not yet finished."

Angeline was going to ask Him what that meant, but she was already under the water and on her way back to the House of Envy.

~ Chapter Thirty-Three ~

Trinzic was fuming. Adlar had ordered him to scrub his entire quarters with only a sponge that was less than half the size of his palm. Adlar had told both Bereck and Trinzic that they needed to perform the most degrading tasks, in order to relieve them of any suspicion. He was also angry because Adlar still had him wearing a uniform that was far too small for him. While he was left to scrub floors, Adlar had asked Bereck to perform rounds with him. Together, they were looking for Ellie and Angeline's bodies. Trinzic felt completely embarrassed that he had been left behind to clean. To pass the time, he complained bitterly to himself. Just to boost his own ego, he would occasionally perform some acrobatic feat, like scrubbing the floor while walking on his hands, and then flipping backwards and landing on his boots.

"Just look at that," he mumbled. "I am amazing. How could they leave me, Trinzic, seeker of all things beautiful and wondrous, to scrub floors? Who do they think I am . . . Simeon?" Shortly thereafter, Trinzic slid across the wet floor and somersaulted over a table. As his feet hit the floor, he heard a loud crash from within a nearby closet.

Trinzic was immediately ready for action. He slid across the floor, splashing water on either side of him as he went. Trinzic firmly grasped the doorknob and pondered what he might find. His best guess was that it was a large insect of some sort that had just hatched. Giddy excitement rose within him. Perhaps it would be something he could show off to Bereck and Adlar when they returned. He grew more anxious when the noise from the closet grew louder. Something very large was moving around in there. He grabbed his sword and prepared to strike it as soon as the door opened. With a lunge forward, he flung open the door and nearly pounced.

He was greeted by a pair of violet eyes staring back at him; Trinzic took a long step back. In doing so, he slipped on the sponge and lost his balance. He tried to correct his footing, but it was too late. Trinzic's vision blurred, and everything began to move in slow motion. Air brushed past him, and the back his head smacked against the tiled floor. He was now lying on the floor completely helpless, looking like an upside-down turtle. He heard feet shuffling and splashing through water, quickly making their way towards him. Soon he felt a presence hovering over him. In the near silence, water was dripping loudly near his right cheek. It was too late for him to run or fight, so he merely turned his head away and closed his eyes.

Cold water droplets splashed on his face; wet hair glided across his nose, forcing him to sneeze.

His head met with the creature, causing it to whisper. "Trinzic, is that you? Are you all right?"

What?! He instantly recognized the voice. *Angeline? How is she still alive?* Trinzic sat up, opened his eyes, and rubbed the back of his head. He stared at her until his eyes came back into focus. As he gazed upon her, he began to wonder if she was real or not. He reached out his hand to touch her. She could see the confusion on his face. She stopped his hand from touching her hair and instead placed it lovingly in her hand. "Trinzic, it's me . . . Angeline."

Trinzic sat up, struggled to his feet, and began to circle around her. He pulled Angeline to her feet, and, with her close to him, he placed a hand affectionately on her cheek. His voice shook as he spoke, "What's happened to you? You have changed. Your eyes . . . I just can't stop looking at your eyes. I don't think I have ever seen anything so mesmerizing."

Angeline blushed for the first time in her life. She had felt embarrassed before, but never had her skin given her away. Her cheeks turned pink against her sandy-colored skin. Trinzic's hand gently brushed her cheek, as he watched the color change. He was in awe of her beauty.

"Trinzic, the stories are true. There is a Creator; I've seen Him. Look at me, Trinzic; He's changed me."

Trinzic's whole body began shaking at her words, and he placed both of his hands over his ears. "Not now! Not now! Why did this have to happen now?" he shouted over and over again.

Angeline took a step closer to him and pulled his hands away from his ears. "Trinzic, what in the world are you carrying on about?"

He gave her a look that communicated pride. Then he confessed, "Angeline, my dear, I believe you. I know you're telling the truth, but you need to understand something. I told Bereck and Adlar that I was going to find you and Ellie. If I give my life over to the Creator now, then they will win."

Angeline stared at him with a baffled expression, and then burst out laughing. She laughed until tears were rolling down her cheeks. Trinzic, on the other hand, was not amused. He scowled at her. "I can't imagine why you find this so amusing. I have my pride, madam. Please stop your ridiculous laughing."

Angeline wiped the few remaining tears from her eyes. She was still giggling when she answered. "Trinzic, ever since we first met, you have proclaimed that you are the seeker of all things beautiful and mysterious. Now that you finally have the chance to embark on the greatest adventure ever, you have become a sniveling, foolish coward, hiding behind your own pride."

Trinzic, embarrassed and angry, shouted back, "Fine, I'll do it! I, Trinzic, am afraid of nothing! Tell me what I need to say."

Angeline immediately stopped laughing. She walked up to Trinzic and cupped his hands in hers. Knowing tears were starting to well up in her eyes, her tone softened. "Trinzic, I'm sorry. I should have never talked to you like a child. I was a fool for so long. My pride and selfish ambitions nearly destroyed me. You saw what kind of person I was. I had no right to call you foolish, when I knew that out of the two of us, I was the greater fool. Please, just be patient, and let me tell you what made me finally let go of my life."

She began to relate all the things that she recently had experienced. Trinzic's emotionless, proud exterior broke down when he heard of Ellie's sacrifice; it reached deep in his heart. Angeline told him everything, except for the flying part; she wanted him to be surprised. As Trinzic listened to Angeline, he thought of all the conversations he had with Aristus, and the countless times he had heard Opella tell her stories. When Angeline had finished, Trinzic was no longer angry, but broken. He realized all the time he had wasted; he finally was ready to hand over his life. He was ready for a real adventure.

Trinzic clung tightly to Angeline's wet sleeves and begged her, "Tell me, how do I become like you, Aristus, Honna, and all the others? I'm tired of making excuses; let's do this right now."

Angeline quickly explained what he must believe and say. Trinzic spread his arms out and dropped to his knees. He looked up and yelled to the Creator, "I think I always believed in you; I just wanted to have the adventures without you. Now, I realize that you hold the key to all things beautiful and wondrous. Take my life, and make it a tool in your hand. I believe in your sacrifice! Take me; my heart is ready to serve." Instantly, Trinzic vanished.

In the same moment, Angeline heard a noise at the door; it was Bereck and Adlar. They both looked at her, but neither one recognized her at first. "Did that idiot, Trinzic, let you in here?" Adlar bellowed. "I don't care what kind of romantic lies he's told you; there are no females allowed in the guard section of the House of Envy!"

Angeline gave him a funny little smirk. "Adlar, I hear you've been looking for me."

Adlar's eye twitched, as he gave her a second look. "Lady Angeline? Is that you?"

Angeline nodded in response. Bereck spoke up next. "Is Trinzic here?"

"No, he's not."

Bereck's face beamed as he turned to Adlar. "Trinzic is going to be so embarrassed. I can't wait 'til he gets back. What's even better is that he would have won if he had finished his cleaning."

Adlar let out an annoyed huff and rolled his eyes. He crossed his arms and walked over to Angeline. He needed to question her concerning Ellie and Julia. Angeline was smiling as he stopped across from her. She wasn't smiling because of Bereck. She only had one reason for her smile; she was debating whether or not she should tell them about Trinzic.

I'll just wait until Trinzic returns and asks me to tell Bereck. Then, I will pause for a long time; and then I'll tell him. She visibly nodded with the conclusion of her thought. Then she turned her attention towards Adlar and focused on everything that the Creator had sent her to do.

⌘

Music played softly as Madam Julia lounged with her head on the Lord Denham's lap. He played with her hair in sync with the flute and harp chords. His voice was sweet and affectionate, as he gently spoke to her. "You are the most enchanting woman I have ever laid eyes upon. Everything about you is so mysterious. I have never owed one person so much. You tried to rescue a woman you had never met; you had her murderer killed for me; you held an exquisite banquet in my honor; and you have managed to capture my heart completely. When enough time has passed to honor Celestra, I would be overjoyed if you would enter into a lasting union with me."

Julia felt a cunning smile spread widely across her face. Her words flowed sweetly from her lips. "My Lord Denham, nothing would please me more."

He almost stood up in his excitement, and his words began to run together. "You continue to amaze me! Please allow me to apologize for my drab demeanor. I would like to impress you with my voice. It may surprise you, but all my friends know me as a master of entertainment and hospitality. Let me sing to you of my love."

Julia relaxed into a nearby chair. The Lord Denham stood up and walked over to the two musicians. From his bags, he retrieved a few pages of sheet music. The melody started off beautiful and slow, and then the Lord Denham began to sing. His voice was that of a seasoned tenor. Julia felt a consuming satisfaction spreading like fire within her chest; the time had come to relish in her conquest.

She made a mental list of her accomplishments. *I have accomplished everything that I set out to do. I am an unstoppable genius. Apollyon, you have served me well. You have even disposed of my sister for me. My life is a glowing gem. Everything, including the Lord Denham and the House of Envy, are completely under my control.*

She continued to watch Denham sing his tribute to her. While he sang, she fell more and more in love with herself and her abilities of deception. She smiled with even more pleasure at the thought of how she had silenced Ellie. Even while the Lord Denham sang, she pinched her fingers together, mimicking the ripping of Ellie's wings. Then she let out a flirtatious giggle to show the Lord Denham that his song had pleased her. Julia fixed her eyes on him, trying to draw him deeper into her snare. When his song had finished, he slowly returned to her, falling to his knees before her. He placed her hand in his, effortlessly lifting it to his lips. His body shook as he knelt before her. Julia looked down at the Lord Denham with hungry eyes; she longed to bask in more of his flattery.

Suddenly, a flash of red caught her eye. She leaned quickly to look around Denham, and what she saw made her sick. Her head spun, her stomach sank, and her throat released an unexpected screech. She was looking right in the eyes of Angeline! Her sister was decorated the same as she had been the night of the banquet. Krenna was also there, cowering behind Angeline. Julia's scream had caused

Lord Denham to quickly jump to his feet. Now, he, too, was gazing upon Angeline and Krenna.

Angeline was first to speak. "Lord Denham, I have come to tell you that my sister Julia has deceived you. She and I were not attacked. She is the one who viciously murdered my servant. I have also come to inform you that a child's blood is not the only one that stains my sister's hands."

Julia frantically searched her brain for anything that could turn things around. "Angeline, I am glad to see that you are alive, but why have you come here, spouting such horrible lies about me? If you tell the truth now, all will be forgiven. You may still even be granted the honor of taking my place someday. Please forget all this foolishness."

Angeline's voice remained steady. "No, Julia." She looked again at the Lord Denham. "I am sorry, but everything I have said is true."

The Lord Denham broke into the conversation and addressed Julia. "I don't care if you killed one of your sister's servants, but there is no way I am going to leave. I love a good fight. I want to hear the rest of what your sister has to say; I think this whole thing is amusing." The Lord Denham waved his hand to signal Angeline to continue.

She moved closer and kept her eyes focused on him as she spoke. "Ellie was only a child, and Julia killed her simply because she didn't like the way in which Ellie answered her questions. As for the other victim, Krenna will have to tell you about that."

Krenna was now visibly shaking. Her teeth chattered together, as she started. "L . . . L . . . Lord

Denham, I am Madam Julia's servant. I . . . I . . ."
She paused as she caught a glance from Julia, whose
eyes screamed, "If you say anything, I will see to it
that your life ends."

Krenna then felt Angeline's reassuring hand on
her shoulder, giving her the security she needed
to continue. "I have obeyed every evil command
that this woman has ever given me. I have kept her
secrets and put up with her constant abuse. I am
loyal, but my loyalty does not extend to the cages.
I knew that if ever Madam Julia were caught, she
would try to drag everyone else down with her.
Lord Denham, I want you to know that I played
no part in the assassination of your fiancée, Lady
Celestra."

On hearing Celestra's name, the Lord Denham
rushed up to Krenna and angrily grabbed both of
her shoulders. His face was livid with rage, and he
began to shake her. "It can't be true! Explain yourself immediately, or I shall kill you myself. Speak!"

Krenna was terrified. Denham had stopped
shaking her, but was now staring at her; mere inches
from her face, with hatred and humiliation in his
eyes. Krenna closed her eyes in fear, and her words
flew quickly as she explained, "Over a month ago,
Madam Julia requested that I bring her information on eligible lords. Out of hundreds, she picked
you, but you were engaged. She had me gather all
the information I could on you. Then she had me
fetch Kenrick, a member of the guard. I know she
hired him to murder your fiancée, because Kenrick
bragged of being a notable assassin and divulged

a few small details about his mission. He thought that I had offered myself to Madam Julia as a prize for him if he succeeded. I knew then that I was just something disposable to her." Krenna opened her eyes and looked pleadingly at Lord Denham, tears running down her cheeks. "Please, I swear, I had no part in your fiancée's death. It was all her; please don't hurt me."

The Lord Denham wasn't even looking at or listening to Krenna anymore. His rage was directed solely at one person. He pushed Krenna aside and turned to find Julia, but she was gone. Denham turned to Angeline and, through clenched teeth, he hissed. "Where did she run?"

Angeline had not been paying attention. The confusion on her face told him that she hadn't seen, and he ran off enraged, searching wildly after her. Angeline prayed that she would get a chance to find her sister first before the Lord Denham satisfied his anger on her. She ran with purpose, hoping she would not be too late.

~ Chapter Thirty-Four ~

In the House of Envy, there was one room dedi-
cated to the safekeeping of each palette's excess
wealth. Only the supreme madam and the captain
of the guard were given keys to this room. Angeline
sensed that her sister would stop there before
making an escape; she was right.

Upon reaching the bolted door, she found it
unlocked. She pulled the door open and crept
inside, closing it carefully behind her. Orb lanterns
illuminated the gold glittering in piles on the floor.
Angeline easily spotted Julia and called to her softly,
"Julia, it's me, Angeline. I have come to help you."

Julia's back straightened. Her wings became
stiff, and she turned around, her voice cold and
hollow. "Angeline, you are more cunning than I
ever expected. It was ingenious of you to question
Krenna, but foolish of you to follow me."

Angeline put up her hands defensively, as her
sister steadily walked towards her, uttering a low,
guttural hiss. Angeline spoke quickly, "Julia, listen
to me; this is important. I was just like you, but
the Creator made me into a new person. I am no
longer evil and selfish. I have come here to beg you

to change. Please, sister, believe me; this is your last chance." Angeline quickly removed her fish-eye lenses to reveal her sparkling violet eyes.

Julia paused only for a moment to observe what Angeline was doing. Then she looked into her eyes, grabbed Angeline's hair, and began clawing savagely at her sister's face. Angeline flung her arms up to protect herself as Julia screamed at her, digging deep cuts into her arms. "You were always the stupid one. I will never be a servant to anyone. I will rise again to crush you. Your Creator is no match for me. He cannot protect you from my wrath!"

Julia eventually gave up on scratching and instead hit Angeline over the head with a nearby glass vase. Angeline fell to the ground, amidst the countless shards of broken glass. Julia gazed down upon her sister, bleeding and motionless on the floor, and smiled to herself. She grabbed the remaining jewels and exited quietly, locking the door behind her. As the key turned in her hand, she whispered, "Goodbye, Angeline; I hope you starve in there."

Julia quickly turned and ran toward her escape. She bounded down the hallway, keeping close to the walls in order to hide behind one of the pillars at any time. As she departed the House of Envy, she carefully reviewed her plan. *This is easier than I had hoped. I have more than enough wealth to secure a position of power. Everything could still go my way. Soon, I'll be in the carriage house, and I'll find a coachman to bribe. In no time, I will be in Crossford, watching countless suitors battle for my affection in the Coliseum.*

Julia made it to the carriage house easily, not seeing one soul on her journey there. She quickly hid herself and awaited the coachman's entrance. About an hour passed, before someone appeared from the nearby door. The man had his hood up, which caused Julia to question whether or not she should show herself. She watched as he began preparing the carriage and the salamanders for travel, and then she saw her chance. She crept up behind him unnoticed, reached out her hand, and tapped him lightly on the shoulder. The second she touched him, the man spun around, grabbing hold of her wrist. Now facing her, he pulled back his hood, which caused Julia let out a surprised chuckle.

"Adlar, I must say you gave me a touch of fright. What are you doing here?"

Adlar spoke casually as he answered. "My lady, I have come to prepare this carriage for your departure."

Julia smiled. "Good old Adlar; always so efficient and dependable."

He politely thanked her, and then he set about preparing the carriage. Julia climbed into her seat and impatiently waited for him to finish. When he was done, Adlar climbed into the carriage with her. He carried with him a rope, a sack, and a long strip of cloth: then he sat there, motionless.

"Adlar, if you're trying to scare me, it's not working. Put those silly things away and drive this carriage before you anger me." He still didn't move or say anything. Now Julia was getting scared. "Adlar, what are you planning on doing with those?"

Outside, she heard the carriage house door open and close. That's when Adlar sprung out of his seat and grabbed her tightly. She struggled violently, but to no avail. He tied the rope around her wrists and bound her hands behind her back. She kicked viciously, but he managed to tie her tightly to the metal ring on the floor.

She hissed and spat at him as she ranted, "If you plan on handing me over to Denham, I swear I'll tell him everything. I'll make sure that you go down with me. How dare you think you could betray me, you old fool!"

"You never change, Julia . . . so predictable. That's why I brought these." He placed the gag cloth in her mouth, as she glared at him with hatred searing in her eyes. "Julia, you really should be more careful with the lives you choose to take. The reason you're here right now is because you killed that little girl. I want you to know that I liked that child, and it's not very often that I like people."

He pulled out his poison-tipped dagger, and carefully grabbed Julia's ring finger. "Because I know you'll talk, I'm afraid I'm going to have to poison you. Only a prick, so the Lord Denham will know I delivered you alive; it's truly a mercy. If only you knew the horrible things that he had planned on doing to you." Adlar visibly shivered at the thought. "Farewell, Madam Julia."

Adlar pricked her finger. Julia's eyes were still wide as he set the bag over her head. Adlar gave her one last sympathetic look before leaving her alone.

The Lord Denham was at the front of the carriage, giving instructions to the driver.

He turned to face Adlar. "Is she in, ready?"

Adlar nodded. "She is tied and ready to be delivered to your family."

The Lord Denham's eyes were empty; his words fell flat and lifeless from his lips. "What did I ever do to deserve this? I made a fool of myself. She has taken everything from me. What could I possibly do to her that could make up for all this?"

Adlar shrugged, "Nothing, my lord."

The coachman signaled that he was ready. The Lord Denham said nothing more to Adlar. He merely glided past like a shadow, opening and closing the door to the carriage, with only a small squeak emanating from the rusty hinge.

Adlar stared thoughtfully at the carriage, as it moved like a ghost out of the large carriage house. "Julia, you were like a spider weaving an intricate web to catch your prey, but it was you who became entangled in your own silvery threads. This carefully constructed tomb was of your own design; I merely closed the door."

⌘

Angeline was confused and disoriented in the darkness. She reached out, groping the hard surface around her in an attempt to get a better understanding of where she was. Broken glass punctured her skin, as she crawled on her hands and knees. Eventually, her bloodied fingers felt the coolness of the metal door, and she used the handle to pull herself up.

Now that she was standing, she remembered where she was and everything that had happened. Two main thoughts plagued her: she was trapped alone in the vault, and her sister had rejected the Creator. She felt like a failure. She slumped back down, rested her face on her knees, and wept.

Her hands were clutching the painful gashes on her arms, when a cool breeze blew across her forearms, and, with it, a momentary hint of the sweet smell of grass. Her heart leapt with hope; she knew something good was about to happen. Cold, water droplets ran down her neck, and then a comforting hand came to rest on her shoulder. The hand was cool and damp. Angeline almost didn't want to look up; she was too excited. Perhaps she was dreaming.

Then she heard a familiar voice. "Hello, my beautiful lily; a woman as beautiful as you should never be left alone to shed tears. May I partake in a few with you?"

Angeline's whole body hurt, but for a moment she forgot about the pain. She grabbed Trinzic by his dripping wet shirt and pulled him down to the ground. Then she wrapped both arms around him and hugged him as tightly as her injured limbs would allow, crying into his shoulder for a long time. In between sobs, she looked into Trinzic's sparkling new green eyes for comfort.

"Trinzic, the Lord Denham will kill my sister, and she will be lost forever to the Core. I was no different than her. I could be in her place right now!

I was just as stubborn and evil. Trinzic . . . why me? Why did the Creator change me?"

He listened to her repeat the same thoughts over and over again, but he patiently waited for her to stop crying before responding. "I'm afraid the answer to your question, my lovely maiden, may be simpler than you realize. I think the only reason why the Creator rescued you, and not your sister, is because you asked Him. You were willing to be changed; she wasn't. Look at me. It took me much longer than you to trust in Him. Angeline, you were the one who opened my eyes to the truth, and I'm grateful to you. You may not have helped your sister change, but you did help me."

Angeline listened intently to everything Trinzic said. His words calmed her, and she knew his words were true. Her anxiety faded and, for the first time, she examined the new Trinzic. His hair was light yellow, almost white, and his skin was the color of milk. She couldn't stop looking at his eyes; they were brilliant emerald. She lightly touched his face. "Trinzic, you look beautiful."

Trinzic started to laugh. "Beautiful, huh? I've been called handsome, charming, witty, and enchanting, but I have to say that I've never before had a lady call me beautiful."

Angeline realized she was staring far too intently at him. She pretended to look at something else, but then she felt her hand throbbing. Carefully, she began pulling shards of glass out of her hand. "Trinzic, why did you come back? What mission did the Creator assign to you?"

A large smile spread instantly across his face, and he cleared his throat. "Well, the real world was more amazing than I could put into words. It was so exquisite that I almost decided not to leave, but I knew that an adventure was waiting for me here. I wouldn't be able to live with myself if I missed out on a challenge."

Angeline knew there was more, and that Trinzic was just pausing to build dramatic effect. She couldn't help but ask, "So, what was your challenge?"

Trinzic knelt before her. "You." He kissed her hand and winked.

Angeline's heart skipped a beat. She was excited, but she wasn't sure that he was serious. "Trinzic, you just winked at me. How am I supposed to take you seriously? Are you just trying to get a good laugh out of me?"

His face changed. He grabbed both her hands firmly and looked into her eyes. His voice was clear and steady, lovely and sincere. "Angeline, the Creator told me that He created us for each other. No other woman was designed for me. You have always been beautiful to me from the moment we first met. When you're near me, I feel as though I could do anything. I know that together we could change this dark mountain forever. Will you be united with me? The Creator said that you would bring forth my greatest adventure. I am ready to start on our beautiful journey together. Angeline, will you be united with me? If you are not ready, I will not try to force you with guilt. The Creator said the decision is up to you."

Angeline pondered all that Trinzic had said. She gazed into his new green eyes. Angeline had always felt a special connection with Trinzic. She, too, knew that he was her match.

Trinzic, in his excitement, was becoming unnerved by her silence. In reality, hardly any time had passed. He tried searching her eyes to see if he could figure out what she was thinking. When he couldn't stand the silence anymore, he spoke. "Oh! I'm such a fool! You are bleeding, depressed, and trapped. What a horrible moment to confess my love for you; I'm a better romantic than that. Give me another chance! I can do this right."

Angeline was now ready to give him her answer. "Trinzic, you have given me wise counsel, cried with me, opened your heart to me, and you've always brought joy to my life. I know a lifetime with you will be an exciting adventure. Any other man would bore me. Trinzic, seeker of all things beautiful and mysterious, I would be delighted to be your wife."

Trinzic's white face flushed. She had succeeded in causing Trinzic to be speechless. He took a moment to regain his wit, while Angeline stared at his red cheeks. After the scarlet color had vanished, he found his words. "Well, I suppose we will never be united if we remain trapped in here. Sit back and watch, as I entertain you with my lock-picking skills." Trinzic pulled some wire and a knife from his wet boots. First, he opened the panel covering the lock, which exposed the inner working parts. His fingers moved quickly as he dismantled it. When he had finished, he handed the parts to her and swung the door open dramatically. "I have saved the day! You are now free, my beloved." He reached his hand out. Angeline's hand slid delicately into his, and together they walked away from the vault door.

She turned her head, looking deep into his green eyes. "What is left for us to do?"

Trinzic's thumb rubbed the back of her hand as they walked. "Nothing; all is done. Bereck will rescue Honna and bring her home. We are now free to leave this retched establishment, if that is all right with you?"

Angeline sighed. "I am ready to leave this place. The House of Envy no longer has a claim on my heart. I want to go home."

Side by side, they walked silently through the empty halls of the House of Envy. As she left, Angeline tried to remember the message the Creator had given for Aristus. She hoped in her heart she would know what to say. She knew that words could never fully express all that Ellie had given her. Through Ellie's sacrifice, Angeline finally understood what it meant to love.

A crystal city lay glistening in the distance. A little girl ran, hoping to unravel the beautiful mystery before her. Her heart raced with anticipation; she wondered what adventure awaited her. The child looked down at the ground for a moment to check her feet and ran into someone's legs. The girl looked up to see a man who lifted her up into his arms. He held her closely to himself.

It was the Creator, and His voice boomed with pride. "Ellie, you are a true child of light. My light shines through you like the sun. I love your spirit and your servant's heart. You have done amazing things in my name, and, for that, I am very proud of you. I want you to know that your friend Angeline is now one of my children because of your sacrifice."

Ellie hung tightly to the Creator and replied, in a singsong voice, "Your city is so beautiful. I can't believe that I actually get to see it. Are you going to take me there now?"

The Creator lovingly threw Ellie high into the air, and her laugh echoed in the openness. "Ellie, my child, you know the Celestial City is perfect. It is a place of eternal bliss; a place full of countless, joyful adventures. Here, there are no tears, no hunger, no pain: everything is how it was meant to be; and you are welcome to stay here. You have worked hard and have accomplished much, but I have come to ask you something before you enter the gates. Would you be willing to return to the mountain?"

Ellie politely floated back down and looked inquisitively at her Creator. "Why would I go back? I have made it to the end."

The Creator smiled lovingly down on her. "There is still work left for you to do in the mountain. I will paint two pictures for you; the first being the Celestial City. Upon entering the city gates, I will carry you on my shoulders and lead you through the streets. You will live life the way that it was meant to be lived, experience joy that you never knew existed, and you and I will spend time just being together. It will be more amazing than words could ever express.

"The other choice will be filled with hardship, sorrow, and loss: but I will be with you, helping you, and enabling you to rescue people out of the darkness. The choice is completely up to you. Either one is a good decision."

Ellie shuffled her feet. "I really want to live forever in the Celestial City, but I also loved being a part of your plan in the mountain."

The Creator picked Ellie up and held her tightly. "My child, what have you decided?" Ellie whispered her answer into his ear. He hugged her tightly and lifted her up onto his shoulders. The Creator's voice resonated, "That is a good choice, my child. Let's go. They are waiting for you."

The End

Johnson, Jennifer K
The house of envy

CPSIA information can be obtained
at www.ICGtesting.com
Printed in the USA
LVOW12s1030230717
542317LV00001B/75/P

9 781498 480161